A NATHAN MASON THRILLER

Nightfall in Famagusta

Jackson Beck

Jacksonbeck.com

Also by Jackson Beck

The Sanctuary Cipher

Cabin in the Clouds

Acknowledgements

St Oswald's Church, Winwick
Ivan Butler
Gladstones Library
Janet
Emma
Chris

When the reward hinges on the risk

1

Auckland, New Zealand

NATHAN MASON and his girlfriend, Loretta, were driving to her parents' home on the outskirts of Auckland. It was early May and the start of the New Zealand winter. The North Island, particularly north of Auckland, is blessed with a temperate winter climate. It can be wet but very rarely cold enough for frost or snow.

'I feel quite nervous,' said Nathan.

'Ah, you poor little thing,' Loretta replied. 'There's nothing to worry about. I think you'll get on with my parents; they're very down to earth.'

'Really? Tell me a bit more about them.'

'Well, my dad is seventy-two and my mum sixty. As you know, my dad is Cypriot and my mum is a Māori.'

'How did your dad end up in New Zealand?'

'Well, I know he used to have lots of business meetings all around the world, so I presume he came here once, liked it and decided to move here.'

'Business meetings all around the world? He sounds like a high-level minister for the foreign office. What was his job?'

'Well, he had businesses.'

'What sort of businesses?'

'The type that take you all around the world,' Loretta replied.

'What, like a drug dealer you mean?' Nathan said, smiling.

Loretta slapped his leg. 'I'll tell him you said that.'

Nathan faked a movement of the steering wheel. 'Hey, that's dangerous. Not while I'm driving and, no, I'd rather you didn't tell him that. Seriously, though, what type of businesses?'

'I don't know an awful lot but I know he had lots of jewellers shops and real estate agencies and other things. I was always interested in the real estate agencies over here. It's all I've ever really known.'

'So why did your dad ask to see us?' said Nathan.

'Because I've been talking about you a lot. I guess he wants to see what kind of guy his daughter has hooked up with.'

'Oh great, so it's like an interview to have the pleasure of seeing his daughter.'

'Yes, and you'd better pass with flying colours.'

'Tell me about your mum.'

'Well, she's beautiful, kind-hearted, generous and she's passed all her attributes on to me.'

Nathan sniggered and, as a result, suffered another slap to the leg. 'Is your mum a businesswoman too?'

'No, not at all. She's not interested; she's old-fashioned and believes her role is to look after her husband, daughter and home.'

'Well, there's nothing wrong with that,' said Nathan.

'I know. I love her to bits. She's held our family together.'

'I can't help noticing that the houses around here are pretty big,' Nathan said, changing the subject.

'I know. Take the next left.'

They were travelling on a long straight road heading away from Auckland, in a part of the city that could be called the stockbroker belt. Very exclusive houses that were set well back from the road, with long tree-lined drives surrounded by huge, landscaped gardens, with rockeries and other areas of interest. The wet leaves were blowing across the road on the back of a stiff south-westerly breeze.

'Not far to go now,' Loretta said. 'You'll shortly see two white stone pillars on the left. That's the house. You'll have to stop and press the intercom for the gates to open.'

'Okay, I think I can see it now.' Nathan pulled into the entrance and pressed the button.

A female voice answered: 'Hello.'

'Hello, it's Nathan and Loretta.'

'Oh, please come in. I'll open the gate for you now,' said the lady with enthusiasm. Both gates slowly opened.

'Was that your mum?' asked Nathan.

'Yes.'

'She sounded so young.'

'She is compared to my dad, by twelve years.'

They were on a long straight tarmac drive, which took them up to the side of a huge, cream-coloured and extremely attractive bungalow. At the side of the bungalow was a turning area in front of the garages. In the centre of this area was a small, turfed island with a large spectacular fan palm tree. Nathan could see what appeared to be lights wrapped around the tree, which seemed to be distributed on to its fronds.

'I bet that's spectacular in the dark,' said Nathan.

'Oh, the palm tree; yes, it's beautiful. He only turns it on for special occasions like Easter or Christmas. I remember it as a child, so for me it's always been there,' Loretta said.

'Good memories then.'

'The best,' she replied.

Nathan pulled up outside the garage and they both jumped out of the car. They were walking towards the side entrance door, hand in hand, when it opened.

'Hi Mum,' shouted Loretta as she ran ahead to give her mum a big hug. 'This is Nathan,' she said as he approached. He looked at Loretta's mother and could see where his girlfriend got her beauty from.

'Pleasure to meet you,' said Nathan.

'The pleasure is all mine, and please call me Maia. My husband's in the lounge. Please call him Stelios. We've been dying to meet you.'

'Likewise,' replied Nathan, knowing that it was a bit of a fib. Loretta was right, Maia was an attractive woman. She was of average height and, with her olive skin, you would have taken her as a fifty-year-old, not a woman who had just had a landmark sixtieth birthday.

Maia led them into the lounge, which was a beautiful room with ornate carved furniture and an open aspect across meadows. It also had a beautiful sea view. Stelios arose from his easy chair. A small man, approximately five feet seven inches, Nathan towered over him as he approached. They shook hands. Stelios had a firm grip for a seventy-two-year-old with an overweight physique.

'Welcome, young man, it's great to meet you at last.'

'Thank you, and please call me Nathan.'

'If you agree to call me Stelios.'

'It's a deal,' said Nathan. They were off to a good start. Loretta walked over and gave her dad a kiss on each cheek.

'Please sit down,' Stelios said. They sat down on an exceptionally large cream leather sofa.

'Would you like a drink Nathan?' asked Maia.

'White coffee please.'

'Loretta?'

'Same for me please Mum.'

Maia walked off to the kitchen.

'I'm sorry I haven't been to see you earlier but I understand you needed time to recover from the road traffic accident,' said Nathan.

'Yes, it did take quite a while to get over that, then we decided to go to Cyprus for a couple of months, so this is really the first opportunity for us to get together,' replied Stelios.

'And are you recovered from the accident?'

'Maia is, but she's a lot younger than me. I still don't feel right. It's time for me to slow down a little. I've worked all my life since I was fourteen years old. I'm just tired.'

'Well, if you don't mind me saying, you both look very well.'

'That's truly kind of you Nathan. I like you already,' said Stelios with a hearty laugh.

'Nathan was admiring the palm tree Dad,' said Loretta.

'He has good taste too,' Stelios replied, with another loud laugh. 'I had that imported from Cyprus many years ago. A little taste of home.'

'Can I ask why you moved from Cyprus?' enquired Nathan.

'Yes, you can, but you have to answer some of my questions first,' said Stelios with a hint of a smile.

Nathan feared that the dreaded interrogation was about to start.

'So, tell me Nathan, I understand you're staying with your sister up in Dome Valley.'

'Yes, I am. I came over last year with a view to a possible permanent move.'

'And why did you want to leave the UK?'

'Well, it's a long story and it—'

'Here's your coffee,' interrupted Maia, as she walked into the room with four large coffee cups and saucers on a silver tray, complete with a plate of cakes and some side plates.

'This looks lovely Mum, thank you.'

'It's a pleasure sweetie,' replied Maia.

'Sit down Maia, Nathan's just about to give us his life story,' said Stelios, followed by another loud laugh.

'Dad, don't be so cruel, stop embarrassing him,' said Loretta.

'There you go Nathan, be warned. If you marry my daughter, she's not afraid to speak her mind.'

'Dad, now you're embarrassing both of us,' said Loretta with flushed cheeks.

'Stelios, that's enough mischief for now,' added Maia.

'I'm deeply sorry everyone, that was very mischievous of me,' said Stelios with a cheeky grin on his face. 'It's lovely to see you both together. Now, Nathan, please continue.'

Nathan had decided to abbreviate his introduction. 'Well, I used to be a police officer ... a detective in London, but I got a head injury while playing rugby. I ended up having a stroke and was medically discharged as a result.'

'But you look so big and strong, and you speak so well. There's no indication that you've ever had a stroke,' said Stelios.

'I know, I'm in pretty good shape but I've lost a lot of memories from years ago and that was part of the problem. I'd forgotten a lot of police procedures, even the most basic things, so in effect I was back to square one, like an inexperienced police officer, so they decided to let me go. It was hard at first but then I buried my head in books and knowledge and keeping myself fit.

'So, it was my sister Millie's idea that I think about a fresh start in New Zealand. My parents had died in England, so I had nothing to really stay there for. So now I'm incredibly happy, especially since I met your beautiful daughter, and I'm planning to stay.' Loretta took his hand in a show of support.

'What do you do for a job? How do you earn a living?' asked Stelios.

'I'm fortunate in that I received a significant inheritance when my parents died and I received a payment from the police when I was discharged. My brother-in-law Chris has introduced me to the world's stock markets too, so I spend a couple of days a week working on that.'

'So, is that your brother-in-law's job, a trader/investor?' said Stelios.

'Yes, that's what he does. He used to work on the London Stock Exchange but wanted to get away from the rat race.'

'Well, he couldn't have gone much further,' said Stelios, followed by one of his loud laughs. 'I too am a businessman. I have business connections throughout the world, or I used to have, but the whole thing got a bit too big for me to handle. Now that Loretta's grown up, she's become a good businesswoman in real estate over here.' He turned to look at Loretta. 'I was hoping that you'd be able to start looking at other issues for me. I'm getting too old now sweetie, so if you think you're ready, we need to sit down together and make some plans.'

Loretta got up and walked over to her father. She crouched down in front of him and took his hands in hers. 'Dad, you know that I'll do anything that you want.'

'Then I want you to take over all my business affairs. I want to hand everything over to you. Your mum and I have everything that we need and more, so now it's your turn to take the reins. I've discussed it with her and she's in full agreement with me.'

Loretta stood up and leaned over to give her father a kiss on each cheek and then did the same to her mother. 'I will, of course, say yes, and thank you so much, but all I really know is the real estate business in New Zealand. I don't really know about your other dealings, so please give me a clue Dad.'

'Okay, so you, of course, know Mykanos Real Estate, but there are other companies under the holding group of Mykanos Corporation. There's Mykanos Jewels, Mykanos Mining and Mykanos Pharmacies.'

'What's Mykanos Jewels?' asked Loretta.

'Jewellers shops.'

'How many, and where are they?'

'Off the top of my head, about twenty-five, in Cyprus, Israel, Doha and a couple in Australia.'

Loretta was open-mouthed. 'What's Mykanos Mining?' she asked.

'I have an aggregate mine in Cyprus, a mineral mine in Australia and a couple of others, I can't remember why and where. On the pharmacies front I have about the same number as jewellers and in the same countries.'

'I had no idea that you had all of these interests. How did you amass them in the first place?'

'You know that your grandfather was a very wealthy man.'

'Yes.'

'Well, I inherited MOGL.'

'What's that?'

'Mykanos Ocean-Going Liners.'

'I can't believe it; I didn't know that you used to be a shipping magnate Dad.'

'I sold it years before you were born, Loretta, and invested it into all these businesses.'

Nathan had sat there listening intently and was about to speak when Maia said, 'I think we've talked enough about business, you two. Can't we change the subject? In fact, tell me Nathan, Loretta told me about your exploits last year finding the gold. I heard that the owner has invested a lot of the money from the find into Māori causes.'

'Yes, you're right. The original finder was her son Fred. He'd brought some of the gold home and the remainder he'd stashed in a cabin up in the forest. The cabin belonged to his one and only friend Tawera. When Tawera moved away he allowed Fred to use the cabin and the gold remained unrecovered until I arrived. Anyway, Fred's mother wanted to help some Māori causes in Tawera's name and that's what she did, as well as replenishing the funds of her beloved church.'

'That's fantastic. And how did you find out about it?'

'It was just investigation work really; but it was so sad that three people lost their lives in the process.'

'A terrible thing,' interrupted Stelios.

'It was, and I just walked straight into it. They never found the suspect. He disappeared, they reckon, into the crevasse that they found up there near the cabin. Some sort of fracture in the forest floor probably, as a result of an earthquake many years ago.'

'Fascinating,' said Maia. 'So you had the opportunity to put your detective skills to the test.'

'I did, and that wasn't what I was expecting to be doing when I arrived here. I enjoy doing historical research and that's what helped me.'

'Loretta, there's something I need to ask you,' said Stelios. 'I'm sorry to go back to business but I had a garbled message from one of the tenant farmers at Anapetri Villa in Cyprus.'

'Oh, right, what's the problem?' asked Loretta.

'I don't know whether he'd been drinking but I think it was Andreas Polycarpou, bumbling on about the land and planning applications. I didn't know what he was on about. He rents the land off me, as do all the other tenants, at below the market value. Anyway, I was wondering whether you could contact him and find out what's going on and deal with it. I was going to contact our housekeeper over there but I don't really want to get involved. Like I said before, I want you to take over my affairs and make them your own.'

'Don't worry Dad, I'll sort it. We need to arrange a meeting about this discussion and formalise it.'

'I agree,' replied Stelios.

'Oh, and since you mentioned Cyprus, I was wondering whether Nathan and I could pay a visit to the villa. Maybe a couple of weeks before I take over the Mykanos *Corporation*?' Loretta said, placing the emphasis on corporation.

Stelios looked over at Maia. 'What do you think Maia?'

'I think that would be a great idea. She's going to need the rest before she takes over everything.'

'Ah, thank you,' said Loretta.

'Yes, thank you so much,' added Nathan.

'Let's all eat some cake in celebration,' suggested Maia.

After cake and coffee, Maia proudly took Nathan on a tour of the house and grounds. He was pleasantly surprised to find an indoor pool and hot tub, which was part of an elaborate extension to the rear of the house that had been carried out only a couple of years earlier.

'I can see that you're very house-proud,' said Nathan.

'Oh yes, very. It may be old-fashioned but I always saw it as my role. Stelios was always too busy with business, so it was a natural fit for me. He's never disagreed with any changes or additions that I've made.'

Maia changed the subject very quickly as she linked Nathan's arm as they walked. 'You two look like you're happy.'

'I'm incredibly happy and very lucky,' replied Nathan, smiling.

'She's going to need all the support she can get,' said Maia.

'I'm lucky that I'll have the time to help her as much as I can.'

'She'll also support you,' added Maia, 'and you'll find that she'll be very loyal. She's that type of person and she'll expect that kind of loyalty from you.'

Nathan suddenly felt that he was being warned by a protective mother, which he knew was perfectly natural. He was unsure what to say. 'I understand,' he replied. 'And thank you so much for your hospitality … and this tour of your beautiful home.'

'It's been a pleasure Nathan, and I hope we see more of you in the future.'

'Likewise,' said Nathan, as he gave her a quick peck on the cheek.

They walked into the lounge, where Nathan suspected that Loretta and her father had been talking non-stop business.

'Stelios, I must say I absolutely love your house. It's amazing,' said Nathan.

'Thank you Nathan, it's all my hard work,' Stelios replied with a smile and a wink.

'Whatever,' said Maia.

~~~

The afternoon continued with more conversation, more coffee and with the inclusion of sandwiches. It was early evening before Loretta and Nathan finally left her parents' home. As they drove out of the drive on to the quiet road, Nathan quickly looked at Loretta. She was deep in thought.

'Wow, what an afternoon, and it looks like you just inherited your father's empire. Your inheritance has come early.'

'I know, and I don't know whether to laugh or cry,' Loretta replied.

'Well, why don't you scream instead.'

Loretta didn't need to be told twice. She let out a blood-curdling scream followed by uncontrollable laughter. 'I can't believe it; I'm going to be in control of the Mykanos Corporation.' She was now smiling from ear to ear.

'This calls for a celebration, I think,' said Nathan.

'Yes … er … no,' she replied.

'Why, what's wrong?'

'Let's wait until we get to Cyprus, then we can celebrate there.'

'Why? Are we going that soon?' asked Nathan.

'Well, if you're free, and I'll make myself free, why not? The sooner the better.'

'I'll consult my diary when I get back, although I fear I may have a full itinerary,' said Nathan mockingly.

'Then I fear I may have to take someone else,' Loretta replied.

'That won't be necessary. I'm sure I can fit you in.' Nathan took his left hand off the steering wheel and reached over to Loretta. She took his hand and kissed it. 'What was that for?' he asked.

'Because I'm so happy.'

'So am I.' Nathan took her hand and kissed it.

~~~

Nathan dropped Loretta off at her apartment in Auckland before making his way back to his sister's in the north at Dome Valley. They had agreed that they had things to do in preparation for their visit to Cyprus. Loretta was going to arrange the flights through her office in the morning. They would both be prepared to leave at short notice.

That evening, Nathan spoke to his sister Millie and her husband Chris about the afternoon's events at Loretta's family home and the plans they were making to go to Cyprus. Chris agreed to keep watch on Nathan's stock market portfolio while he was away. He had made a passing comment that 'he liked the idea of playing with someone else's money for a change'. If Nathan didn't trust Chris implicitly, the comment could have been unnerving, but Chris had taught him all that he knew and they had built up an extraordinarily strong and trusting relationship, much to Millie's delight. They were both delighted to hear that Loretta was taking over her father's concerns and agreed that a couple of weeks' holiday in Cyprus was what the couple deserved.

Nathan went to bed early and used his laptop to start researching Cyprus. He was in his element as he loved researching a location, knowing that he was going to visit soon. He looked at the churches, the archaeological sites, the museums and anything associated with the history of the area. He had been to the island on a couple of occasions for a family holiday but they had always stayed on the west coast near Paphos.

This time he and Loretta would be staying at the Anapetri Villa in Anapetri village on the east coast. Positioned between Famagusta and Palakori, Nathan couldn't help noticing that the villa was positioned about a mile to the south of the border with the Turkish-occupied territories, under their control since 1974.

He decided to look on Google Earth, which enabled him to get a good visual idea of what the area was like. He saw that if you headed south from Anapetri you would come across Protaras and Ayia Napa, the latter being a holiday resort for the hedonists, young families and off-duty British troops. Known for its nightlife and club scene, it wasn't a place that Nathan planned to visit.

Going north again, past Anapetri and into the Turkish north, he came across what was once the glamorous resort town of Varosha, part of Famagusta. This was the modern beach resort of its day, with high-rise hotels and apartment blocks, restaurants and bars, supermarkets and banks. A thriving, bustling community until August of 1974 when the Turkish military arrived, Varosha was abandoned by its thirty-five thousand residents, the vast majority being Greek Cypriots. The town was fenced off as part of the demilitarised zone between the north and south and it had been looted and left to rot. Nathan could see that it was slowly returning to nature. Trees had broken through the concrete, and grass and weeds had taken over some of the roads. The town was cordoned off to all except official visitors, with a series of staffed outposts positioned strategically throughout its entirety.

Nathan found the images disturbing, so he came away from Google Earth and just did some local searches on the village of Anapetri. He was pleasantly surprised to see that it had a lovely little church, a coffee shop, a small bar-like pub, a restaurant, two shops, council offices and a playground for small children. It was a picturesque village and he was looking forward to his visit, especially in the company of a beautiful woman like Loretta.

2

THE FOLLOWING day Nathan spoke to Loretta just before lunch. She was going to visit her parents that afternoon to discuss business. 'Shall we go on Friday,' she said.

'I presume you mean to Cyprus.'

'Yes, sorry, we can fly from Auckland to Doha in Qatar, a couple of hours on the ground, then fly straight to Larnaca. What do you think?'

'Sounds great to me. We'd probably need a few days to get over the jet lag. It's a fair old flight.'

'Yes, I know, but the way the return flights are falling, we should still be able to have a good two weeks in Cyprus before we return,' said Loretta.

'I'm really looking forward to it. Have you booked it yet?'

'My colleague Grace is just about to do it. I thought I'd call you first to make sure that you can go so soon.'

'Then go ahead, of course I can,' Nathan replied.

'Okay, I'll call you after my meeting with Dad.'

'Okay, speak to you later.'

Nathan came off the phone. He was really looking forward to going to Cyprus but he was also concerned about Loretta's meeting with her father. He couldn't quite put his finger on why but it could be because he was a little anxious that Loretta may be taking on something that she would regret. Something that she may find too difficult to manage. He knew he was being presumptuous and that Loretta probably had a perfectly good management team alongside her, but he couldn't help feeling the way he did.

Later that afternoon, Loretta called Nathan and asked whether he could come that evening to her apartment in Auckland. He said he would be there by seven.

Loretta's apartment was in a good location, if you worked in the city like she did. It was only a stone's throw from the Sky Tower, famous for its firework displays, which made the city one of the first to annually welcome in the new year. She had a view of the harbour, with rows and rows of boats and yachts, all overlooked by the impressive harbour bridge.

As Nathan approached that evening, he turned into a service road that led to the underground car park. The barrier was down. He had the option to enter a four-digit code, which he couldn't remember, so he pressed the intercom button for Loretta's apartment. She answered, 'Hi, passphrase please.'

'Hello, it's me, and I have some wine.'

'Please enter,' was the reply. Loretta pushed the button on her handset to lift the car park barrier.

As Nathan drove down a ramp, he was surprised at the quality and quantity of the cars. Mercedes, BMW, Jaguar, Porsche, among others. He suddenly felt conscious as he parked his black Toyota RAV4, which wasn't even his, it was his sister's. As he got out, he looked back at the RAV and smiled to himself. None of these cars had gnarly off-road tyres like the RAV. He could drive on dirt tracks and beaches, and he did.

He stepped into the lift and pressed the apartment number on the aluminium control panel. The lift's operation was smooth, until it came to a juddering stop at Loretta's level. The doors slid open with a swish and she was standing there waiting for him. He stepped out of the lift and they embraced with a long passionate kiss.

'Now that's what I call a welcome,' Nathan said. Loretta took his hand and they walked the short distance along a corridor to the door of her apartment. She touched the reader with her entry proximity card, the lock clicked and she pushed the door open.

It wasn't the first time Nathan had been to her apartment but it always smelled as if everything was brand new. It was modern, it was bright, but it still had a very cosy feeling. With two bedrooms, a large kitchen, two bathrooms, one of which was en-suite, and a large lounge/dining room, it was a good size and well proportioned.

They stepped inside and Nathan passed Loretta the carrier bag containing the bottle of wine. She kissed him again. 'Now make yourself comfortable. I'll bring in the wine and nibbles.'

Nathan did as he was told and went into the lounge. He looked at the sofa and then took a seat in one of the two easy chairs. Loretta followed him in shortly after with two large glasses of wine and a plate of assorted cheeses and biscuits. She put them on to a small table between them and sat down. 'Help yourself,' she said. Nathan took a sip of his wine and then ate a chunk of cheese.

Loretta spoke first. 'We're booked for Cyprus; we're flying out on Friday. Flight departs at 11am.'

'Fantastic, I can't wait. I've done my research and there are some places I'd like to visit.'

'Oh, that's great, but there's been a slight change on my part.'

'Why, what's happened?' asked Nathan, concerned.

'Oh, it's nothing to worry about, but I'll have to take my laptop and a few work bits and pieces.'

'How come?'

'I had the meeting with Dad this afternoon.'

'Yes, I was going to ask you about that. How did it go?'

'Well, put it this way, I was with him for three and a half hours and it went roughly like this. He went through a list of business interests country by country. Each group of companies such as pharmacies has a national manager. For example, there's a national manager in Cyprus for jewellers, then there's one for real estate and one for mining. This is replicated through six other countries. So, in each country each manager reports back to an accountant who prepares a set of accounts, which is then emailed to the group accountant here in Auckland. The group accountant then prepares an overall set of accounts for the Mykanos Group.'

'Wow, that sounds pretty complex,' said Nathan.

'Just a bit,' replied Loretta. 'The whole process is crying out to be rationalised. But I can't quite make out what's wrong with Dad. I don't think he's unwell but he has memory issues. He's found it difficult compiling this information for me. He can't even remember the names of some of his national managers.'

'It's called old age Loretta; it comes to us all. I can see why he wants to hand it all over to you. It needs a young agile mind to oversee all this and a good management team to back you up. Have you seen any of these accounts, either individual or as a whole?' asked Nathan.

'I had a look at the group figures for last year, but until I drill down into the individual businesses it's pretty difficult to identify which are the not so profitable ones and in which country. He's given me a memory stick with all the contact details of every shop, mine, business premises, and all the accountants that he deals with. I reckon it's taken a while for him to compile all this so that he can hand everything over to me. He's been planning it for months.'

'Well, you're lucky that you don't have three or four brothers to share it with, then it could get messy. On a serious note, though, this is a massive project to take over and run. You really are going to need a good management team to help you to bring the business up to speed. And before you say it, no I'm not pitching for a job, but if there's ever anything that I can help you with, I'm at your service and I'll support you one hundred per cent.'

'Thank you, that means so much to me, and I would like you to be involved in some aspect if you fancy it,' said Loretta with a serious look on her face.

'What were you thinking of?' replied Nathan.

'You could be the group security consultant.'

'I wasn't actually looking for a job.'

'I know, but it appears to me that all these premises that I'm taking over are going to need some sort of security procedures in place, and a review of their alarm systems and CCTV. Don't forget, we're talking about jewellers and pharmacies here, and god knows what else.'

'I presume they'll already have systems in place, especially the jewellers and pharmacies,' Nathan suggested.

'Well, you would think so, but my dad doesn't seem to know. I guess only the local managers would know that, but perhaps it should or could be a job for the national managers in consultation with our security expert.'

Nathan thought for a second as he took another sip of wine and nibbled a piece of cheese. 'Okay, of course I'll help, but I don't need to be on the payroll as long as you cover all my expenses. I'll be happy with that.'

Loretta got up from her seat and walked over to Nathan. She planted a big kiss on his lips as she cradled his head in the palms of her hands. 'Thank you so much. This means that our trip to Cyprus can be all expenses paid by the company,' she said.

'Well, that's really great, thank you, but I thought it was a holiday at your parents' place.'

Loretta laid down on the sofa. 'It is, but I thought that perhaps while we there we could visit some of the businesses in Cyprus and see what the problem is with the tenant farmers on the villa land.'

'Okay, that's fine with me, but it would be nice to do some relaxation, sightseeing, swimming, sunbathing … that type of thing.'

'Oh, I'm sure we'll find the time to do all of those things and a few more,' Loretta said in what Nathan thought was a seductive manner.

'You can be very persuasive, you know.'

'Yes, I know. My dad said I inherited it from my mum at an early age.'

Nathan smiled to himself and thought she had inherited her mother's good looks too. He felt incredibly lucky. 'I've been doing some research on Anapetri,' he said.

'Oh right, what do you think?'

'It's a beautiful village; did you know that the little Greek Orthodox church is nearly one thousand years old?'

'Well, I knew it was old but it's not something I've ever had any interest in.'

'Then we shall make a point of visiting it,' said Nathan.

'You're such an anorak, Nathan Mason,' she said, laughing.

'I know, and I don't care. There's also an archaeological dig going on just outside the village, so maybe we could look at that.'

'Mm, I'm not so sure about that.'

'Why's that then?' asked Nathan.

'Well, in that part of the world, an archaeological dig is usually a cover story for a dig for the disappeared,' Loretta replied.

Nathan thought for a second. 'Ahh, you think it may be a dig to search for people that were killed during the war.'

'Yes, it's possible. We tend to steer clear of those places. If they find anything, it can get quite emotional and upsetting for the locals.'

'Right, point taken, tread carefully near any archaeological sites. Or, better still, stay away,' said Nathan.

'Yes, I think so. There are lots of other places that we can visit. We could go shopping in Nicosia or we could visit other parts of the island – Larnaca, Limassol, Paphos.'

'Oh, I love Paphos,' said Nathan. 'We used to go there as a family when I was a child. There are lots of historical places to go to in and around the town. Do you not fancy going to anywhere in the north of the island?'

'Not really. My dad always used to say not to cross into the occupied territories. He's never forgotten when the Turks invaded, so he always encouraged us to stay away.'

'Did your dad lose much when they took over?'

'Yes, he had some shops in Varosha, the tourist part of Famagusta. He doesn't like to talk about it though, it upsets him.'

Nathan decided to change the subject. 'How are you going on with your packing?'

'I'll do it tomorrow,' she replied.

'Yes, I'm the same. Who are we flying with?'

'Qatar Airways, business class.'

'I feel excited, like a little boy,' said Nathan.

'Me too, but like a little girl,' Loretta replied.

Nathan got up from his chair and lay down facing her on the sofa. She put her arms around him and dragged him close. They kissed. 'Will you stay over tonight,' said Loretta.

'Oh, if I have to,' said Nathan mockingly.

'Oh well, you can leave now, I don't want to keep you,' she replied, playing him at his own game.

'No, it's okay, I'll grace you with my presence.'

'Seeing as you're not driving, get some more wine from the kitchen.'

'Okay,' Nathan replied. As he stood up, she smacked his backside. 'What was that for?' he asked.

'For being so considerate as to grace me with your presence,' she said, smiling.

A couple of hours later, after more wine, snacks and a movie on Netflix, the couple retired to bed. The following morning Loretta rose early and went into the office. She planned to finish early that afternoon to finish her packing.

Nathan rose early too and was on his way back to Fern Heights. He intended to get all his packing done before lunchtime so he could spend the afternoon with Chris going over his portfolio on the stock market. Tomorrow was the beginning of their long flight to Cyprus.

3

THEIR FLIGHT to Cyprus was better than expected. On the longest leg from Auckland to Doha they enjoyed a selection of wines and food, before both catching a good seven-hour sleep. The leg from Doha to Larnaca was much shorter and without the sleep. During the flight, Loretta resorted to mocktails as she would be driving when they arrived.

Upon landing and following luggage collection, they made their way through arrivals to one of the car hire desks. A car had already been booked back in New Zealand, so the paperwork was just a formality. They walked out of the terminal building and crossed a road to the car hire park.

'Wow, it's warm for early evening,' said Nathan.

'Yes, for May they expect mid-to-late twenties, but it's been in the low thirties,' Loretta replied.

'I hope the car has good air conditioning.'

'Yes, I hope so too.'

'What car are we looking for?' asked Nathan.

'A silver Hyundai Tucson SUV. I think I can see it straight ahead.'

Loretta pushed the button on the fob and the lights flashed on the car that she had spotted. They walked up to the car, loaded their cases into the rear and, with Loretta behind the wheel, they were on their way to Anapetri.

The early-evening drive from the airport was spectacular. They drove along the coast road part way before joining the A3 heading for Ayia Napa. The coast road was breathtaking, and at certain points a low crash barrier was all there was between the tarmac road and the sheer cliff edge. Looking south, the sea shimmered in the evening sunlight, as several small fishing boats sat with rods outcast, awaiting the evening's catch.

As they joined the motorway, the contrast was considerable. Birds of prey could be seen overhead, circling on the thermals as the road undulated through the rocky terrain and man-made valleys cut through hard sand-coloured rock. Up on the dry barren hillside and overlooking the sea, several wind turbines were barely moving in the light evening breeze.

As they left the motorway and passed through numerous small villages, Nathan dared to open his window and contaminate their air-conditioned bubble. The humid air had a floral scent with a hint of pine, indicating that they had now travelled inland and away from the salty-aired coast. As they cut across the south-eastern horn of Cyprus they passed the town of Palakori. A short while later they arrived at Anapetri Villa.

Nathan got out of the car and opened two wrought-iron gates. Loretta drove through and Nathan asked her to stop so he could close them behind her. 'You could have left them open,' she said as he jumped back in.

'Force of habit,' he replied.

Anapetri Villa was a very appealing building. It was finished in a terracotta cement render with white metal window frames and timber doors. A good-sized two-storey house with a garage to the side and a red tiled roof, it was surrounded by huge palm trees, with the occasional clump of highly scented purple-pink bougainvillea intermixed with the occasional prickly pear cactus.

They pulled up outside the garage and Loretta went over to a small key safe, which was partly hidden behind a downpipe. She twisted the wheels to a four-digit code and the small door sprung open to reveal a bunch of keys. She took them out, closed the key safe and went to open the front door. They carried their luggage into the house.

It was absolutely stifling inside so Loretta ran around switching on all the air conditioning units downstairs. 'Let's take our luggage straight up,' she said.

As they walked up the stairs it became even warmer. Loretta rushed into the master bedroom and switched on the air conditioning unit, then they began to unpack. When they had finished, they both flopped on to the bed. The room was nice and cool now and they both lay there as the feeling of jet lag swept over them.

'We can't go to bed yet, as tired as we are,' Nathan said. 'We must get into the routine and establish a normal sleep pattern. Show me around the house and gardens.'

'Okay, I will but, if you don't mind, I'm just going in the shower to freshen up,' Loretta replied.

While she was in the en-suite shower, Nathan thought about joining her but he didn't know whether she had locked the door or not when she went in. Then, as he was thinking about whether she would appreciate him barging in on her, he fell asleep.

Ten minutes later he was awoken with a start as Loretta was wringing the water out of her hair on to his face. He took hold of her firmly and pulled her towards him. All she was wearing was a damp towel. Nathan's hands began to wander.

'Now don't be getting any ideas. You have a shower and I'll go and pour some wine,' said Loretta.

'Okay,' he replied.

After his shower Nathan joined Loretta, who was out on the patio. The light was fading now but she was lying on a sunbed in a bikini. The backdrop was the infinity swimming pool. The image of the pool and the sea laid out beyond, plus the endless mass of water, was a sight to behold. It was striking, and so was Loretta. Nathan joined her, wearing his flip-flops, shorts and T-shirt. She handed him a large glass of red wine. He took a sip and thought it was the best wine he had ever tasted. A couple of hours later and the jet lag had got the better of them, so they called it a day.

The following day they were both up by 9.30am and, although not fully recovered from their travels, were feeling much better. Loretta gave Nathan a guided tour of the house prior to them going for a walk to the village before it got too hot. He was fascinated by the small village church, which was just how he had viewed it on the internet, but the smell and the atmosphere was something that the internet could never replicate. They made their way back to the villa.

'Shall we go down to the beach?' said Loretta.

'Yes, that would be great.'

They walked past the swimming pool, where the land noticeably but gradually fell away for about one hundred metres. Suddenly they were at a cliff edge looking down on the beach. The views were spectacular, the sea turquoise blue and the sun directly ahead of them. Nathan peered down over the edge of the cliff face. There was a drop of about fifty metres, then a small cove of white sand. It was spectacularly beautiful.

'This way,' said Loretta, taking Nathan by the hand. There was a timber staircase that zig-zagged from the top cliff edge right the way down to the beach.

'Wow, this is handy,' said Nathan.

'Yes, my dad had it built many years ago.'

'So, it's a private beach.'

'Sort of. The only way to get to it is either by boat or down this staircase. The locals can have access to it if they want but it very rarely gets used.'

Nathan was wearing swim shorts with his T-shirt, so as they finally reached the beach, he pulled off his shirt, kicked off his flip-flops and ran into the sea. The depth was shallow, with a fine gradient to deeper water. The sand was soft under his feet and there were small fish swimming around, which swam away as soon as he approached. He walked into an area where the water was significantly warmer, so he bent his knees to submerge his chest, shoulders and head. He resurfaced, swimming on his back, shouting for Loretta to join him.

'I haven't got my costume on,' she replied from the beach, hands on her hips.

Feeling suitably refreshed, Nathan swam back towards the beach until he had to stand. Loretta admired his fine muscular physique as he left the water and walked towards her.

'That was so refreshing,' he said, as he brushed his blonde hair back from his face with his hands.

'I'm sure. I take it that you like it here then.'

Nathan looked around and outstretched his arms. 'This is paradise, what more could I want? I have a beautiful location and a beautiful woman.'

Loretta put her arms around Nathan's neck and kissed him passionately. As he tried to pull her closer, she squealed, shouting, 'No, you're cold and wet,' and pushed him back.

He picked up his T-shirt and walked hand in hand with her from one end of the cove to the other. 'This is so private, it's priceless,' he said.

'I know, I think that's why Mum and Dad don't want to sell it; it really is an escape when they come here.'

'It's hard to believe that just forty-odd years ago this little island was at war and one of the main victims of that was the holiday resort of Varosha. It's such a shame that it's remained cordoned off to the public ever since; it's only a couple of miles north of here,' said Nathan.

'I know, incredibly sad. I heard that someone had recently compared it to Pripyat, the town next to Chernobyl. I think what they were saying was that nature was reclaiming both towns.'

'Yes, I noticed on Google Earth,' he replied.

'Come on, I'll make us some sandwiches for lunch,' Loretta said.

They made their way back to the villa. In passing, Nathan decided to dive in the pool, then realised he needed a change of shorts and T-shirt for lunch. As he walked through the hall, he noticed an envelope sticking through the letter box. He grabbed it and took it to the kitchen for Loretta, before running upstairs for a quick shower and change.

Loretta opened the envelope. It contained a handwritten letter from Andreas Polycarpou, one of the tenant farmers, who had a house and smallholding on Anapetri Villa land. Attached to the letter was a formal typed letter from the Municipal District Administration of Palakori and a photocopy of a proposed plan to turn Anapetri Villa, its land and its resident farmers into one big landfill site.

Loretta's heart sank and she walked into the lounge and sat down. She looked at the handwritten letter. Andreas was asking for a residents' meeting at the bar in the village at seven that evening and he had written down his contact telephone number. She put his note to one side and started reading the official letter just as Nathan appeared, freshly clothed after his shower. He could see by the expression on Loretta's face that all was not well.

'Is something wrong Loretta?'

'Yes, I can't believe it. This is a letter from the local council saying that an application has been made to turn Anapetri Villa, its land and houses into a landfill site. They go on to say that because the land or property appears to have had no legal ownership rights issued, they've set in motion a process of compulsory reclamation and even had the cheek to forward a plan of what they're going to do with the land. They're going to turn it into, in lay terms, a rubbish dump, a tip, Nathan; of all things, a tip.' She looked up and Nathan could see she had fire in her eyes. 'Over my dead body,' she said with determination.

'Can I see,' said Nathan. She handed over the documents. Nathan had a quick look through. 'This is pretty devastating. I mean, what do they mean, no legal ownership? Surely that can't be the case. I'm sure your dad will have rights of ownership documentation.'

'He will have. I need to speak to him.'

'What's the time difference between here and New Zealand?' asked Nathan.

'I'm not sure. They're ten hours ahead maybe.' She looked at her watch. 'So it will be nearly eleven-thirty at night. They'll be in bed by now and probably asleep.'

'Then let's leave it until later tonight and call him after this meeting, which I presume we'll be attending?'

'Yes, we need to find out as much as we can about what's been going on,' said Loretta.

'Who's Andreas Polycarpou, by the way?'

'He's one of the tenant farmers. He was the one that spoke to Dad last week. He must be the designated spokesperson for the group.'

Nathan could see that Loretta still had that look of fire in her eyes, a look of steel and determination but also with a hint of concern.

'You know, I remember Mum telling me that Dad bought the land after the Turkish occupation. Although he lost several shops in Varosha when the town was partitioned, I remember her saying he wanted a piece of land for the family, just on the Greek side of the green line. He was adamant that Southern Cyprus would remain Greek, so he built Anapetri Villa on this huge piece of land. He was so upset by the number of Greeks who had lost their homes and their livelihoods, which they just had to leave behind to the Turks, that he decided to try to help some of them out. He had fourteen houses built, with their own farming plots, and he rented them out to displaced families all at a favourable rate. The rate today I believe is something like thirty per cent lower than the going rate. You can imagine the properties are sought-after and never vacant. Numerous families have been raised in those houses and a lot have remained and never lived anywhere else.'

'And what do the farmers grow?' asked Nathan.

'From memory, pomegranates, oranges, lemons, limes, grapes, strawberries, artichokes, onions, butternut squash. They formed a cooperative and all their products are sold at the local markets. These people survive off the land and, even in the winter months, they sell marmalade, different jams and wine.'

'So, we're talking about fourteen households with families and all of their livelihoods.'

'Correct,' said Loretta, now with a tear in her eye. 'And we're responsible for all of it. It's Dad's legacy, so we've got to stop this landfill from going ahead.'

Nathan walked up to Loretta and hugged her. As he did, he talked quietly in her ear. 'Please don't get upset but let's try to formulate a plan of action.'

'Yes, I agree, we mustn't let our emotions take over. So, we have the tenants meeting tonight. We need to find out as much about the landfill proposal as possible.'

'Yes,' agreed Nathan. 'We also need any names and contact numbers at the council so we can lobby them if we need to, and details of the local MP or whatever the equivalent is called over here. What about a solicitor, Loretta? Who does your dad use in Cyprus?'

'Off the top of my head, I don't know, but in the master bedroom there's a wall safe behind a mirror.' Loretta picked up the villa keys from the kitchen unit. 'I'd like to bet that one of these keys fits it. There could be some documentation in there.'

'Okay, let's have a look.' They both walked up the stairs and into the master bedroom. They were standing in front of a large rectangular frameless mirror. 'How does it come off?' said Nathan.

'It will just unhook but it's heavy.'

Nathan grabbed each side of the mirror and raised it slightly to lift it off the bracket. It came away quite easily and he placed it to one side, leaning against the wall. The space revealed a small metal door with a keyhole, which was flush to the wall.

Loretta was fumbling with the bunch of keys before selecting one. 'I think it's this one,' she said, inserting it into the lock, turning it and opening the door. There did appear to be several documents in the safe. She grabbed them all and sat down on the bed and started to sift through them. Nathan sat next to her but left a distance between them so as not to appear too intrusive should any private documentation come to light.

There were several receipts, for jewellery and from the housekeeper, there were invoices from the pool attendant and the gardener. Loretta opened a large manilla envelope and pulled out the contents. The covering letter was from a solicitor in Nicosia regarding the possible purchase of land in Paphos. 'Bingo,' she said. 'He has a solicitor in Nicosia.'

She passed the letter over to Nathan. 'Yes, this looks promising and it's to do with land too,' he said.

'I'll give them a call now,' Loretta suggested, so they went down into the kitchen to use the land line and she made the call to Dimitri Stakis Associates. Then, inconveniently, the front doorbell rang just as she started to speak. Nathan made his way to the door and, when he opened it, there was a tall Cypriot-looking man about Nathan's age with a concerned look on his face. He was wearing a black sweat-stained T-shirt, light-blue denims and workman's boots.

'Can I help you?' said Nathan.

'Yes, hello, my name is Andreas. Would it be possible to speak to Miss Mykanos please?' he said in heavily accented English.

'I'm sorry, she's on the telephone at the moment. I'm her partner. Can I help?' As soon as Nathan said it, he wondered whether that was the right thing to say. He supposed they were partners but, because they didn't live together or work together, he wasn't sure.

'It is about the meeting tonight. I was just wanting to make sure that you had received my note,' said Andreas.

'Yes, we have, and we'll be there. I'm pleased to meet you Andreas. My name is Nathan.' The two men shook hands.

'All of my neighbours are very upset; their futures are now uncertain after all these years.'

'We understand and we're working on it now. We look forward to seeing you all later,' said Nathan.

'Okay goodbye, we'll see you later,' said Andreas, and he walked away.

Nathan walked back into the kitchen just as Loretta hung up. 'What did you find out?' he asked.

Loretta looking relieved puffed out her cheeks. 'Yes, they're a solicitor for the Mykanos Group, one of many, no doubt. The lady I spoke to said she does recall documentation relating to Anapetri Villa. She said she'll go into the archives, because a lot of their documentation still remains unscanned. I'm booked in for a 10.30am appointment tomorrow and I have to take identification. They also need written confirmation from Dad saying that I'm taking control of the group.'

'Well, when you speak to your dad, ask him to get his solicitor in Auckland to email the one in Nicosia. What are they called?'

'Dimitri Stakis Associates,' replied Loretta. 'And yes, you're right, that would be the quickest and correct way to do it. Will you come with me?'

'Of course I will. We're partners, didn't you know?'

'No, not until now,' she replied.

'Well, that's what I just told the guy at the door.'

'Who was it?'

'Andreas, one of the farmers, just making sure that we're going tonight.'

'We've got to reassure them that everything will be all right once we've located the ownership documents, and I think we should hold fire on contacting the council until we have the relevant documents.'

'I agree, but did you say *we've* got to reassure them?'

'Yes, you did after all tell Andreas that we were partners,' she said, with a knowing smile. 'Now you have to perform the role.'

'That sounds a bit demanding Miss Mykanos.'

'It could be, and I hope that you're up to it.'

'I think you'll find that I'm fit for purpose Miss Mykanos.'

'Stop calling me miss; that's what the locals call me,' she said, looking offended.

'Okay, I'm sorry,' he said as he leaned over and gave her a kiss.

'Right, I'm going to make some sandwiches. Let's eat outside,' she said.

'Okay, I'll get the table ready; shall we have some of that gorgeous red wine?'

'You can. I'll just have some flavoured water with a slice of lemon,' she replied.

That afternoon they talked, then went for a swim in the sea, before returning to the villa for cold drinks. Nathan could see that Loretta was concerned and he suspected it was about the upcoming meeting.

~~~

That evening they walked up to the local bar in the village. As they approached, they could see a large group of people outside, all sat together around several tables. It looked like a pavement café and had a beautiful overhead pergola covered in vines with huge bunches of red grapes dangling down at random. There were people smoking, drinking tea and coffee. Some of the men were drinking beer out of bottles. Children were playing joyfully in the square as a little dog ran around after them yapping to its heart's content.

As they got closer, Andreas suddenly appeared and pulled out a couple of chairs from the throng of people. That's when Nathan and Loretta realised that all the people sat outside were the tenant farmers. Andreas positioned the chairs against the wall of the building, facing the others. Nathan felt as if they were being put up against the wall to be executed.

'Welcome Miss Mykanos and Nathan,' said Andreas, gesticulating towards the people sat in front of them. 'These are the Anapetri tenant farmers.' There was complete silence.

Loretta stood up and introduced herself. 'I'm Loretta Mykanos and, please, I insist that from now on there's no more Miss Mykanos, please call me Loretta.'

'Ms Mykanos, we're very concerned. Have you seen the letter from the council?' stated a man from within the group.

'Yes, I have, and I'm as shocked as you are.'

Andreas suddenly reappeared and presented Loretta and Nathan with a glass of red wine each before pulling a chair over to join the group. Loretta decided to sit down, as she didn't feel right standing in front of them as if asking for servitude.

Nathan eyed the group. These were obviously industrious people, the majority of whom appeared to be mid-thirties to mid-forties, with the occasional elderly couple. It was one of the elderly men who stood up next to speak. He spoke slowly with a heavily accented voice.

'My dear Ms Mykanos, I know your father very well and there is many a time we have spent up at this bar drinking wine and putting the world to rights. Knowing the man that he is, he will be very upset to hear of the proposed plans. He built the houses for displaced Greek tenant farmers, out of the goodness of his heart. People were homeless, destitute. Your father saved fourteen families. Please, please do not abandon us now.' He sat down and the group of people around him cheered and patted him on his back. Loretta cleared her throat.

'We're not abandoning anybody. Please remember that our family home, the villa, is also part of this landfill site plan.'

A younger man spoke out this time. 'How can they make a compulsory reclamation when you are the rightful owners of the land?'

'First of all, I would like to confirm that we are the rightful owners of the land and, under Cypriot law, they can't take the land without giving us the going rate for it and everything upon it.'

The young man persisted. 'So, if you prove that you are the rightful owner of the land, are you going to sell?'

'Definitely not. Everything will remain the same.'

This time a woman, who had a small girl on her knee, put up her hand and at the same time said, 'Ms Mykanos, on the papers we have received, the council have said that the land is without an owner. Can you explain what that means, if you say you are the legal owner?'

'I can only assume that the council has been unable to locate any records of the land belonging to our family. You have to remember that the land was purchased just after the war, when the green line was instigated, so I can only think that the records of ownership were displaced. We're in the process of trying to locate them,' said Loretta.

At this point, Andreas intervened. 'Ms Mykanos, if the documents that you are referring to are lost, our livelihoods will be gone and we will all be homeless. I understand that you could lose the villa and the land but, respectfully, you are a very wealthy family and this would not be a significant loss for you.'

'You're correct in one sense,' replied Loretta. There were a few gasps from the group. 'The financial loss to the family would be one that we could handle but what I couldn't handle is the thought of good, hard-working families losing everything, everything that my father had provided in the first place. So, my message to you is that the last thing I want for any of you is to suffer and, believe me, we'll do our very best to make sure that your families and work lives continue uninterrupted.'

'Is there anything that we as a group can do, or maybe I can help in some way?' asked Andreas.

'At this point can you please leave it with us. If you don't mind being the go-between Andreas, then if there are any developments, I can forward them to you for distribution among the group. We have a meeting in the morning with our solicitors in Nicosia. We're hoping that they'll confirm that they have the land deeds and then we'll ask them to act on our behalf and deal with the council to get this action dropped once and for all.'

Andreas stood up and asked, 'Does anyone have any further questions?' The younger woman who spoke earlier raised her hand.

'Yes?' said Lorretta.

'Please, Ms Mykanos, try your hardest. None of us wants to be out on the streets with no money and with children to feed. I have been unable to sleep since we found out about the proposals for the landfill site, so I beg you, please.' Tears rolled down the woman's face as she was comforted by her child and neighbours.

Loretta walked over and crouched down in front of her. She took hold of the woman's hands. 'I assure you I'll do my very best.'

The weeping woman leaned forwards and hugged Loretta. 'Thank you, and thank you from all of us. We trust you Ms Mykanos, we trust you.' The three words 'we trust you' weighed heavily on Loretta and she was unable to stop a tear from appearing in her eye.

There were more questions and answers but all in all the meeting went as well as it could have. There were some very upset people who just walked away before the meeting had concluded. The majority were hoping and praying that the council's action to reclaim the land would be defeated once it came to light that the Mykanos family had documentary evidence that it was the lawful owner.

Andreas invited Nathan and Loretta to walk to his house to see what he was growing. Nathan thought this was a good idea. If this was going to be a protracted affair, it was important to know the subjects at the heart of the matter. Loretta hoped that she had made it clear that this was about the people and their livelihoods, not the Mykanos's land and villa.

The three of them walked up a slight incline as they left the village square. It was a lovely evening and the light was starting to fade. Swallows dipped and dived above their heads, picking up the last of the evening's flying insects before darkness. They were on a narrow dusty road that was patterned with the colours of different fruit that had fallen from the low trees on either side of the road and been crushed by passing vehicles.

Ahead of them was a long stretch of seventies-built houses. They were all the same structurally but they had different coloured doors and rendering. These were the tenant farmers' homes. It was very quiet. In the background there was music coming from one of the houses but it was nearly drowned out by the noise of the cicadas clicking away like crickets in the roadside trees and shrubs.

It was still very warm, with no breeze. Nathan could feel beads of sweat beginning to form on his forehead. He looked at Loretta, who looked cool and in control, but he could tell that she was concerned. The weight of responsibility sat heavily on her shoulders.

'This is mine. Please come in,' said Andreas.

They walked through a small, gated garden to the front door. Andreas pushed the door open and they passed through an entrance hall and into the lounge. It was sparsely decorated, with little furniture, but was clean and tidy. They walked through into the kitchen.

'This is my wife, Helena, and my baby boy George.'

Helena was discreetly breast-feeding George. 'Hello, I am afraid I am a little busy at the moment,' she said.

'Don't mind us. Andreas is going to show us around your plot. I'm Nathan and this is my partner, Loretta Mykanos.'

'Hello Ms Mykanos, it is very good of you to come around and see us.'

'Please call me Loretta.'

'And please call me Nathan.'

'I will pour you both some wine when you are ready,' said Helena.

'That's very kind,' said Loretta as they followed Andreas out to the rear of the house. They stepped through the rear door on to a small patio area. Ahead of them were four straight lines of trees, all heavily burdened with fruit. To the left were oranges and to the right limes.

'This is fantastic. I've never seen trees with so much fruit. What's the secret?' Loretta asked.

'Follow me,' said Andreas.

They walked into the orchards on a pathway that separated the oranges from the limes. Andreas bent down and picked up a handful of soil from beneath a tree. 'When Mr Mykanos bought this land, he must have known it was probably the most fertile on all the island.' He opened his hand and Nathan, and Loretta took a closer look in the fading light. 'If you have fertile soil and you mix it with the mulch of the leaves created by the soil, you double its fertility.'

'Are you serious Andreas?' said Nathan.

Andreas just opened his arms, smiled and said, 'Look around you. The proof is on the branches, it works. This is the most fertile soil in Cyprus, which is why we are all able to live off the land. We can collectively make enough money to see us through the winter months until the spring, then the fruit starts to grow again. Follow me.'

They walked back towards the house. At some point a staircase had been fitted to the rear of the house, leading up to a small wooden terrace. There was also access to the main bedroom from the terrace. The three of them climbed the stairs and they had a spectacular view. The sun was about to go down but what little light was left in the sky enabled them to see across the adjacent tenants' plots towards the sea.

'It's like as oasis,' said Loretta. 'All the different-coloured orchards.'

'It is beautiful, I know. We are very lucky. If you look straight ahead past our orchards you will see the roof of Anapetri Villa.'

The villa could be seen through the trees that surrounded it. It was illuminated by a dim yellow light that came on when darkness fell.

'You really get the scale of how big this plot of land is from this aspect,' said Loretta. 'Thank you Andreas, for showing us around.'

'It is my pleasure. Please come down and have a glass of wine before you leave.'

The three of them joined Helena, who was in the lounge with a bottle of red wine and four small wine glasses. She poured each of them a glass and handed them out. 'Yamas!' she said. 'Yamas!' they all replied.

After twenty minutes of small talk Nathan could see that Loretta was looking as if she had other things on her mind and he knew she was desperate to speak to her father. He therefore promised to keep Andreas informed and they thanked their hosts for their hospitality and wine. After hugs, kisses and the shaking of hands, Nathan and Loretta started to make their way back to the villa.

The narrow road was poorly lit and, in between street-lamps, they relied upon the moon to illuminate their way. Walking hand in hand, Nathan suddenly stopped and turned towards Loretta. He kissed her passionately on the lips.

'What was that for?' she asked.

'Because I thought you deserved it after the meeting earlier. That wasn't an easy situation to be in,' said Nathan.

'Thank you for being by my side,' she replied with a smile, then returned the kiss.

When they arrived back at the villa, Nathan decided he was going to have a swim while Loretta went to call her father. He changed into his swimming shorts and he could hear Loretta speaking to her dad as he dived into the pool. A few minutes later she came out on to the patio area, still on the telephone. Nathan climbed out of the pool and joined her on an adjacent sun lounger.

'So, are you sure Dad? Okay, we have a meeting at their office in the morning, so I'll let you know how it goes. Okay, thanks Dad, love you too.' Loretta hung up.

'What did he say?'

'Well, he's pretty upset about the whole thing. In fact, he was more annoyed than I've heard him for many a year. He doesn't sound too well. His voice is very throaty, like he has a bad chest. Anyway, he said Stakis Associates will be in possession of all the documents relating to the purchase of this land, the building of the villa and all the houses. He's going to notify the solicitors in Auckland to inform Stakis that I'm now in control of the company. He's also asked me to employ them to act on our behalf and to deal with the council's attempt at the compulsory reclamation of the land.'

'Do you feel a bit better now?' asked Nathan.

'Yes, I do. When he said that Stakis will be in possession of all the documents, what a relief. It's debatable whether or not we need to go there for the meeting. I could instruct them over the telephone.'

'Yes, you could, but I think it would be a good idea to get copies of all the relevant documentation for our records. And you did say you wanted to go shopping in Nicosia,' said Nathan.

'Yes, you're right. We'll leave at nine in the morning.'

4

THE FOLLOWING morning, Loretta and Nathan reached Nicosia early for their ten-thirty meeting, so they visited a small coffee shop just around the corner from the solicitor's office. After two coffees and a shared Danish pastry, they made their way to the office. The building was nothing special from the outside, made from local stone and with a front door that looked as if it had been upcycled from the local jail.

Loretta pushed the doorbell. A lady answered the intercom in Greek and Loretta said, 'It's Miss Mykanos for a ten-thirty appointment.'

Nathan elbowed her and pointed to her face, smiling. 'You just said Miss Mykanos. I thought you hated that.'

'I do, but now I'm on official company business,' said Loretta with a wink.

The receptionist spoke in English this time. 'Yes, please come in.'

The electric lock buzzed and Loretta pushed the door open. They walked into the entrance lobby, where a sign on the wall directed them to the first floor. They ascended a grubby staircase to a landing area, where there was a door with an elegant, polished brass sign, which read Dimitri Stakis Associates. Loretta opened the door and Nathan followed her in. There was a small reception desk with an attractive young receptionist with long raven-black hair, who welcomed them: 'Good morning.'

'Good morning,' replied Loretta.

'I will take you through to Mr Stakis,' the receptionist said, rising from her chair. 'Please follow me. Can I get you a drink?'

'A sparkling water please,' said Loretta.

'Same for me,' added Nathan.

They walked into a quite large room, very brightly decorated with white vertical blinds that fluttered in front of the open windows. The room was surprisingly cool.

'Good morning, Miss Mykanos,' said the man behind a large mahogany-coloured desk. He stood up and offered his hand. Quite elderly in appearance, he looked to be in his early sixties and had thinning black hair.

'Good morning Mr Stakis, this is my partner Nathan,' Loretta replied, shaking his hand.

'Good morning and welcome,' Mr Stakis said, shaking Nathan's hand. 'Please take a seat. First of all, I would like to congratulate you, Miss Mykanos.'

'Please call me Loretta.'

'I will if you call me Dimitri.'

'Of course,' she replied.

'I understand that you have taken over the Mykanos group of companies. I received an email from your solicitors in Auckland.'

'Yes, that's correct. I'm planning a strategy of visiting all our business interests with the help of Nathan. I think my father may have neglected several of our national managers and I believe he's been waiting for the right time for me to take over. I'm planning to inject some new impetus and ideas and to reconnect with all our employees at some level.'

'This is good news,' said Dimitri. 'So I take it that people who are employed by your group need not fear for their job security. People are worried in these difficult times.'

'No, any business that's producing the right percentage profit-wise should be encouraged and conditions improved in appreciation,' replied Loretta with confidence and authority.

'How many business premises do you have in Cyprus?' asked Dimitri.

Loretta had a slightly puzzled look. 'You're testing me, Dimitri.'

'I don't know what you mean,' he said with a smile.

'You're trying to establish whether we have any businesses in Cyprus that you don't know about and whether we could be using another solicitor.'

'Not at all,' he replied, still smiling. 'You are very shrewd but at some point in the past I am sure your father may have dabbled with another solicitor.'

'Not that I'm aware of. You're our only solicitor in Cyprus and that's the way I want it to remain,' said Loretta.

'Thank you, your business is greatly appreciated. Now my assistant informs me that you are wanting to look at all the documents relating to your land at Anapetri,' said Dimitri.

'Yes, that's correct.'

'This morning she brought the last of them up from the archives. They are in the two boxes on the shelf there.' Dimitri stood up and took the boxes from the shelf, placing them on the table in front of them. Now these documents are from the seventies, so they are not yet scanned on to our system, but I do have a headline list of what the boxes contain.' He started to tap the keyboard of his computer.

'Okay … Anapetri,' Dimitri continued. 'So, we have fourteen sets of plans or drawings for individual farm lets. Fourteen sets of original lease documents. Fourteen certificates of registration or, in other words, title deeds for the property. So, it looks as if we have all the documentation to the fourteen lets on your land.'

'Do you have the documents relating to the villa and the purchase of the land?' piped up Nathan.

Dimitri looked as if he was scrolling down a list. 'No, I can't see anything relating to the land and, come to think of it, I do not remember ever seeing anything relating to the purchase of the land or any plans or approvals for the villa.'

The receptionist interrupted Dimitri as she entered with a tray that held three glasses of water and passed them around.

'It may be a good idea if we had a quick look through … erm, Maria, will you please go through these boxes and see if you can find any documentation relating to the purchase of the land at Anapetri and the construction of Anapetri Villa.'

'Yes, of course,' Maria replied. 'It should not take too long. There are just fourteen envelopes and some loose documents.' She placed her empty tray on top of the boxes and carried them out of the room.

'It is very strange that I do not recall seeing anything relating to the villa,' said Dimitri. 'You know the early seventies was a very difficult time here in Cyprus. When the Turks invaded there were many of us Greek Cypriots that were displaced and lost a lot of land.'

'That's why he bought the land in the first place. It wasn't just for a home, it was to help people who were displaced,' said Nathan.

'That's right,' confirmed Loretta. 'The idea was to hand the farm lets out to people who had lost their livelihoods so that they could start again, and they'd be charged below the going rate.'

'I will be quite honest with you; I have a had a quick look into one of the boxes and I noticed that Mr Mykanos has stated that the rent rate should always remain thirty per cent below the going rate at any given time. I think from other things that I know about him, there is one word to explain him ... I think the word is a philanthropist.'

'Well, I never thought of him like that but, yes, I suppose he is,' Loretta agreed. 'But it does bring me on to the question in hand. These fourteen families, Anapetri Villa and all the land that they stand upon is now under threat. I'll email you a copy of the letter from the local council but, in a nutshell, they want to make a compulsory reclamation of the whole plot on the basis that it's not under lawful ownership. They have no record of a land purchase and no certificates of registration of immovable property known as the title deeds,' said Loretta, with passion.

'And to add insult to injury, they want to turn it all into a landfill site,' added Nathan.

Dimitri's demeanour changed upon hearing this news and his mood seemed to darken. 'Which council is this?' he asked.

'It's the Municipal District Administration of Palakori,' said Nathan.

Dimitri got up from his chair and walked over to one of the windows. He pulled one of the cords, which retracted the vertical blinds to reveal a view over the city. 'You know, about a half a mile from here is the Turkish border. Their actions on invading this country can never be condoned but neither can our actions and the way that some of the Turks were treated. The Turkish troops were coming to liberate their people. Sorry, I am procrastinating. What I am trying to say is that sometimes the enemy is within, and this is such a case. I presume that you want me to act on your behalf to try to stop this diabolical act from proceeding.'

'Yes, it must be stopped at all costs,' said Loretta.

'Then we must locate the proof of ownership documentation. Please excuse me a second.' Dimitri walked out of the room to speak to his receptionist.

Loretta turned to Nathan. 'Thanks for being here with me. I really appreciate your support; it gives me strength.'

'You don't need my support, you're a brilliant business-woman but, having said that, I'll always be by your side as long as you want me.'

'I want you; we're a formidable partnership, you and I, and you're just as passionate about this land as I am.'

'I must admit the whole concept of the farm lets, about how and why it was set up, is really appealing, and the fact that it's been working for over forty-five years is phenomenal,' said Nathan.

'We have to fight for the land and the families,' Loretta replied.

'And we will.'

Dimitri returned and closed the door behind him. 'My assistant has been through our records. There is nothing relating to the land purchase.' He sat down behind his desk.

'I'm wondering whether he may have used the solicitor in New Zealand,' suggested Nathan.

'I don't think so. I don't think we had a solicitor in New Zealand then,' said Loretta. 'I might be wrong but I think the home in New Zealand was purchased several years after the land at Anapetri. The thing is, I'm not sure. I'm going to have to call him, so I'm going to do it now as it's not too late there.'

'Okay. If you don't mind, can I have a look in the boxes with your assistant?' Nathan asked Dimitri.

'Yes, please come with me. We will leave Loretta to her phone call.'

Nathan followed Dimitri out of the office and into a small boardroom at the rear of reception. The assistant looked as if she had just put the lid on the second box as they walked in.

'Maria, have you had any luck?' Dimitri asked.

'No, I am afraid not. These documents all relate to the fourteen properties.'

'Dimitri, do you mind if I take a quick look through just so I can familiarise myself with what's in each docket,' said Nathan.

'Please go ahead.'

Nathan pulled out one of the envelopes, opened it and spread the documents out on the desk. There was a plan drawing of the house and land. There was a more detailed plan of the house, including room dimensions, windows and door sizes and locations. There was an inventory of the fitted specification, covering items such as foundations and framework, wall plaster, walls, rendering, internal and external doors, kitchen cabinets, bedroom cupboards, floor and wall tiles, paint, sanitary fittings, wiring, plumbing, water supplies, boundary walls and driveway. There was a quantity of documents that were typed in Greek and marked with a very official-looking stamp. There were documents from the builder. Agreements with the builder. Purchase price of the house. Delivery documentation. Title deeds for the property. And lease documentation between the Mykanos Group and current occupants.

'That is what is replicated in each envelope. I have found nothing else,' said Maria.

'Okay, thank you,' said Nathan, as he walked back into the office with Dimitri.

Loretta was still on the phone, speaking to her mother. 'If he remembers or you find out anything, please call me straight back. Love you too, bye Mum.'

She ended the call and looked quite concerned. 'Dad hasn't been very well; he keeps complaining about headaches and Mum said he's got memory issues. This may be the reason he's handed everything over to me so suddenly. I knew there was something wrong. I should have stayed at home.'

'Your dad is in good hands Loretta,' Nathan assured her. 'He'll still be there when we get back. It's important that we sort out this problem while we're here. Did he mention where the documents are for Anapetri?'

'No, he said he thought they were all here with Stakis Associates. He said he needs to think and then he'll get back to me.'

'I am sorry to hear that your father is unwell,' said Dimitri. 'But this confirms my theory that at some point he has had another solicitor here in Cyprus and the documents will be lodged with them.'

'Well, I hope he remembers, as there's so much at stake,' Loretta replied.

'Loretta and Nathan, I propose that I put Maria to work on contacting as many solicitors on the island as possible to locate these files. I will do this free of charge, and please inform your father that I wish him well.'

'That's very kind of you,' said Loretta.

'In the meantime, can you please keep me informed? I will not be making any approach to the council without the relevant documents. We will, as you say, not have a leg to stand on.' Dimitri shook hands with both Loretta and Nathan and they exchanged pleasantries.

Loretta and Nathan left the office and, as they walked outside into the bright hot sunshine, Loretta took hold of Nathan's hand. 'Let's take a walk around the shops while we're here. Don't forget, we're on holiday … well, a working holiday.'

'That's fine by me,' said Nathan.

'I knew Dad wasn't well, you know. I could tell he was putting on a brave face at our last meeting, and this sudden decision to hand everything over to me …'

'I don't want to sound too harsh but, if your dad is ill, then surely he's doing the right thing passing everything over while he still has his faculties, so to speak.'

'Yes, you're right. It's just that I've never known him to be ill before. He's always been so healthy and fit. All this anxiety won't be helping him either. I hope Stakis finds out where all the documents are so we can start defending our corner.'

They walked down a street that was gradually becoming populated with shops instead of office premises.

'Shall we have an early lunch?' said Nathan.

'Yes, but first of all there's a shop I'd like to visit.'

'Okay,' said Nathan.

They crossed over the road and walked past a coffee shop, with tables protected by parasols. The tables were occupied by groups of Cypriot men, who appeared to be playing dominoes, smoking and drinking strong black coffee.

'It's just here on the left,' Loretta said.

Nathan looked at the sign above the shop, which read 'Mykanos Jewellers'.

'Don't say anything,' Loretta said as they walked in via a small, windowed corridor with displays of silver and gold bracelets, rings and necklaces. The shop was air-conditioned and a refreshing break from the growing heat outside. There was a woman and a young female assistant behind a long, glass display counter.

'Kalimera,' said the older of the two.

'Good morning,' replied Loretta and Nathan in unison.

'Is there anything I can help you with?' the lady asked.

'Do you mind if we just have a look around?' said Loretta.

'Not at all. Please let me know if you find anything of interest,' said the lady, smiling.

Loretta was looking at the displays and the quality and price of what was on offer. Nathan was looking at the cleanliness of the shop, how it was laid out and whether there were any CCTV cameras on show. He walked over to Loretta and stooped over to whisper in her ear. 'Perhaps this isn't very fair, being a secret shopper. Perhaps you should let them know that you're the owner.'

'I agree. I will in a moment but I rather like that gold pendant.' She was pointing at a small gold teardrop-shaped pendant that appeared to have a small diamond mounted at its base.

'Yes, it's very petite,' said Nathan. 'It would suit you.'

Loretta turned to the shop assistant. 'Could I possibly have a closer look at this please?'

The younger assistant came over with a set of keys, opened the display cabinet and handed Loretta the pendant. The older lady suddenly appeared next to her. 'It's very pretty, isn't it,' she said.

'It's absolutely beautiful,' replied Loretta.

'We also have it in platinum or silver,' replied the younger assistant.

'Oh, but I do love it in this colour gold. It's not too yellow, just how I like it.'

'Then please let me buy it for you,' said Nathan with a smile.

'Oh, would you? That would be lovely, thank you.' Loretta handed the charm back to the young assistant, who moved back behind the counter with her colleague. Loretta mouthed the words 'thank you' to Nathan, then kissed him on the lips.

'It's my pleasure, and a token of my appreciation for organising this holiday,' said Nathan.

They walked over to the counter by the till and Loretta said to the young assistant, 'Can I ask, do you enjoy working here?'

The girl looked a bit perplexed, before replying, 'Oh, very much so. The majority of work around here is in retail, and if you are lucky enough to get a job in a jewellers, you are at the top of the tree,' she said with pride.

The older lady intervened. 'I think we are lucky to be working for such a good employer. They are nationwide and employ lots of people, so you do have a feeling of stability.'

Nathan presented his card for payment and entered his pin number into the card machine.

'I should probably have told you earlier,' said Loretta, 'but my name is Loretta Mykanos, and this is my partner, Nathan Mason. I'm the owner of Mykanos jewellers.'

The two stood there open-mouthed, before the lady, who was starting to lose her composure, said, 'Can I get you some coffee or cold drinks? I am sorry, I did not realise. Can I ask how Mr Mykanos is. He used to make a point of visiting us whenever he was in Cyprus.'

'No, we're fine for drinks. It's just a quick visit, and my father is well, just getting older. Do you see much of your national manager, Aris?'

'Yes, he usually visits a couple of times per week and we speak on a daily basis. He is based at the other shop just around the corner. I am sure he will be delighted to meet you.'

'I'll catch him again in the next couple of weeks. This is just a quick visit to Nicosia. We're actually here on holiday.'

'Well, I hope you are enjoying your stay.'

'Yes, thank you,' replied Loretta.

The younger shop assistant handed Nathan his credit card when the payment had gone through. She then passed him the necklace box, which was in a small, dark-blue, plastic bag with 'Mykanos' emblazoned on the front in ornate gold lettering. Nathan took it from her and she looked him in the eyes and said, 'Thank you for your business,' in very good English, while giving him a shy smile.

'Thank you,' said Nathan, smiling back as their hands briefly touched. They said their goodbyes and left the shop.

'The young lady had eyes for you,' said Loretta.

'I do have this effect,' said Nathan, while Loretta used her shoulder to push him lightly in a playful gesture.

'Shall we find somewhere to get lunch?' he suggested.

''No, if you don't mind, let's get back to Anapetri and have lunch in the bar in the village.'

'That's fine with me.' He handed her the small plastic bag. 'It was a good choice,' he said.

'Thank you so much.' She kissed him on the lips.

On the way back, Loretta drove through the city, which gave them the opportunity to look at the divide between Greek Cyprus and Turkish Cyprus. Guard posts, United

Nations troops, streets cordoned off by permanent barriers, and a large Turkish flag on a hillside looking down on the city from the occupied territories.

5

BACK AT the sleepy village of Anapetri, Loretta parked the car in the square. They walked over to the bar and took one of the tables outside under a parasol. It was extremely hot but in the shade of the parasol it was manageable. Almost immediately a young man wearing a white apron came out of the bar and asked whether they wanted drinks. Nathan ordered a beer and Loretta a sparkling water. When he returned with the drinks, Nathan ordered some hummus with pittas, and haloumi and tomato sandwiches with a portion of fries.

Loretta opened her handbag and took out the blue plastic bag. She removed the box and opened it, revealing the lovely necklace. 'Can I put it on for you?' asked Nathan.

'Yes please,' she replied. Nathan stood behind her, undid the clasp and refastened it around her neck. It was very attractive and the diamond sparkled when it caught the sunlight. Against Loretta's olive skin, which seemed to be getting darker by the hour, the fine gold of the teardrop and chain took on a rich standout glow. 'How does it look?' she asked.

'Spectacular,' he replied. At that moment, the waiter came back with a large tray containing their food and drink, then proceeded to lay the items out on the table.

'That's great, thank you,' said Nathan.

'You're welcome,' replied the waiter.

'What's our next step?' asked Loretta.

Nathan knew what she was referring to. 'Well, fingers crossed, and with a bit of good luck, we're going to get a phone call from Stakis Associates informing us that they've located the missing documents.'

'And if we don't?'

'Then a lot of people are going to lose their homes and their livelihoods. The Mykanos Group – i.e. you – are going to lose the Anapetri estate and villa, the private beach and any goodwill that the locals currently hold towards you.'

'This is slowly turning into a nightmare,' said Loretta.

'The documents must be somewhere; we've just got to locate them. I think you should ring your father again. You should quiz him and get as much information out of him as possible. He's got to give some clues or lines of enquiry for us to follow, even the slightest thing that may point us in the right direction.'

'Such as what?'

'Any known associates or good friends who he may have confided in at the time. There's also something else that's been bothering me. In the 1970s, when the solicitor was dealing with several houses being developed on your land, wouldn't that solicitor want to know that you had proof of ownership and planning approval on that land in the first place?'

'I see what you mean but you could say the same for the council. How could they pass approval plans on properties built on land, when ownership of the land was in doubt in the first place?'

'Because it wasn't,' said Nathan.

'What do you mean?'

'There's no way that the council would allow the development of that land for houses without knowing who the landowner was. Think about it. Your dad or his representative would have had to apply, and part of the application process must be to prove that you're the owner of the land in the first place. And if you couldn't prove it there's no way you would get approval.'

'Yes, I know what you mean, and I understand that, but you would think that Stakis would have proof, since he acted on our behalf with regards to the building and selling of the houses,' said Loretta.

'So, we're left in the position where the council says they don't have the documents and neither do Stakis Associates. It's a bit like being passed from pillar to post. Someone isn't telling the truth.'

'What's bothering me is that these houses were being built at such a difficult time. The upheaval must have been considerable in this area – people being moved, resettled, houses and businesses being looted – so the documents could have been destroyed accidentally or on purpose,' suggested Loretta.

'Then we must contact the council offices in Palakori and try to find out what happened between 1973 and 1974, other than a war, and see whether they can explain where the documents have gone. Let's start making some phone calls when we get back to the villa.'

'Yes, I agree. We need to get proactive; we can't just accept this,' replied Loretta.

After lunch, the couple drove back to the villa with a plan in mind and a renewed determination. As they walked into the kitchen, Loretta's mobile rang. 'Hi Mum, is everything okay?'

'Yes, it's okay. I've been speaking with your dad. I think he's remembered a few more things about the paperwork for Anapetri Villa, so I've written them down and I wanted to let you know what he said.'

'Okay Mum but, if you don't mind, I'm just going to put you on speakerphone so that Nathan can hear you too.'

'Okay,' Maia replied.

'Hi Maia, how are you two doing?' Nathan asked.

'Hi Nathan, I hope you're enjoying Cyprus. Stelios is a bit under the weather. He's having more problems with his memory but I'll tell you what he told me just a few minutes ago.'

'Okay Mum, go ahead,' said Loretta.

'He wanted to let you know that all the documentation relating to the purchase of the land and building of the villa was originally lodged with a solicitor in the Varosha region of Famagusta. But he said he moved them when the Turks first invaded. He never expected them to come as far south as Famagusta but he moved them anyway because he thought they would be safer there.'

'Where to?' asked Loretta impatiently.

'He said he moved them into the real estate agency because it had a very secret safe in the basement and he thought it would be better there.'

'Which real estate agency? Where?' said Loretta with even more impatience.

'The Mykanos Real Estate agency. He said it was about fifty yards down the road.'

'Down the road from where Mum? For goodness' sake.'

'The solicitor's in Varosha, in Ermou Street,' Maia replied. 'Your dad is so upset. He said the premises was probably looted or burned out with very little chance of recovery. He said we may lose all the land and villa and houses.'

'Yes, it's not looking good,' said Loretta. 'Can I speak to Dad please?'

'I'll get him, but he isn't very good on the phone these days. Just give me a second.'

About a minute later, Stelios was on the telephone. 'Hello sweetie, how are you?' he said in a very croaking and weak voice.

'All the better after hearing from you,' Loretta replied. 'What's been the matter?'

'I've been unwell, sweetie … correction … I am unwell. I've been meaning to talk to you about it.'

Nathan got up to leave the room so they could talk in private. Loretta gave him a sad smile in appreciation as he walked out. Nathan grabbed a beer from the fridge and walked outside on to the patio. The sun was burning hot on his skin and the heat was stifling. He headed straight for the parasol and sat down in its luxurious cooling shade.

He suspected that Stelios was about to inform Loretta about his illness and it didn't sound good. He thought about the conversation with Maia. That really was disastrous news, all the documentation that they were looking for being in the basement of a real estate agency in Varosha, a ruin of a city in a militarised zone and effectively off limits to all but official visitors since 1974.

Nathan shook his head and looked around him at the orchards, the swimming pool, the villa, then he looked across at the row of houses whose rooftops could be seen peeking over the orchard trees. This was a truly beautiful and peaceful location. It was hard to imagine that the green line that cut the country in half, resulting in deaths and imprisonment, was only half a mile away. He wondered what was going to happen to the occupants, both adults and children, when they were told to vacate their homes on the Anapetri Villa land. He couldn't help thinking about Andreas, Helena and baby George. What a lovely family they were, surviving and living off a strip of land just like their neighbours.

Could the documents still be there? Would it be possible to retrieve them? He suddenly dismissed the idea and took a sip of beer. He was a bit upset with himself for even entertaining the thought. His mind was distracted, when a large dragonfly with a bluish body landed on the table in front of him. It was stunning, with almost transparent wings that carried its long body away as Nathan leaned a little too close.

Loretta appeared with a glass of water and sat next to him. He was waiting for the bad news, which wasn't long in coming.

'My dad has cancer of the oesophagus,' she said, her voice trembling. The tears poured down her face and she leaned into Nathan.

He put his arm around her and said very softly, 'I'm so sorry, Loretta.' She didn't reply. She just cried and cried, and Nathan just sat there comforting her as best he could.

~~~

Later that afternoon Nathan pressed Loretta on her conversation with her father. The cancer was very advanced and he only had weeks to live. When Nathan heard this, he knew that the holiday was over and they had to return to New Zealand. When he suggested this to Loretta, she was hesitant.

'This sounds bad on a couple of levels,' Loretta said. 'Firstly, I don't want you to come back with me. I need to be alone with my thoughts and it means I may get some work done on the plane on the way back.' Nathan felt deflated and disappointed. 'But also,' she continued, 'I'd like you to make representations to the council on our behalf to see whether there's any possibility of them reconsidering and, if not, starting a campaign against their proposals.'

Nathan considered this for a moment. 'I'd rather that we were together on this but I understand your urgency in wanting to return to see your dad. When will you be leaving?'

'I'll call the office and ask them to book the earliest flight to leave tomorrow.'

'I'm so sorry, but you must do what you're comfortable with. I'll do as you ask and try to make some headway into this whole land saga.'

'Thank you, I really appreciate all this that you're doing for me and the family. I do feel as if I'm dropping you in it. It seems like this holiday was never really meant to be.'

'I know, but it's a good job we came, otherwise we may never have known about the seriousness of the situation. At least we have a plan,' said Nathan.

'Please ensure that you don't put yourself or anyone else at risk. I know how you like action and adventure Nathan, but please stay well away from Varosha, otherwise it will end up with you being in jail or dead. The Turkish military won't hesitate to shoot if they see you in there. So please, under no circumstances must you go in there.'

'Okay,' replied Nathan nonchalantly. He leaned over and kissed her on the forehead.

'And when you speak to the council, you'll have to convince them that you're a member of the family, otherwise they won't entertain you.'

'Okay, I'll think of something.'

Loretta then spent the remainder of the afternoon and early evening on her laptop. Nathan asked her whether she fancied walking to the bar in the village but she was preoccupied with work and her father. Her office had secured a flight home in the morning, so she wanted to spend time packing.

'I'm sorry I haven't made anything to eat,' said Loretta. 'I've just lost my appetite. Why don't you go to the bar on your own. You might bump into Andreas and you could get something to eat there.'

'I'd prefer if you came with me,' replied Nathan.

'I know, I'm sorry, but I just need a little time on my own.'

'I understand.'

Nathan hugged and kissed Loretta before walking out of the villa and heading for the bar. As he walked down the drive and turned left, it was still noticeably hot and humid, although the sun was now low in the western sky. The dust lifted into the air off his trainers as he walked alongside the gravelly road. Ahead he could see a young man on a moped approaching him in a cloud of dust. Nathan shielded his eyes as the moped passed but looked up in time to see the youth waving and smiling at him. Nathan did a double take as he was sure there was a dog on the seat behind the rider, before he disappeared in a cloud of dust and two-stroke engine smoke.

As Nathan approached the village he could see there didn't appear to be anyone sitting outside the bar, so he continued on until he came to the small stone church. He pushed open the heavy wooden door and the smell and the atmosphere was noticeable as he stepped inside. Candle wax and furniture polish were the prevalent aromas. He sat down on one of the wooden benches facing the tiny altar. It was cooler in the church, the thick stone walls acting as a mild refrigerator in the summer and an insulator in the winter months. It was deathly quiet and peaceful.

On either side of the altar, on the semi-circular wall, there were two large iconic paintings in black and gold of Jesus and the Virgin Mary. Standing on the middle of the altar was a large brass ornate cross. Although not particularly religious, Nathan suddenly found himself whispering the Lord's Prayer, then asking for help in his quest to find the missing documents. When he had finished, he took one quick look around the church, then left.

He thought about walking back to the villa. He was slightly upset at the fact that Loretta didn't want his company on the return flight and wanted her space from him this evening. Then he perked himself up by reiterating to himself that they weren't married, just a couple trying to deal with everyday life with its trials and tribulations, so this was no time to be feeling sensitive. Loretta had to go and be with her dad, and he had to try to find the missing documents.

As he approached the bar, he noticed that someone was sitting outside under the trellis. As he got closer, he was delighted to see that it was Andreas, so he walked over and shook his hand. 'Can I join you, Andreas?'

'Please do,' was the reply.

Nathan had no sooner sat down than they were approached by a man in an apron. 'What can I get you?' he asked, looking at Andreas.

'Just my usual please. Nathan, would you like to join me with some local red wine?'

'That's fine by me,' replied Nathan.

A moment later the man reappeared, poured two glasses of wine and left the bottle on the table.

'Thank you,' said Nathan.

'Yamas,' said Andreas, holding up his glass.

'Yamas,' replied Nathan, as he did the same. The two glasses came together with a clink.

'How are Helena and George?' asked Nathan.

'They are very good thank you. This morning we went to the market at Palakori. There is a shop that sells agricultural equipment, so I bought some new pruning shears, a spade and a rake. Then we decided to have lunch at a small café, which was going well until George was sick all over the table and Helena. We ended up paying and leaving quickly. What about yourself? Are you enjoying your holiday?'

'We were until we found out that Loretta's father has cancer.'

'Oh no, that is terrible. How serious is it?' said Andreas with genuine concern written all over his face.

'Very serious, I'm afraid. From what Loretta said, he doesn't have a great deal of time left. So, she's returning to New Zealand in the morning.'

'That is very sad, shocking news, so the last thing you want to be dealing with at the moment is this land issue.'

'On the contrary,' said Nathan. 'Loretta has asked me to carry out enquiries with the council to see whether we can get this land grab quashed.'

'Oh, so you have located the missing documents?' asked Andreas enthusiastically.

Nathan took a moment. 'Look, what I'm going to tell you must be in the strictest confidence. I don't want your neighbours or anyone to find out and start a panic.'

'I promise on the life of my wife and son,' said Andreas. Nathan thought this was a bit extreme but at least he knew he was taking the issue seriously. The waiter returned with a bowl of bread, oil and olives, as more wine was consumed.

'Andreas, the news isn't good. We've been to our solicitors in Nicosia. He holds all the land and building documents for your and the other tenant farmers' homes. Unfortunately, he doesn't have the documents for the land proving that it belongs to the Mykanos family.'

Nathan could see that Andreas was deflated but continued. 'To cut a long story short, we've since found out that the documents are lodged in a safe in the basement of a real estate agency in Varosha.' Andreas looked shocked and repeated a word in Cypriot that Nathan didn't understand but assumed to be some sort of curse.

'That is not good,' said Andreas. 'The likelihood is that the building has been looted and stripped of its worth and now has a big tree growing in the middle of it. The Turks took Varosha as a bargaining chip in 1974. You have read about how it used to be a glamorous seaside town. It has numerous high-rise hotels and blocks of apartments. There was something like thirty-five thousand mainly Greek Cypriot residents all forced to leave on the promise of return that never came. Varosha was cordoned off to the outside world and now displays signs that say forbidden zone, with a picture of an armed soldier. Nature is returning to the streets as some are overgrown with bushes and trees and, like I said, some buildings even have trees growing inside them, bursting out through the windows for sunlight.'

'You know a lot about Varosha,' said Nathan.

'It is our country's history. It was part of our education at school.'

'I've never seen it, only in books and on the internet,' said Nathan.

'It is a crazy place. You have seen what the town looks like nearest to Chernobyl … it was called Pripyat. It was left abandoned after the radiation leak from the reactor.'

'Yes, I've seen it on the news and different documentaries,' said Nathan.

'Well, Varosha is very similar to Pripyat, except the danger is not radiation, it is bullets from Turkish guns. They have watchtowers along the beach and, I understand, at random places throughout the town centre. Intruders stand a good chance of being shot.'

'You paint a very grim picture Andreas.'

'It is a very grim place Nathan, and very dangerous.'

Andreas was suddenly distracted and stood up to extract his mobile phone from his tight denim jeans pocket. 'It's Helena. George has woken up and he has a temperature. I am sorry Nathan, I will have to go.'

'Not a problem. Let's meet again tomorrow night.'

'Yes, that is fine and, again, I am sorry about tonight.'

'Don't worry, family comes first. Go and help to get the little man sorted out.'

'Thanks Nathan, bye.' With that Andreas ran across the road before suddenly turning around and shouting, 'If you do not mind paying for the wine, I will pay tomorrow.'

'Yes, you will,' replied Nathan, laughing.

Nathan sat back in his chair and took a deep breath. The night air was infused with a hint of jasmine, which grew wild in the grass verges and was in flower at this time of the year. The scent seemed to drift through the village on the slightest of breezes. He poured himself another glass of wine and was briefly distracted by six local men who were in the bar watching a game of football on the television. They all cheered loudly, so presumably the local team had scored.

His thoughts returned to Stelios, his cancer and their terrible predicament. He liked Loretta's parents and got the impression that they liked him. He knew that Loretta was in knots and desperate to get home to New Zealand. He also knew that he had to try his best to recover the missing documents. He didn't like admitting it to himself but he was thinking of going into Varosha. After all, the documents could be there, couldn't they? Trying to dismiss the thoughts as folly, he got up from his seat, walked into the bar and paid for the wine. There was probably two small glasses' worth of wine left in the bottle so, as he passed the table, he picked it up and made his way back to the villa.

On arrival, he walked through the front door and made his way into the kitchen. 'Loretta,' he shouted.

'In the garden,' was the reply.

He picked up two wine glasses from the kitchen and made his way out on to the patio. Loretta was sitting there, a book and magazine lay on the table. Nathan placed the glasses on the table and shared the remnants of the bottle of wine.

'What happened to the rest of it? Did you drink it on the way back?' Loretta asked with a smirk.

'I was having a drink with Andreas but he had to leave. Baby George has a temperature.'

'Oh dear, poor thing. I hope he's okay,' she replied with concern.

'I'll give them a call in the morning. They probably have their hands full right now. How are you feeling?' Nathan asked.

'Still trying to come to terms with the news and trying to put on a brave face, but I just want to be with him. If you don't mind taking me to the airport for seven-thirty in the morning, it would be appreciated.'

'How much?'

'What do you mean, how much?' Loretta held Nathan's gaze until he gave her a beaming smile. She looked down at the table. 'I'm sorry Nathan, but with all this news about my dad, I'm just not in the mood.'

'That's a shame. I could have done with a shoulder massage.'

'I'm not in the mood for your jokes either.'

'I'm sorry, it was bad timing and in bad taste.'

Loretta looked at Nathan with a tear in her eye. 'Yes, it was.'

Nathan leaned over to put his arm around her in an apologetic manner. Loretta pushed his arm away, got up and walked into the kitchen. Nathan sat there. He was sorry that he had been insensitive towards her and he didn't want her to be upset. He remembered a saying that his mum used to use: 'Never let the sun go down on an argument.' Well, the sun had already gone down but she had meant never end the day after an argument without making up. He got up and walked into the kitchen, where Loretta was pouring herself a glass of milk as he approached. He took hold of her hand and she turned around. 'I'm so sorry,' he said.

'So am I,' she replied coldly.

'Are you going to bed?' asked Nathan.

'Yes,' she replied as she turned and left the kitchen.

Nathan went back outside and sat down in his chair. He was having mixed thoughts. *Should I be going back with her? Why should I try to help her find the documents? It's as if she doesn't really care about me. Is she just using me? Perhaps I should just go home myself and, as for thinking of going into Varosha, that was ridiculous.*

Then his thoughts turned to Andreas, Helena, George and the tenant farmers. If this proposed plan went through, they would be on the street, destitute, without any form of income. Morally, the right thing to do would be to try to help these families. He felt confused, as this wasn't a predicament of his own making; in fact, it was nothing to do with him. He had been sucked in by Loretta, the woman he loved, and he didn't know whether she loved him in return.

Nathan felt as if his head was going to explode. For the first time in his life he was hesitant as to his next move. If only his parents were alive. He could speak to them like he used to. Ask them for advice. They always seemed to know what the right thing was to do or say. But they had been taken by a snivelling drug user who couldn't control his car.

He could feel himself becoming annoyed. He needed a release. He stood up, removed his T-shirt, shorts and boxer shorts. He left his flip-flops on as he made his way over to the swimming pool, then kicked them off as he approached. He stood at the side of the pool, his tall, naked muscular physique tensing as he jumped in at the deep end. He turned to look at the villa and thought he saw the blinds move in their bedroom but he wasn't sure. He didn't expect Loretta to come running out in her bikini to join him, so he just swam length after length after length, alternate breaststroke then crawl. He didn't know how many lengths he had done, he just intended to swim until he was tired.

Eventually, after about twenty minutes, he was short of breath and had to stop. He climbed out of the pool and walked back to the patio. He noticed a large white bath towel had been placed on the table. This meant a lot to him. Perhaps Loretta's attitude towards him was softening. He dried himself and dressed. He lay down on the lounger with the damp towel on top of him. He now felt chilled and relaxed. He fell asleep.

6

*I*N THE *heart of England, somewhere near Cheltenham, Nathan grabbed the body and pulled it into the pig pen. When the pigs realised that someone had entered their domain, the adult males appeared from their sties. He closed the gate quickly but quietly so as not to make too much noise. As he walked away, he could hear the pigs grunting and gorging on the large luxurious slab of meat. Nothing would be wasted, down to the last bone or tooth. He walked into the forest. He had blood on his hands.*

Suddenly, he was in New Zealand, on a small hill in the middle of a forest. A sign read URUPA Māori burial ground. The warm air vented from the fissure in the earth's crust. He looked into the blackness of the crevasse, then pushed the body in. He walked away, stepped over the sign and stooped down to wash his blood-soaked hands in a small stream. He splashed the ice-cold water on his face.

Nathan awoke with a start. He had slept on the sun lounger all night and, as the sun arose in the east, he realised that the sprinkler irrigation system that watered the palm trees and flower beds had sprung a leak in one of the black hose lines and was spraying a large arc. It was only a fine spray but he was absolutely soaked. He must have been lying there asleep for quite a while with the jet of water spraying the area between his chest and neck.

He got up from the bed and followed the wet line along the patio floor, which eventually led to a small rose bush bed, where he spotted the small hole in the hose. He filled his cupped hands with pea gravel from the flower bed and covered the hole where the water was emanating from. He stood there staring at the pea gravel, watching it change colour as it became soaked in water. He couldn't believe he had slept on the sun lounger all night … and this two-part recurring nightmare, it was horrible.

He looked down at his wet clothes. He felt a mess, so he turned around and made his way back to the patio. Loretta was watching him from the kitchen then she stepped on to the patio.

'Good morning. What happened to you?' she asked. Nathan thought she sounded slightly more cheerful than she had the night before.

'Good morning.' He walked over and pecked her on the lips, to which she was receptive. 'I fell asleep on the sun lounger and was awoken by a spray of water from the irrigation hose. It's sprung a leak.'

'You poor thing. By the looks of your face and arms the mosquitoes have had a field day.' She quickly changed the subject. 'You still okay to take me to the airport?'

'Of course. When are we leaving?'

'About half an hour. I'll make you some scrambled eggs while you have a shower.'

Nathan was pleased that at least they were back on speaking terms but he wasn't looking forward to staying in the villa on his own. After he had showered and dressed, he made his way to the kitchen. Waiting for him were scrambled eggs on toast with English breakfast tea. Loretta was eating her breakfast and sending an email on her laptop at the same time. She looked up at Nathan. 'I'm sorry we fell out last night, and you didn't need to spend the night on the sun lounger, you could have come to bed.'

'I didn't intend to sleep out there. I just fell asleep.'

'I have some cream for mosquito bites.' She produced a small tube, which looked like a travel toothpaste. 'You just put a small amount on each bite and it reduces the swelling and, more importantly, the itching.'

'Okay, brilliant, thank you. Is this one of your mother's remedies by any chance?' said Nathan.

'Sort of. It was one of her friends who started to make and sell her own Māori naturally made products. Mum used to help her for a while, bottling lotions and things like that. She wouldn't accept any pay in return but she seems to have got a lifetime supply of mosquito cream and honey lip balm,' said Loretta with a smile.

'Great, I'll give it a try,' Nathan replied.

'I was up late last night; I stupidly opened my laptop and went on to the Mykanos database. Dad has kept me so shielded from all the businesses for so many years. I was in my own little world, concerning myself with Mykanos Real Estate, when realistically it's not even five per cent of the total business empire.'

'Loretta, granted you're going to have your work cut out, but I suggest that you concentrate on your father for a while. When you get home, enjoy your time with him. Make the best of it, ask as many questions as possible about anything, not just about work but your childhood, his childhood, your grandparents. Because, when he does eventually pass, you'll realise that you wish you had asked him this or asked him that.'

Loretta took Nathan's hand and then reached over and gave him a lingering kiss on the lips. 'Thank you, you're so wise. I know that you're speaking from previous experience and the loss of your parents. I'll take your advice. Now, you must take mine. I don't want you putting your life at risk to try to locate these documents; I just want you to do everything that you need to do here, then come back to New Zealand. I know you don't want to work for the company but I really need you.'

'For what? Business or pleasure?'

'Both,' she replied, and they kissed again.

The journey to the airport was uneventful. Loretta talked about her childhood and what life had been like growing up in New Zealand. Nathan did the same, except his memories were all based around Cheltenham in England. Loretta didn't want him to go with her to the departure lounge, so they said their goodbyes from the car in the drop-off zone once Nathan had obtained a luggage trolley for her.

~~~

Nathan made good time on the way back from Larnaca Airport. When he arrived back at the villa he changed into his swim shorts and dived into the pool. For mid-morning the water was surprisingly warm, in fact a bit like a warm bath. After a quick swim he jumped out, put his flip-flops on and made his way down to the beach. As usual he had the place to himself. Leaving his flip-flops on the sand he walked into the sea. It was bracing but pleasantly so and, once his shoulders were under the water, it was very relaxing. He formed a star shape by lying on his back and just floated.

The sea was so calm, with just the occasional bobbing up and down of a tiny wave making its way to shore. He began to think about Loretta. They had left on good terms and she told him in no uncertain terms how fond she was of him. But he still wasn't sure whether his strong feelings for her were reciprocal. He admitted to himself that he loved her. He loved her personality, he loved the way she looked …

He was suddenly distracted by a helicopter flying across the bay. He didn't get chance to identify whether it was Turkish, British or Cypriot. He wondered whether they could see him, a small speck in the ocean. Did he look like a lonely man on an empty beach? One thing was for sure, he was on his own, but he wasn't lonely. Thoughts were buzzing through his head about the view from the helicopter. A bird's-eye view. Would it be possible to get a bird's-eye view over Varosha? He realised he needed a drone.

Nathan made his way back to the villa then made a call to Andreas. Helena answered the phone and Nathan asked her whether George was feeling better this morning. She confirmed that he was fine. He asked for Andreas and she said he was in the back but that Nathan was welcome to come round. He said he would be there soon.

Before he left the villa, Nathan called the local council. When he was eventually transferred to the planning department he explained who he was and the reason for his call. He was informed that the planning officer dealing with the application to develop their land was currently on annual leave. He was, though, invited to view the plans in their entirety and agreed a noon appointment. He put the phone down and shook his head. *The relevant planning officer is on leave. How fortuitous. Well, I'm sure there will be someone standing in for him.*

Nathan quickly got changed, closed up the villa and made his way around to Andreas's home. As he walked into the village square, he noticed an elderly lady with a broom who was brushing the outdoor seating area of the bar. She brushed the floor, then the seats before throwing down a bucket of water to wash away any residue that remained on the stone-flagged floor. With the heat, it would be fully dry within about ten minutes.

There was another elderly lady dressed in black, wearing a black headscarf. She was opening the church and she looked Greek Orthodox. She too had a broom in her hand and, as she brushed the floor around the entrance to the church, she was enveloped in a cloud of dust. It didn't seem to bother her though; she just continued until she was satisfied with her work. No doubt she performed such duties on a daily basis.

Nathan walked up the road, which was covered in squashed fruit, and approached the house of Andreas and Helena. Helena was standing at the front door with George in her arms. He was wearing only a disposable nappy and she was rocking him slowly, but he wasn't happy.

'Come in Nathan,' Helena said. He walked in and immediately noticed a cooling breeze, which swept through the house.

'Good morning Helena. I can't get a breeze through the villa like this. I always have the air conditioning on.' As soon as he said it, he felt guilty and privileged.

Helena must have sensed his embarrassment. 'Oh, we have air conditioning, but we only use it when it's really hot. In the meantime, I stand in the doorway with George to keep us cool.'

Really hot, like now, you mean, Nathan thought to himself. 'How is the little man?' he asked.

'He is okay. He has his moments but, overall, he is a good little boy.' She kissed George gently on the forehead. 'Go through Nathan. I told him you were coming. He will be down at the far end waiting for you.'

'Thanks Helena,' Nathan said, as he made his way through the house to the patio and orchard area. He walked down the narrow path through the fruit trees. 'Andreas, are you there?'

'Yes,' Andreas replied. 'Just come down to the end.'

At the end of the path Nathan noticed that the orchard changed into a small vineyard. Bunches of succulent-looking red grapes were hanging from the small vines. Andreas appeared with a pair of pruning shears in in a gloved hand. 'Welcome again, my friend.' He put down the shears and removed his glove to shake Nathan's hand.

'How are you, Andreas?'

'I am very well, thank you. Would you like a seat?'

'You have seats out here?'

'Of course.' Nathan followed Andreas down a side pathway until he came to an area at the end of the vineyard covered by a small tarpaulin. This was supported by a couple of old dead vines, beneath which there were two chairs and a table.

'Come, take a seat in the shade,' said Andreas. Nathan sat down and Andreas sat beside him.

'This is very cosy,' said Nathan.

'This is my hideaway, if I want some peace and quiet or just some respite from the sun. Perhaps you would like some liquid refreshment.'

'What did you have in mind?' Andreas put his hand in a box underneath his seat and pulled out a bottle of wine. 'Woah, it's a bit too early for me, Andreas.'

'You must try.' Andreas pulled out two small glasses from the same box, placed them on the table and filled them up with red wine. Nathan wasn't looking forward to tasting the wine so early but it would be bad manners to refuse. He was pleasantly surprised. The wine, although slightly warm, had no bitterness and was slightly sweet.

'Do you like it?' Andreas asked.

'Actually, yes I do.'

'I told you this was the best soil on the island.'

'Is this your wine?' asked Nathan with surprise.

'It certainly is, but I am very foolish with my wine.'

'What do you mean?'

'I will give you an example. I sell it to the bar in the village and, when I go there, he sells it back to me by the glass at double the price.' They both laughed.

'How is Loretta this morning?' asked Andreas.

'Well, that's one of the reasons that I'm here. I've dropped her off at the airport and she'll soon be on her way to see her dad.'

'Yes, it is very sad,' said Andreas. 'Is there anything I can do?'

'Yes, there is,' replied Nathan.

Andreas eyed him with an inquisitive look on his face. He took a sip of wine. 'What is it?' he asked.

'I need you to take me to Famagusta,' said Nathan.

'You're not talking about Varosha are you?'

'Yes.'

'Why?'

'You know why Andreas; I need to do a recce.'

'What is a recce?'

'Reconnaissance. I need to have a look. I'm thinking of going in there,' said Nathan.

'No, you must not. It is madness. I have already told you.'

'I know what you said but I just need to go take a look.'

'Then I will take you to see it and, when you do see it, and see how dangerous it is, I am sure that you will change your mind. Why would you want to risk your life? It makes no sense.'

'I need to help the Mykanos family. Loretta has taken control of the business group and she has her hands full at the moment. Plus, her father would be devastated if he were to lose this land and its occupants. You know how much it means to him, and to you for that matter, and to your neighbours. All your livelihoods rest on the outcome of this land grab but, if we can find these documents, we can stop it in its tracks.'

'And what will Loretta say when she finds out that you have been into Varosha and been shot or arrested?'

'I would rather wonder what she might say if I go into Varosha and retrieve the missing documents,' replied Nathan.

'Like I say, I will take you there and hopefully it will put you off from ever doing anything so stupid.'

Nathan was feeling a bit aggrieved and wasn't quite sure that he appreciated the tone that Andreas was taking with him. However, not wanting to antagonise him, Nathan softened his tone. 'I just need to see. And I would really appreciate it if you would take me.'

'Very well then. When do you want to go?'

'This afternoon, if possible. I'm going to the council offices at lunchtime to view the plans.'

'Okay. If I pick you up at two then?' said Andreas.

'Yes, that's fine. Is there anything I need to bring?'

'Just your passport and your wallet,' said Andreas.

~~~

Later that morning Nathan visited the council offices at Palakori, where he was shown plans for the development of the villa site. It was unrecognisable. A huge crater was the focal point, with a couple of small office buildings on the area where the villa currently stood. The farmers' houses were all gone and the general area was a raised platform. The public could park their cars and drop their refuse into a series of large open-topped containers positioned at a lower level, which could then be easily

99

loaded on to the rear of a truck. There were ten processing plants around the site to deal with recyclables, electrical items, white goods, garden waste and even food. Whatever was deposited in the containers would be moved to the relevant area and processed on site.

This was a slick operation but it would wipe the village of Anapetri off the map. The dust, the smell the vehicles. It was inconceivable how the area would survive and what effect it would have on the immediate environment, even though the whole idea of the project was to improve it. The village had to suffer for a greater cause. Looking at the plans, Nathan couldn't help noticing that the writing seemed to be in English, Greek and Russian. He couldn't understand why there was a Russian option but thought no more of it.

He managed to speak to a junior planning officer, who was a few levels lower on the food chain than the person who he would have liked to have met. He came away with the distinct impression that the council had been looking for land where private ownership was in doubt. Unfortunately, Anapetri Villa and its land was the largest and most suitable for the project. The wheels of compulsory reclamation were in progress and the only thing that would stop it was proof of ownership of the villa and land.

Nathan came away with all his fears confirmed. But seeing the plans in black and white and now knowing how much people had to lose, he was more determined than ever. He was going to try to recover the documents from the forbidden zone in Varosha, the ghost city of Cyprus.

7

AT TWO-FIFTEEN Andreas called to collect Nathan, driving his rusty white Isuzu pickup. Nathan had a small backpack, which contained a couple of bottles of water, his mobile, wallet and passport. They headed north to the crossing point at Deryneia.

During the journey, Nathan took the opportunity to fill Andreas in on his meeting at the Palakori council offices. 'It's just as we expected, Andreas. Unless we can produce the documents proving the Mykanos family owns the land, within a matter of months they'll be bulldozing your house and your living to the ground.'

Nathan's approach had changed. He needed help and he was tired of pussyfooting around, while Andreas sat there seemingly accepting defeat. 'I'm going into Varosha,' Nathan said. 'Not today, like I said; this is just a recce to see if it's possible, but I will need your help, Andreas.' He looked at Andreas and noticed the sweat trickling down the side of his face. He wasn't sure whether it was the thought of going into Varosha that was making him sweat or simply because it was another very hot afternoon.

'I am helping you now Nathan.'

'I know, and it's appreciated, but I want you to help yourself as well.'

'What do you mean?'

'This is your livelihood, your home, everything that you've worked for. It doesn't mean any of those things to me, it's just the right thing to do. I want to help you and the other families, including Loretta and her parents.'

'I will not go into Varosha,' Andreas exclaimed. 'If I get captured and sent to prison, it does not bear thinking about. What will Helena and George do then? It scares me Nathan, it scares me for my family. You do not have a wife and child, you do not have the same responsibilities.'

Nathan held his tongue and thought about his reply. This was a crucial moment in their short friendship and he couldn't afford to lose him. 'Andreas, I don't expect you to come into Varosha with me. I just need your support and knowledge of the local area. Without that help and support I won't be able to do this. I have to go in there and do this. Imagine if those documents are there in an abandoned basement.'

'Imagine if they are not, or they have decomposed, or been looted by the Turks,' replied Andreas.

'Well wouldn't you want to know the answer to that question when you're being evicted from your home? Don't you think you would be saying to yourself at least I should have tried?' Nathan was immediately concerned that he may have gone at Andreas too hard.

'We are approaching the checkpoint. Just have your passport at hand,' Andreas said.

'Okay,' replied Nathan.

They approached the control box; the barrier was down. Andreas leaned across, took Nathan's passport and handed it over with a piece of paper. There was a brief unintelligible conversation then Nathan heard Andreas say, 'There are some fresh strawberries under the tarp. Help yourself.' The man handed back the passport and paper.

Nathan was unable to tell whether he was a soldier or a border guard but, whichever he was, he walked to the rear of the truck and lifted a small plastic crate of strawberries. Four of his colleagues came across and were about to help themselves when the guard said to them, 'Do not take any more. I will share mine.' He then stepped into the control box, pressed a button and the barrier lifted. Andreas put the Isuzu into gear, gave a casual wave and pressed the accelerator. They were now in the Turkish Republic of Northern Cyprus.

Everything seemed familiar to Nathan. They still drove on the left, there were frequent small, stone cottages with their front doors open and elderly ladies sitting in their hallways sewing lace or knitting.

'What was the piece of paper that you gave to the guard?' asked Nathan.

'Oh, that was just my insurance document. There are few companies in the south that give cover for the north but you have to have it or they will make you buy Turkish insurance.'

'Okay,' replied Nathan.

'If you look straight ahead you will see the darker-looking properties as we approach on the right-hand side,' said Andreas. 'This is the outskirts of Varosha and the forbidden zone.'

As they approached, a fence appeared on the right, displaying a metal sign in red with a picture of an armed soldier. Beneath the picture in three languages was written in capitals 'FORBIDDEN ZONE'. The perimeter fence was ramshackle, in a poor state of repair. Holes had been filled with oil barrels, tyres, rocks, corrugated iron, barbed wire and vicious-looking prickly pear cacti. All the same, Nathan couldn't help noticing that there were still gaps in the fence. In the forbidden zone he could see low-level apartment buildings, either boarded up completely or stripped of every last piece of timber or metal.

The further north they travelled, the larger the buildings became. Several large high-rise hotels appeared, huge monoliths of the 60s and early 70s, some of them still displaying their hotel signage and some with trees or foliage growing through the windows or from the roof. It was endless building after building. Through the fence could be seen abandoned vehicles stripped of their worth, cracks in pavements and roads with trees protruding.

Nature was taking back Varosha. During the summer months the trees were parched, dry and barely green. They were absorbing every drop of moisture that they were rooting out beneath this concrete jungle. It was the winter months that sustained them and allowed rainwater to penetrate the earth and spread beneath the foundations of both roads and buildings. It was a hostile environment that now appeared to be occupied by birdlife, stray cats and the occasional dog.

'It is a creepy place isn't it,' said Andreas.

'I can't disagree with you there,' Nathan replied. Looking at these old buildings and their condition, he fought off feelings of despondency as he realised the likelihood of him finding the documents were so slim. However, he was still determined to give it a try. He hadn't noticed any sign of any human life on the other side of the fence. He was expecting soldiers on patrol and some watchtowers.

'Just around this corner there is a small car park, which gives us access to the beach that is just outside the forbidden zone,' Andreas informed Nathan. 'If we take a walk along the beach, you can getter a better view of all the deserted hotels along the beach front. It will give you an idea of the scale of the place. You can only go so far because the beach is fenced off.'

They pulled into the car park, left the vehicle and headed for the beach. A young boy approached, carrying a tray of bottled water and soft drinks. The tray was attached to a leather strap that went around the back of his neck, reminding Nathan of when he was a child, and the ice cream sellers in the cinema during the interlude. Andreas just dismissed the boy with a wave of his hand. Nathan did the same. They stepped on to the beach, the sand soft and golden.

'Keep your shoes on,' warned Andreas, 'or you will burn your feet.'

They walked past people who were sunbathing and taking shade beneath their parasols. About a hundred metres ahead, Nathan could see a pile of timber, oil barrels and other items, which formed a barrier along the beach, preventing any further access. There were at least twenty people hanging around the barrier taking photographs of the landscape of the Varosha beachfront beyond.

As Andreas and Nathan approached the barrier, they headed for the point where the sea lapped against the shoreline. The barrier reduced in height as it neared the water and offered the best vista along the coast. Nathan looked in amazement. He could see right down the coastline and, as far as he could see, it was all derelict. There was one hotel on the front that had a several parasols and sunbeds out. He pointed to the hotel. 'I thought this was a forbidden zone,' he said.

Andreas looked at him. 'We believe that the hotel you are looking at is a holiday hotel for the Turkish military.'

'But why have a hotel in the middle of all this chaos? It's madness.'

'It is private and probably very cheap,' said Andreas. 'And I do not think they will have any security issues to worry about.'

Nathan scanned the coastline and that's when he noticed guard boxes strategically positioned every hundred metres or so. In fact, there was a guard post just on the other side of the barrier on the roof of an apartment building. A guard started to show his displeasure at a couple who insisted on leaning on the barrier to take photos. He blew a whistle very sharply to attract their attention and waved them away.

Nathan considered the possibility of guards positioned all over Varosha but doubted that would be the case. He suspected the majority of them would be positioned along the sea front, which would surely be the weakest point, particularly after dark.

Andreas turned to Nathan and asked, 'Do you still want to go in there?'

'First I need an old street map of Varosha,' Nathan replied. 'I meant to call in at a library to see what was available. There's very little on the internet.'

'I doubt you would find one in the library. They have been removed and replaced with maps with Turkish names. But do not worry, I have an old street map of Varosha at home. You can use that.'

'Thank you,' said Nathan. 'There's one other thing. Would you know anyone who has a drone?'

'Yes, the United States military and they can drop bombs too.'

Nathan could see that Andreas had a cheeky smile on his face and a glint in his eye. He didn't smile very often so Nathan enjoyed the moment.

'Actually, yes,' Andreas said with enthusiasm. 'I have a friend who is a hill farmer not far from us. The terrain of his land is very difficult, even for his old jeep, so he bought a drone from Larnaca. It even has its own camera. He has a control stick and a tablet, and he flies it from that, and keeps an eye on all his goat herd, which roams freely. He looks out for predators, foxes and birds of prey, which take the young. He also looks out for anyone on his land who should not be there. It is a great thing.'

'Do you think he would lend it to me?' said Nathan, trying his luck.

Andreas turned to Nathan and started to shake his head. 'No, he would not do it.' Then very quickly, he added, 'But he might lend it to me,' and the smile was back. 'I can see your plan to use the drone to find the building but it is still a very difficult task and, in the dark, it will be impossible.'

'I don't dispute the fact that this is going to be difficult, but I don't believe it's impossible,' said Nathan.

'You are a crazy Englishman.'

'I will admit that I like to take a risk but it's all calculated, my friend, it's all calculated.' The two men high-fived.

'There is a small coffee shop by the car park. Let's have a Turkish coffee,' said Andreas.

The two men walked to the coffee shop and sat down under a parasol. The table was a rickety wooden one that rocked whenever they touched it and the chairs were of a common white plastic type. Nathan was pleased to be out of the sunshine. Andreas ordered coffees and, within minutes, the waiter returned with the drinks and two glasses of water. Nathan took a sip of coffee. It was black and bitter. As if recognising Nathan's displeasure, the waiter returned with a small plate of Turkish sweet biscuits. Nathan found the sweetness of the biscuits complemented the coffee and made it more palatable.

Andreas produced a small, flat, metal tin from his pocket, which he opened to reveal some small cigars. He offered one to Nathan. 'Take one, I think you will like it.'

'Please tell me it's only tobacco and not something else,' said Nathan.

'It is just a miniature cigar. My father used to smoke these. In fact, I go to the same trader in Palakori to buy them from the market, very cheap.'

'Cheap they may be, but are they doing you any good?' said Nathan.

'Probably more harm than good, but here, try one.' Andreas offered the open tin to Nathan, who hesitated but took one anyway. Andreas then produced a Zippo lighter from his pocket and, as he flicked the lid open, Nathan could smell the lighter fluid. Andreas turned the wheel with his thumb and the spark ignited into a flame. He lit Nathan's cigar then his own.

Nathan took a drag. He wanted to cough but he didn't want Andreas to see that he had never smoked in his life. Then the taste of the smoke was in his mouth. It was really strange, like chocolate, and was actually quite nice.

'They go well with this coffee, and also my wine at home,' said Andreas. 'That is why I have a secret area at the end of the orchard. As far as I am aware Helena does not know I smoke. She would get very angry at me for wasting our hard-earned money on such luxuries but they are only a couple of euros a tin.'

The two men sat and enjoyed the cigars, the coffee and each other's company. Before they knew it, an hour had passed and they were ready to return home.

'On the way back, there was a layby I noticed opposite a large terracotta-coloured house,' said Nathan. 'Do you think we could pull in there while I have a casual look at the perimeter fence?'

'Yes, okay, but we must be careful. I will get out with you and we can have a smoke and look casual together.'

'Sounds like a plan,' said Nathan.

They did as planned and pulled into the layby. Andreas jumped out first and walked around the front of the vehicle as Nathan got out. Andreas offered him a cigar and they stood with their backs against the vehicle, smoking and laughing.

From behind his sunglasses, Nathan was observing the construction of the fence in front of him. It was ramshackle, with the usual oil drums and tyres, barbed wire and cactus. But again there were gaps. He diverted his attention to the buildings on the other side of the fence, starting at the highest points and looking for observation posts. He couldn't see any. Working down the buildings he was looking for any signs of life, particularly any occupation by a guard. There was nothing and there were no CCTV cameras. When they had finished their cigars, the two men got back into the vehicle and drove away.

'There's no sign of life or security inside this western perimeter, yet the coastline to the east is bristling with observation posts,' said Nathan.

'They obviously fear an approach from the sea, but do not be deceived. It would not surprise me if they had vantage points looking all along this western perimeter. It is just that we cannot see them,' replied Andreas.

They drove south, retracing their earlier route. They came across another layby and pulled in. At this point they could see right through the wire fence. There were very few buildings, just large areas of open grassland. They were nearing the end of the fence before it turned east towards the sea. It was again noticeable that there were tempting gaps in the fence. Nathan thought that if he went through one of these gaps in the daytime he would stand out and surely be seen from an observation post. However, if he went through at night he would stand more of a chance but it would only take a soldier or guard to be looking through his FLIR night-time binoculars and he would stand out like a beacon.

'Have you seen enough?' asked Andreas.

'Yes, but I really need a bird's-eye view. If I could get a drone up there and try to identify Ermou Street, then I'd have a chance.'

'Have you ever flown a drone before?' said Andreas.

'Never, have you?

'No.'

'I'm a quick learner though,' said Nathan.

'Perhaps I should call my friend this evening to ask if I can borrow it. If he says yes, I could ask him to give us a quick course on how to operate it. We will also need to give him a reason why we want to borrow it and promise to replace it if we lose or damage it,' said Andreas.

'We could tell him that I'm looking at a piece of land to purchase for the company, so I need a bird's-eye view. And I would of course replace it if it were damaged or lost.'

'Okay, I will speak to him later.'

They continued their journey, passed back through the border post without incident and were back in the south.

Andreas drove to his house so that Nathan could collect the map of old Famagusta, which included a street map of Varosha. Nathan then decided to walk home from there after previously agreeing to meet Andreas in the bar at eight that evening.

He walked back through the village and noticed several men sitting outside the bar drinking and smoking. He didn't recognise any of them but he couldn't help noticing that they watched him carefully as he passed and spoke in an Eastern European language, possibly Russian. Perhaps they thought he was a holidaymaker. He certainly stood out, with his light-blonde hair, T-shirt, shorts and trainers. They weren't far wrong; except he was a holidaymaker on a mission.

He made his way back to the villa, where he decided to make himself a ham sandwich and a cup of tea, which he took out on to the patio. After the brief coolness of the air-conditioned villa, the sun-trapped heat of the patio was a shock to the system. He removed his T-shirt and kicked off his trainers. Now sitting at the table, the urge for a hot drink had diminished, so he went inside to retrieve a cold beer from the fridge.

Settled at the patio table, Nathan opened the old map and spread it out. He placed a few pebbles from an old plant pot along the map's outer edge to keep it flat. Looking for Ermou Street in the index, it directed him to square G5, running into G6. It reminded Nathan of the old A to Z maps that his father always kept in his car.

Varosha was shaded slightly darker in colour than the rest of the map. Ermou Street was located in the north-west segment of the town and looked as if it was one of the main thoroughfares in the area. It was one of the denser areas of Varosha and Nathan was unable to decide whether this was a good thing or bad. He searched the surrounding area for any landmarks or points of interest, noticing that at the end of Ermou Street there was a silo. It seemed out of place because the street looked like the main retail area and not somewhere you would expect to find such a construction. Nothing else jumped out at him, so he hoped that the silo was substantial enough in size to function as a landmark and a point of reference.

The problem remained of how he was going to find the Mykanos Real Estate agency in a street of rundown overgrown buildings. The silo could be all he had and was a throwback from when Varosha was being constructed. There was a huge demand for cement to build new towns in the 1950s and 60s. Traditionally, deliveries were received compliments of rotating cement mixers, as it would set rapidly in the hot Cypriot sun. The use of silos allowed the mixing, pouring and adding of other ingredients, such as aggregates and rebar to be conducted on site, on a supply-and-demand basis. As long as the silo was full, its contents could be extracted, moved and mixed as and when required.

There were two small side streets branching off Ermou Street, one giving access to a small car park and the other seemingly a service road to the rear of the shops. The arrangement seemed to be reciprocated for the shops on the opposite side of the street.

Looking at the map, overall, Nathan realised that the car park where they had parked earlier was about half a mile away from Ermou Street but obviously they were on different sides of the divide. They wouldn't be able to launch a drone from the car park without bringing themselves to the notice of the authorities. They would need a private location to launch. He would speak to Andreas about it later in the bar.

Nathan looked at his phone and realised he had a message from Loretta. It stated that she had landed in Doha and was about to board the flight to Auckland. The first leg of the flight had gone well and she was missing him already. She apologised for leaving him in Cyprus but promised that she would make it up to him when he returned to New Zealand. The message was a couple of hours old. Nathan smiled when he read it. *I wonder whether she'll still make it up to me even if I'm unsuccessful,* he pondered.

That evening, after a swim, shower and shave, Nathan made his way to the bar in the village in his favourite shorts, T-shirt and trainers. As he approached, he could see Andreas sitting outside, in his usual place. Andreas waved through a cloud of cigar smoke, which filtered up through the vines above his head and dispersed into the warm, humid evening air. There were a few other people sitting outside, who looked like locals.

As Nathan approached, the man he now knew to be the owner appeared in his white apron and placed a carafe of red wine and two glasses on the table in front of Andreas. The owner gave Nathan a quick wave before returning to his duties behind the bar.

'Your timing is impeccable,' said Andreas, as Nathan pulled up a chair to the table.

'I wish that were always the case,' Nathan replied, 'but I tend to put my foot in it, particularly where Loretta's concerned.'

'Have you heard from her?'

'I had a message to say that she's on the final leg of the flight. All seems okay.'

'Good, well hopefully you can get back to be with her soon.'

'Well, that's the plan, if all goes well here,' said Nathan.

'A glass of wine, my friend?'

'Yes please,' replied Nathan.

Andreas poured two glasses. 'Yamas,' he said.

'Yamas,' replied Nathan.

Andreas appeared keen to speak. 'I have spoken to my friend. If we go to his farm in the morning at ten o'clock, he said he will give you a crash course on using his drone. He is happy for you to use it but he wants it back tomorrow night.'

'That's fantastic,' said Nathan. 'But perhaps not good to call it a crash course.' They both laughed. Nathan took a sip of wine. 'Your wine?'

'Of course.'

'I can tell. I recognise the flavour. You're a man of many skills, Andreas.'

'I know,' said Andreas nonchalantly and with a smile.

'I've been looking at your map of Varosha. I've identified the street that we're looking for, and a landmark, so hopefully I'll be able to fly the drone over the area to see how the land lies. The only issue I see at the moment is a launching area. The car park that we parked in today would be perfect if it didn't have such an open aspect. We'd stand out and end up being arrested by the authorities.'

'Yes, I understand,' said Andreas. 'There are official viewing points but they are watched by the Turks. But I have an idea. There is a small house just inside the forbidden zone. When we were teenagers a few of us gained access just for the hell of it, just to say we had been in there. When we were in the car park today, it all came back to me. It is the only time I have ever been in there. It was frightening. They had more soldiers in those days but we were young and foolish.'

'Would you be able to take me there?' said Nathan.

'Yes.'

'I mean, literally to the house and into the forbidden zone.'

'I have been thinking about this Nathan. You are showing a determination and a concern, not just about the Mykanos investment but also about us, and I admire that.

So, I think it only right that I support you. I will take you there and hopefully we will be able to launch the drone in secret, but if it is too risky we must be prepared to walk away. Our safety and wellbeing must take priority,' said Andreas.

'I wouldn't have it any other way. And thank you for your help. It means so much. What do you think are our chances of recovering the documents?'

'I do not know. Around five per cent maybe? I guess a big step would be identifying the premises, and that will not be easy. I expect them to be empty shells but one consolation is that you should not have any problem gaining access. They are all wide open to the elements.'

Nathan didn't know whether this was a good thing or bad. If the place was wide open, the chances were the so-called secret safe had already been found. He visualised walking into the basement and seeing an empty safe with its door open and only occupied by numerous spider webs. Loretta had said that her father had moved the documents to the basement of the Mykanos Real Estate agency because it had a very secret safe. Depending on how secret, there was still a possibility that the safe hadn't been found. It couldn't be a free-standing floor safe, which wouldn't be secret, so it must have been buried in the floor or wall.

'Are you planning to fly the drone down Ermou Street?' enquired Andreas.

'Well, I thought if I did an overhead pass first to see whether I can spot any security in the area, and if it was all okay, yes, come down to lower level and try to locate the Mykanos Real Estate agency. Do you think there will still be a sign above the premises Andreas?'

'It depends upon how much weather the front of the building gets. If it is in the shade of another building then it is possible, otherwise it could be bleached, decomposed or have just fallen off.'

Nathan was about to continue the conversation when a large black car pulled up directly outside the bar. It was a model that he didn't recognise. The two men watched as two young women got out of the rear of the car then entered the outside area of the bar and took a table right next to them. Nathan thought it was unusual, as there were plenty of unoccupied tables, so why sit right next to them?

Andreas looked at Nathan and briefly raised his eyebrows. 'We can continue the conversation later or in the morning,' he suggested.

The waiter rushed out to serve the two ladies. Nathan couldn't help noticing his roaming eyes and eagerness to please.

'That's fine,' said Nathan, as he was suddenly overcome with the waft of strong perfume; the scent was very floral and fresh. He wondered whether the two women bathed in it before they came out. He turned to look at the women and saw they were probably not long out of their teens and were both very attractive. One of the women ran her hand through her jet-black shiny hair, using her deep-red manicured nails as a comb. They both appeared to be wearing false eyelashes and dark eyeliner that terminated with a flick in the corner of each eye. Nathan couldn't help noticing that Andreas was giving the women far too much attention. 'How are Helena and baby George?' he asked.

Andreas visibly shook his head to take his mind off the two attractive women and returned to the real world. 'I am sorry, I was miles away,' he said.

'I noticed,' said Nathan with a smile.

'I am a lucky man; they are both very well. Although Helena thinks I am mad for coming here and buying my wine at extortionate prices.'

'Have you thought that perhaps she's correct?'

'I know she is correct but, what the hell, maybe one day soon I will put my prices up. Yamas,' Andreas said, lifting his glass of wine.

'Yamas,' replied Nathan, who was then surprised by the two women in chorus shouting, 'Yamas.'

The evening went from strength to strength. There was plenty of wine consumed and quite a few cocktails. Nathan was flattered, as the two women had paid particular attention to him. One of them had even left him her mobile number. The women later left in the same car they had arrived in.

'That was fun,' said Nathan, as the black car pulled away.

'It was fun for you,' replied Andreas.

'I think I could get used to this Cypriot hospitality,' said Nathan.

8

NATHAN WALKED back to the villa. He was in a good mood after an enjoyable evening and was looking forward to tomorrow's drone learning and flight. But at the back of his mind was the niggling doubt as to whether or not it was the right thing to do. It was as if he were on some sort of conveyor that was leading him to Varosha, and he either couldn't or didn't want to get off. It was a strange feeling but he was committed now and there was no turning back.

Back at the villa, he slipped the key into the front door lock and pushed the door open. Almost immediately he noticed a smell he wasn't expecting. After being in the company of two highly florally scented young ladies, he was now confronted by a smell of body odour and stale cigarette smoke. Although merry with the evening's wine consumption, he was immediately on his guard. He stood stock still and listened for a couple of minutes. Because he couldn't hear anyone moving around the villa didn't mean there was no one in there now, hiding and waiting to make a move.

He removed his trainers and, with stealth, slowly made his way into the kitchen. The moon was shining through the patio doors, which offered a reasonable amount of light to illuminate the room. He could see that the area was clear of intruders as he made his way to the patio doors. He noticed that the main sliding door was unlocked and presumed that was the entry point for the uninvited guests. Immediately next to the doors there was a large, glazed vase-shaped container with two golf clubs protruding from its neck. He removed one of the clubs carefully and, with the confidence of knowing he now had a weapon, turned around to start a search of the villa.

Retracing his way back through the kitchen to the hallway, Nathan thought he heard the sound of some movement, just a faint shuffle, but he couldn't make out where exactly it had come from. Now in the hallway, it was much darker. He padded his way across the tiled floor towards the lounge. The door was open and he quickly peeped around the corner before bobbing back. He repeated this movement three times but it was too dark to see. His heart was pumping as he deliberated whether or not turning the light on was the best decision. He could feel the sweat running down the side of his face and the middle of his back. There could be someone behind the door, so he stood and waited.

Nathan eventually decided to put his arm into the lounge to switch on the light. As he did so the door was immediately slammed against his arm, causing a searing pain to travel up to his shoulder. He pulled his arm free and, in doing so, fell to the floor and dropped the golf club. As the door opened, a large, barrel-chested, unshaven man appeared. He jumped on Nathan and, with a strong arm, forced him into a headlock.

As his assailant tried to stand him up, Nathan quickly grabbed the golf club, moved his torso to one side and reverse-stabbed at the man with the shaft of the club. He could feel the impact in the man's stomach and, as he went higher into the ribs, he felt something give way. The attacker shouted in pain, just as a second intruder rushed down the stairs towards them. Nathan, now released from the headlock, had time to swing the club at his initial attacker's head. The noise on impact was sickening but the effect was immediate, as the man collapsed on to his knees with blood gushing from a serious head wound.

Nathan turned quickly as the other man approached. He stood his ground as the man withdrew a large knife from a sheath on his belt. The intruder started to shout in a foreign language, which sounded to Nathan like Russian. Nathan reciprocated and shouted, 'Get out while you can and take him with you.'

'The land papers,' the attacker replied in an aggressive broken English accent. 'Give them to me now or I'll cut you open.'

Nathan stepped back into the lounge doorway to make space between himself and his attacker's shiny and dangerous-looking knife. The man suddenly became preoccupied with his partner, who was still on his knees, but now in a large pool of blood. He stood him up and put one arm around him for support.

'I will come back for the papers and kill you,' the man snarled, as he started to hobble his way to the front door with the burden of his injured partner. For a brief second Nathan thought about attacking him with the golf club while his back was turned but it didn't seem right, as they were about to leave.

As the two assailants left the villa, Nathan shouted after them, 'Come back again and there will be a small army waiting for you.'

The man turned, and still propping up his partner, who was now looking in a very poor state, hissed back, 'You are going to need it you bastard.'

Nathan watched them as they walked down the driveway. As they reached the road he could see in the moonlight as a silver car appeared and took them away. Nathan stepped back inside the villa and closed the door. He let out a huge sigh of relief as he looked towards the lounge door and the light partly illuminating the hallway. He switched on the hallway light and was horrified at the amount of blood on the floor and also on the walls, which obviously occurred when he hit the first attacker with the golf club.

The club was still in his hand. The head of the seven iron was red with blood and a large piece of skin had attached itself. The shaft was bent at a slight angle. Nathan realised the seriousness of his actions but it had all been done in self-defence and, in his opinion, using no more force than necessary. Although the amount of force used was always a moot point in a court of law. He hoped that the Cypriot police would see it his way.

He walked into the kitchen and used his mobile to call Andreas. He sounded as if he had been awoken from his sleep but, when Nathan explained what had happened, he said he would come around straight away.

Nathan sat down in the kitchen. He couldn't believe what had just happened to him. The Russian-sounding guy had said he wanted the land papers, presumably the same papers that Nathan was searching for. But it all seemed so extreme, to go to those measures just for some land documents. Then he realised what he had just considered. If he were prepared to risk his life for these documents, then so would others.

There's more value to this piece of land than meets the eye, Nathan thought. *And this Russian connection has cropped up again. First, the planning application, which is partly in Russian, then there were the Russian men sitting out at the bar, and now this. Could it be that the Russians want to destroy the documents so there's no proof of land ownership, and then buy the land at a favourable rate from the council?*

If that was the case, and he had to presume that it was, then the situation was much more dangerous than he had previously thought.

There was a knock at the front door. Nathan could see through the door's side window that it was Andreas, so he opened the door.

'Are you alright?' said Andreas with a concerned look.

'I'm okay but look at this mess.' Nathan showed Andreas the blood-drenched floor and splattered walls.

'Oh my god, you must tell me what happened, but first I will call the police.'

Nathan explained everything to Andreas before he called the police. Shortly after, two uniformed officers arrived before a man in a suit appeared, who Nathan presumed to be a detective. He introduced himself as Pavlos. A man in his late forties, of medium height and with thinning black hair. He came across as a no-nonsense kind of guy but he was pleasant enough. He went through the formalities of taking the personal information of Nathan and Andreas before asking for details of the incident.

'So why do you think that you were attacked here in the villa?' Pavlos asked.

'He was looking for the land papers,' Nathan replied.

'And what are the land papers?'

'Well, there appears to be a dispute going on now regarding who owns this large piece of land. It covers many acres. I can't remember how many. On the land is not only the villa but the smallholdings and associated housing, which was provided by the owners, the Mykanos family, and there's also access to the beach. Unfortunately, there's no proof of ownership as the relevant documents are missing.'

'So, what is in dispute exactly?' said Pavlos.

'The municipal council is saying that the Mykanos family are not the rightful owners as there are no land ownership documents. On that basis their intention is to make a compulsory reclamation of the land and sell it to the Russians, who plan to build a huge landfill and recycling plant.'

'How do you know that the Mykanos family legitimately owns this land?'

'Mr Mykanos has informed me that he purchased the land but he can't recall the location of the documents.'

'Are you telling me that Russian nationals have entered this villa with the intention of finding and retrieving documents for the purpose of, what, destroying them?'

'That's exactly what I'm saying. If proof of ownership isn't provided, then this land will be cleared of buildings and people and sold to the Russians.'

Pavlos lifted his eyebrows in disbelief. 'Is all this not a bit far-fetched?'

'Then how do you explain what has happened here tonight? And why was a Russian man demanding land papers from me?'

Turning away to look at the blood-stained hall, Pavlos crouched down for a closer look. 'Tell me how this happened Mr Mason.'

'I came back to the villa and, as soon as I opened the door, I could smell that someone had either been inside or was still here.'

'You have a keen sense of smell, Mr Mason,' said Pavlos sarcastically.

'Yes, actually I do. Anyway, I stood in the hall to listen but I couldn't hear anything, so I made my way through to the kitchen towards the rear patio door.' Nathan then explained how he had started to search the house but had been attacked when he tried to turn the lounge light on. 'The intruder must have been standing behind the door because he pushed it closed as far as he could against my arm. The shock and pain made me drop the club from my other hand, then this large man appeared in the doorway and jumped on me.'

'Did he say anything at this point?' asked Pavlos.

'No, he just got me in a headlock and, as he stood me up, I was able to grab the golf club from the floor. I thrust the club into his stomach then into his ribs and he screamed in pain and released me. Then I took a swing at him with the club and cracked the side of his head. He went down on his knees. By this time, his partner had come down the stairs and was violently threatening me with a large knife. That was when he said he wanted the land papers but, when he saw the state his partner was in, he changed his priorities, although not before telling me that he was coming back for the papers and to kill me.'

'What is your involvement here Mr Mason?'

'I came here with Loretta Mykanos for a holiday. Unfortunately, she had to return to New Zealand because her father is very ill. I offered to stay to try to locate the missing documents.'

'So, you are working on behalf of the Mykanos family then?'

'Yes, I'm trying to resolve the problem. I've been to the council to look at their proposals for development and I'm contacting local solicitors to see whether I can find out where the land documents are lodged.'

'Surely someone in the organisation would know where the documents are held,' said Pavlos.

Nathan hesitated. He certainly wasn't going to tell Pavlos that they were in Varosha and he was planning to go there to get them. 'Like I said before, Mr Mykanos is very unwell and can't remember. It was a long time ago, in the 70s.'

'Not a good time for our country. It seems a lot rests on the finding of the papers. You are under a lot of pressure, Mr Mason. I hope they are paying you well.'

Nathan was about to reply that he was doing it for free but decided it wouldn't bring anything to the conversation. 'I get by,' he replied.

Pavlos took a description of the men involved in the attack, and details of the getaway vehicle. The two officers who had initially attended had left upon the arrival of a female scenes-of-crime officer, who took possession of the golf club. She then took several blood samples from the wall and carpet and dusted some fingerprints from the patio door frame and glass. Before leaving, she did a thorough sweep of the house and took a series of photographs of the hallway.

Pavlos wrote down his contact details on a small piece of paper and handed it to Nathan. 'If you find out that anything has been taken, give me a call on that number and I will include it in the crime report. I notice that your arm seems to be swollen and bruised. Do you have any other injuries?'

'No, just my arm,' replied Nathan.

'I would get it looked at, if I were you. There could be some bone damage there.'

'Yes okay,' replied Nathan, knowing full well he had no intention of spending any of his valuable time waiting at a hospital accident and emergency department.

'If there is anything else, please let me know,' Pavlos said as he stopped in the doorway on his way out. 'Oh, and just one other thing. Be careful who you speak to in the village bar.'

'Why do you say that? And how do you know who I've been speaking to?' replied Nathan.

'I drive through the village in the evenings. I always look to see who is sitting out and enjoying themselves. I noticed you two with the two girls. I know that one of them has been linked with some unscrupulous characters in the past.'

'It is nothing to do with me,' interrupted Andreas. 'It is him they are interested in. I am happily married.'

'What sort of unscrupulous characters?' asked Nathan, with a look of concern etched across his face. 'Could they be involved with what's happened here tonight?'

'It is not for me to say but I will be carrying out my investigations. In the meantime, keep safe, lock your doors and at any sign of further problems call us. Goodnight.' Pavlos left the house and closed the door behind him.

Nathan turned to Andreas. 'What was all that for? What are you scared of?'

'If Helena gets the wrong idea, I will be in for a severe tongue-lashing,' said Andreas.

'So, it's not the fact that one of the girls mixes with the wrong crowd that bothers you, it's the fact that your wife may find out.'

'Yes, and she will. It is a very small village and people talk.'

'But we didn't do anything wrong, we just had a few drinks and conversation,' said Nathan.

'Helena will not see it like that.'

Nathan sensed that there was a bit of a trust issue between Helena and Andreas and wondered whether Andreas had been involved in an extra-marital relationship in the past.

'Well, I've got to start clearing this place up. Thanks for coming around and calling the police,' said Nathan.

'It is the least I could do. Now I will help you to clean up, then you can spend the night at ours. The sofa in the lounge opens up into a double bed.'

'There's no need, Andreas. Honestly, I'll be fine.'

'I think to play it safe you should stay at ours tonight, just in case you get a repeat visit.'

Nathan contemplated for a moment. 'I think the chances of anyone coming back tonight are slim but, thanks, I'll take you up on your offer.'

The two men cleaned the villa. It was the entrance hall that required most attention, although the bedrooms had been trashed and the contents of all the drawers piled up on the beds. Mattresses had been displaced, wardrobes emptied, even the pile of clean laundry in the airing cupboard had been thrown across the landing.

While Andreas was finishing downstairs, Nathan lifted the mirror off the bedroom wall. The safe was there and still intact. He put the mirror back in its place. The intruders had made a mess but they weren't that thorough.

When the villa was tidy again, Nathan made sure everywhere was secure before picking up his overnight bag, locking the front door and walking with Andreas to his home.

9

THE NEXT morning, Nathan arose from his sofa bed at around eight o'clock. He was feeling stiff from the incident the previous night and his right forearm was still swollen and now severely bruised. Andreas came into the lounge, gave him a couple of towels and directed him to the shower room.

Helena had prepared some omelettes and toast. When Nathan was refreshed, he joined them in the kitchen. George was sitting in his high chair, with baby rice spread across his face and hands. The tray in front of him was awash with milk and a rusk-type substance. Helena was trying to feed him with a white plastic spoon.

'Good morning,' Helena greeted Nathan. 'How is the victim this morning?'

'Not as bad as the other guy,' replied Nathan.

'What a terrible experience,' Helena continued. 'I have never heard of such a thing. Well, only on TV. The people in the village will be horrified when they find out.'

'I'm a crime magnet. Everywhere I go something seems to happen.'

'Then please do not stay too long,' joked Andreas.

'Andreas!' said Helena, scowling at him.

'I am only joking. He knows that. How is that arm this morning?'

'Sore and stiff but I don't think anything is broken.'

'Would you like me to bandage it for you, Nathan?' asked Helena.

'No, it'll be all right, but thanks for the offer. You're doing enough for me already.'

'Well, would you like something to ease the pain?' she insisted. Before Nathan had time to answer, Helena had produced a bottle of Panadol from her shoulder bag, which was strung across the back of her chair. She handed him the bottle and Nathan smiled at her before swallowing two tablets with a sip of freshly squeezed orange juice.

'Thank you Helena, you're a good woman.'

'I am but sometimes taken for granted.'

Nathan sensed the barbed comment and couldn't help noticing that she glanced in Andreas's direction when she said it. He smiled inwardly as he thought to himself: *I need to change the direction of this conversation. Helena isn't happy with Andreas. Surely, she hasn't heard about the girls visiting the bar last night already, or he's in her bad books for something else. God help him if she finds out he's going into Varosha. She'll kill him, if not with her hands, then with her tongue.*

Nathan handed the bottle back to Helena and said, 'You really didn't need to prepare breakfast for me. I could have gone back to the villa. Mind you, I haven't got an awful lot of food in. I was planning to use the bar in the village more.'

As soon as Nathan mentioned the bar, Helena looked uncomfortable and Andreas shuffled in his seat. *I've just put my foot in it again. Got to think of something quickly*, Nathan thought. 'But I need to get lots of fresh food in for barbequing. I love barbequed food … king prawns, tuna steaks—'

'Swordfish souvlaki,' interrupted Helena. 'It is a Cypriot speciality. Cubes of swordfish, peppers, onions and anything you like, all on a skewer and cooked over the barbecue.'

'That as well,' said Nathan. 'The three of you are invited to the villa. My treat.'

Nathan noticed that Helena didn't seem too impressed with his offer. 'Nathan, if you do not mind, could we have the barbecue here in our garden? I think I would feel safer, especially with George.'

'I'm sorry, I wasn't thinking. After what happened last night, I can understand your concern. Let me buy the supplies, anyway. I take it you have a barbecue to use?'

'Of course,' interjected Andreas. 'We are Cypriot. We get our barbecues as a matter of priority in this country. It is a standard charcoal one but it is big enough to roast a pig on.' The two men laughed. Helena just forced out a brief nod in agreement. It was obvious to Nathan that she was still cross with Andreas.

Helena stood up and announced, 'Right, I am going to take George upstairs to get him cleaned up.'

'Okay, well I'm leaving shortly, so again a big thank you for everything, and I'll see you this evening,' said Nathan.

Helena smiled at him. 'You are welcome and, yes, we will see you later.' She lifted George out of his high chair and carried him off, close to her chest.

The tension in the room seemed to ease as Andreas watched his wife walk away. Nathan leaned towards him and, in a quiet voice, said, 'Is it the bush telegraph?'

Andreas hesitated for a second before he realised what Nathan meant. 'I think so. I heard her mobile ping earlier. It was probably one of her nosey friends reporting me for being out and about and in the presence of another female. Sometimes in such a small village, life can be very claustrophobic.'

'But you wouldn't have it any other way, would you Andreas?'

'No, I would not. Believe it or not, we are very happy here.'

'I believe it,' replied Nathan, as he patted Andreas on the back.

After breakfast they agreed that Andreas would collect Nathan, then drive them up to his friend's farm. But as

Nathan walked back to the villa, he started to feel uneasy. The threat he had received the night before was playing on his mind. Rightly or wrongly, he was having flashbacks to his sister's house in New Zealand, when on a couple of occasions he had realised he was in danger and was being watched from the nearby forest. He was on his own then as he was now. Although there was no comparison to the differing environments, he recognised all too well the familiar feelings, those gut feelings that were an early indicator to be on his guard.

He walked through the village. All was very calm. There was an elderly lady, complete with black apron and head scarf, who had hung an Afghan rug out on her washing line and was beating it hard with her yard brush. The very slight breeze was carrying puffs of dust across the road in Nathan's direction, so he increased his pace to try to avoid the fog. An image came into his head of Andreas smoking one of his cigars, while Helena beat him with her yard brush, repeatedly shouting, 'You cheated on me.' He smiled to himself.

He was suddenly back in the real world as a car slowly passed by. It was an old BMW that had been pimped up with blacked-out windows, chrome wheels and a chrome exhaust the size of a drainpipe. He noticed that the driver's window was open, just enough for him to see a shaved head. Nathan was watchful as the car pulled to a stop in the bend of the road, about fifty metres ahead.

He suddenly felt very vulnerable. Just ahead, in the adjacent banana plantation, he could see a steel rod lying on the ground. It looked like it had been dislodged but would have originally been used as a securing point for the black plastic water pipes that wormed their way around the plantation as part of the irrigation system. He decided that, if the car was still there as he approached, he would pick up the steel bar in passing, just in case he needed it.

The car still sat there on the corner with its engine running. Nathan was half expecting the door to open as he approached and was about to go for the steel rod but the car suddenly pulled away, not at breakneck speed but at a rate that indicated that the driver was lost or had just been enjoying the view. *False alarm. Just me letting my imagination run away with me.*

As Nathan approached the villa, the memories of last night's attack and struggle returned. He unlocked the front door and looked at the floor by the entrance to the lounge. They had done a good job of clearing the blood from the tiled floor. As he looked at the walls, he was pleased to see there were no remains of blood spots or smears. He was thankful that they had been painted with waterproof emulsion, which made them easy to wipe clean.

He had a quick look around the villa to make sure everything was how he liked it. By the time he had made himself a coffee, changed his T-shirt and put his dirty washing in the washing machine, Andreas was knocking at the door.

10

ANDREAS WAS driving Nathan to his friend's farm in the white rusty Isuzu pickup.

'What's your friend's name, Andreas?'

'His name is Mavros but he is known as Mav. He is a good man. We have known each other for many years. Goats are his business, in particular their milk, which goes towards one of our major products that is exported all over the world—'

'That would be halloumi,' interrupted Nathan.

'Yes, my friend, you are correct.'

They were heading in a westerly direction and graduating up a large hillside. They were no longer on a tarmac road surface but a dusty gravel track and they seemed to snake slowly up the hillside, leaving clouds of dust in their wake. Nathan noticed that the small olive

142

trees that seemed to grow everywhere and at random along the side of the track were caked in fine dust, almost giving the impression of a giant cake decoration sprinkled with icing sugar.

'I'll just pull over here for a second, then jump out and take in the view,' said Andreas. He pulled over and they both got out of the vehicle.

They were looking towards the east, the direction from which they had just travelled. The view was spectacular. Having only driven a couple of miles, they were now looking down on the village of Anapetri. Nathan could follow the coastline along the villa land, then north to the southern end of Varosha. 'This really is a sight to behold,' he said.

'I know, I quite often just come up here for the view. But this is the time of year to appreciate it, especially on a clear morning like this.'

'It's stunning, it really is,' confirmed Nathan.

'Well, let's continue. Mav's place is just over the hill in the valley.'

'Okay,' said Nathan, and they got back into the Isuzu.

They continued to the crest of the hill and once again Nathan was amazed at the spectacular view just laid out like a canvas in front of him. It was a true valley with sheer sides speckled with the occasional olive tree and rocky outcrops forming overhanging ridges. And goats. They were everywhere and in the most ridiculous places. Standing on a rocky shelf with a huge drop beneath it.

Walking up hillsides along the narrowest of paths. Down at the floor of the valley where some had climbed on the outhouse roofs and farm buildings. *Why do goats climb?* He never understood.

Next to the outhouses, Nathan could see a large grey metallic-looking barn. And next to the barn was an attractive, large, stone farmhouse with a perimeter fence. The garden consisted of patches of grass, a couple of palm trees and a vegetable growing area. Even more spectacular was a large palm tree forest in a perfect square, which looked like an oasis in a desert.

'This is all Mav's,' said Andreas, gesticulating with an outstretched arm.'

'What, all of it?' exclaimed Nathan.

'Yes, as far as the eye can see.'

'And what's with the palm tree oasis?'

'He grows and sells them to landscapers, builders, garden centres and anyone who wants one,' replied Andreas.

This guy must be some kind of entrepreneur. I can't wait to meet him, thought Nathan.

They made their way down the winding track. The Isuzu pickup was perfect for this type of environment and, before they knew it, they were pulling up outside the house in a cloud of dust.

'Just to forewarn you,' said Andreas, 'Mav is a man of few words. I have got to know him over the years. He is not being rude or disrespectful, it is just the way he is, so please do not be offended if he does not greet you with open arms.'

'I'll bear that in mind,' replied Nathan.

The two men got out of the truck and Nathan followed Andreas to a side entrance. The heat was intense, there was no breeze of any kind down in the valley bottom and the humidity was considerable.

'Mav!' shouted Andreas loudly.

A strong deep voice from the rear of the house grunted, 'Around the back.'

They made their way via a gravel path. Mav was sitting at a circular wooden table on which, in the middle, was a camouflage-coloured drone. Mav stayed seated as they approached.

'Mav, this is Nathan, who I was telling you about.'

Mav didn't speak. He just stuck out a hand, which Nathan shook. 'Hi Mav,' he said.

'Hello,' was the reply in a deep guttural voice. 'You want to use my drone.'

'Yes, if you don't mind,' said Nathan.

'I mind,' Mav replied. Nathan thought he could see a semblance of a smile but Mav was hard to read.

'We can bring it back this afternoon,' said Andreas. Mav then turned to look at his drone, which had pride of place on the table. He picked it up with one hand and used his dirt-stained index finger of the other to start pointing out its component parts.

'This antenna, this camera, this receiver, this batteries, this speed controller, this flight controller, this motors, this propellors, this handset and this tablet. You can borrow, too. It has the flight control software on it. I plug this handset into the tablet, clip them together and you can watch the pictures and fly it from the joystick on the handset. Here is the power button on the drone.'

Mav stood up and Nathan saw that he was a squat man, powerfully built, in his mid-thirties. 'If we move into the shade so we can see the pictures on the tablet,' Mav suggested. They stepped back towards the house and huddled around the tablet and handset. Within seconds the drone was airborne and making its way along the valley. Nathan was amazed at the quality of the pictures. He watched carefully as Mav used the joystick to manoeuvre the machine left, right, up and down before it returned to a perfect landing on the table in front of them.

'Now I will take time to train both of you how to use it. I do not want it coming back in bits, otherwise you pay me for a brand-new one.'

They spent the next two hours trying to master the controls before Mav proudly announced, 'You are trained. Always keep the drone in your sight and limit your flight time to no more than fifteen minutes. It will then need a full charge before you can use it again and that could take two to three hours. I want it back late afternoon. I use it to check the herd every night before dark.'

'Okay,' they both replied.

'Thank you,' said Nathan. 'Your help is much appreciated.' He picked up the drone and Andreas took the controller and tablet. Mav just gave a nod in reply.

Nathan and Andreas were making their way back to the Isuzu when Nathan's mobile rang. It was Loretta. He placed the drone on the front passenger seat. 'Hi, how are you?' he said.

'Tired. It was a long journey but at least I'm here. I'll be staying with Mum and Dad.'

'How is he?'

'Worse than I expected. The cancer is very aggressive. It's already weakened his voice somewhat and he's very weak. I don't think he has long left. I'm so shocked at the speed that all this is happening, and I'm sorry I left you in Cyprus.' Loretta began to cry.

'Please stay strong. And you left me because you needed to be with your dad. You did the right thing.'

'Thank you for your support. I really don't know what I would do without you,' she replied through the sobs.

'Hopefully you'll never be without me.' Immediately Nathan regretted what he had just said. *Oh no, that sounded too heavy.*

There was a slight delay before Loretta replied, 'I hope so too.' Nathan had the urge to get on a flight to New Zealand and be with her at her time of crisis.

'Anyway, how are you getting on with the council about the land issue?' Loretta asked.

'It's slow going. I'm thinking about starting a stop the landfill campaign and maybe putting something in the local newspapers to try to raise support.' Nathan didn't like lying to Loretta but he was just trying to buy himself some time.

'Okay, and I know I'm repeating myself, but I don't want you going into Varosha. Okay?'

'Yes, okay. How's your mum bearing up?' said Nathan, trying to change the direction of the conversation.

'You know Mum. She's pretty tough but I can tell that she's really cut up about it. It's the speed of events. Her life has been turned upside down in a week and now she has to contemplate going forward in a life without my dad. It's all so sad.'

'I understand. I'll get back to you as soon as I can. I just need a few more days to sort things out.'

'Okay. Mum's calling, so I have to go. I'll call you tomorrow. Miss you.'

'Miss you too,' replied Nathan, before hanging up.

'That sounds like bad news,' said Andreas.

'It is. Her dad is deteriorating quickly. It doesn't sound like he has long left.'

'I am sorry. That is so sad. He is a great man and has done so much for us. And what is this about a stop the landfill campaign?'

'Well, it was just a little lie. If I can't find the documents in Varosha, then I'll start a campaign.'

'Assuming that you are not in prison or lying on a cold slab,' said Andreas.

'You need to start feeling a little more positive, Andreas. What could possibly go wrong?' Nathan knew he was tempting fate with his words but he wanted to show Andreas that his intention was to continue until he had exhausted all possibilities.

'You are a crazy Englishman and you should not be out in the midday sun,' said Andreas with a smile.

'Quite true, my friend, quite true. So, let's find some shade and lunch.'

'Okay, did you bring your passport?'

Nathan fumbled at his combat shorts pocket, undid two buttons and produced his passport for Andreas.

'Okay, let's go to the little beachside café by Varosha, the one we stopped at the other day,' Andreas suggested.

'That's fine by me,' replied Nathan.

11

O N THEIR way to the café, Nathan and Andreas passed through the border control without incident. Nathan had ensured that the drone was hidden from the view of any border guards by covering it in the footwell of the Isuzu with an old piece of sack cloth that he had found pushed underneath the seat. On this occasion, Andreas wasn't familiar with the guards, so his oranges remained in place beneath the tarpaulin.

They pulled into the car park near the café and made their way across a paved area to the outside seating, making sure they had suitable cover at the table in the form of a parasol. After quickly consulting Nathan and a sticky menu card, Andreas ordered two chicken kebabs and two Americano coffees. There were a few people sitting at adjacent tables, tourists enjoying a late lunch or some respite from the searing heat on the beach.

Nathan looked at Andreas and kept his voice in a low tone so that they couldn't be overheard. 'The area where you used to gain access,' he gesticulated towards Varosha, 'is it nearby?'

'Yes, you see where the wall turns to the right and disappears, then it reappears just a little further on?'

'Yes.'

'Well, that is like a cul-de-sac. The outside walls of the properties actually form the perimeter walls of Varosha. It saved them from building a new fence. That is why the doors and windows are either bricked up or boarded up.'

'So how did you get in?'

'There is a very narrow gap between two buildings. The gap is big enough to get through. It is about a shoulder's width. It is fronted by a piece of metal framework with interlaced barbed wire, so it appears secure. But the metal frame has a central strengthening piece of box section, which slots into a slab of concrete. We used to be able to just lift the frame out, place it against the wall, squeeze through, then reposition the frame. Unless anyone saw us going through, there would be no sign that we had entered.'

'It sounds perfect, but what about watchtowers?'

'I do not think there are any on this side. Because this area is well lit at night and is populated by day, they do not really think there is a threat. Having said that, there is still a chance of being seen, and carrying a drone and all the other bits with it we would stand out as suspicious.'

The waiter arrived with two chicken kebabs with salad, two pittas, a large portion of French fries and two coffees. Andreas meticulously forked the chicken pieces off the skewer into the pitta, Nathan followed suit. The waiter returned with a bowl of tzatziki and a spoon. Andreas promptly poured the tzatziki into the gaping open mouth of his pitta, smothering the chicken pieces with the help of the spoon. He then topped it all off with a handsome portion of salad leaves and sliced tomatoes.

'Are you hungry?' said Nathan.

'Yes, just a touch, and I do love the way the Turks cook their chicken kebabs.'

'I've got to admit,' said Nathan, 'I feel really nervous about going in there,' nodding his head towards Varosha.

'Me too. I always get hungry when I am nervous.'

After Nathan had loaded his kebab and took his first bite, Andreas said, 'I've got a plan.'

'Fire away,' replied Nathan.

'If I drive the pickup to this end of the cul-de-sac, you load everything out on the Varosha side so people cannot see what we are doing. I lift the bonnet, making it look like we have broken down. You walk up the cul-de-sac to the entry point and I will quickly go and park the car and come and join you.'

'That sounds like a good plan. I know there's a big risk that we'll be seen but I understand that, no matter where we try to enter, it's always going to be a bit of a lottery as to whether we'll be able to make it in undetected. But we've come this far so we have to give it a shot, don't you agree?'

'Okay,' replied Andreas a little nervously.

The two men finished their meals and drinks and paid the waiter. They walked back to the pickup and prepared everything for a quick exit, before making their way to the cul-de-sac. Nathan could feel the tension as they arrived, then, like a military operation, they both left the vehicle.

Nathan, with his arms full and his load covered with a sack cloth, made his way quickly up the cul-de-sac. He noticed the small fence between the two buildings almost immediately. Meanwhile, Andreas had lifted the bonnet but at the same time was covertly watching Nathan make his way up to the section of fence.

Nathan placed his valuable load on the floor and approached the fence. Slipping his hands through the barbed wire, he gripped the steel cross-member and attempted to lift the section of fence out of its concrete base. It wouldn't move. He tried again, this time improving his grip and bending his knees, but it wouldn't budge. The sun was burning the back of his neck and the sweat was running down his forehead into his eyes as he tried one last time. His face turned red with the unbridled effort of his attempt to extract the box section. It didn't move. He turned around to see whether Andreas was available to help.

Andreas had been watching Nathan struggle so he pulled a half-metre length of angle iron from beneath the pickup's tarpaulin, with the intention of quickly running it up to Nathan to use as a lever to lift the fence. To his horror he saw two Turkish police officers approaching on foot. He was standing there with a large piece of iron in his hand, while the police approached with caution, hands on their side-arms, ready to aim and shoot if threatened. *Think quickly. What are you going to say?* Andreas thought.

One of the police officers came closer and drew his side arm from his holster. Shouting in Turkish, Andreas was unsure what to do. 'It is okay, it is for my car. The starter motor has stuck, it happens quite often. I strike it with this piece of metal and it releases, then I will be on my way.'

The second officer ordered a slight withdrawal as Andreas approached the engine compartment. He struck the starter motor with a clunk, then withdrew to the tarpaulin and threw the angle iron into the back. 'I'm just going to try the ignition,' he shouted. He jumped in, turned the key and the engine started. He turned the engine off and jumped out, then approached the two officers, smiling and with one hand in the air. 'It is okay. I have fixed it,' he said.

'Move on,' said the second officer as they walked by with a menacing swagger and a look that could kill. Andreas breathed a huge sigh of relief and mopped the sweat from his brow. He looked towards Nathan. He was down in a crouched position, with the sack cloth nearly covering him and the drone. He was well disguised among the litter and general detritus of everyday life but would undoubtedly have drawn attention should the police officers have looked in his direction.

When Nathan did appear, he gave Andreas the thumbs-up, which Andreas returned, although he seemed to be hesitating. *There must be something wrong. Why isn't he moving the pickup?* thought Nathan. He therefore decided to cover himself with the sackcloth again just in case the police officers reappeared. He could see through the weave of the fabric and was watching Andreas carefully. Suddenly, Andreas jumped into the pickup and drove off but Nathan knew that he had planned to park it nearby for a quick getaway.

A couple of minutes later, Andreas appeared on foot, as bold as brass, wearing a high-vis vest and carrying a spade on his shoulder; for all intents and purposes, a manual worker going about his business. He approached casually but with purpose.

'That was nerve-wracking,' Andreas said, with a stressed look on his face. 'I thought we were captured.'

'What on earth were you doing under the bonnet with that piece of metal?'

'Pretending that the starter motor had stuck. It was all I could think of at the time, but it used to be a problem until I got it replaced.'

'So, you fooled them into thinking you had broken down. Brilliant, absolutely brilliant. That's what you call thinking on your feet.'

'I know and it is not a position I want to be in again,' replied Andreas.

Nathan gave him a hearty pat on the back, and said, 'Now, give me that spade. We need to lever that fence up. It's rusted into the concrete.'

'I noticed that you were struggling,' replied Andreas. 'Let's do this as quickly as possible. We are standing out like a pair of beacons.'

They approached the small section of fence. Andreas pushed the head of the spade under the frame and both men pulled the handle up so the spade acted like a lever. It worked and the fence gave way as the box section came loose from its concrete socket. In no time at all they had lifted it to the side and squeezed through, along with the drone and its attachments. Andreas then relocated the section of fence, removed his high-vis, placed the spade on top of it and left it in the long grass.

They quickly moved down the alleyway between the two buildings. Fortunately there were no further obstructions, other than the grass, weeds and the occasional tin can. The alleyway opened out to what was previously a communal area surrounded by apartments. Extremely tall trees seemed to have grown from an oasis in the centre. Weeds, flowers and cordyline, plus a concoction of cacti had grown around the base of the trees, nearly filling the area completely.

Andreas pointed to the trees and, in a quiet voice, said, 'That will be the swimming pool.'

Nathan was surprised. *I'll bear that in mind. Stay away from the undergrowth. There will be a sheer drop hidden in there.* Looking around, he was shocked at the desolation, the neglect. *This is one scary place in daylight, so god knows what it would be like in the dark.*

Although they appeared to be in a residential area, not far to the east could be seen a series of tall buildings, towering above the others. They were the beachfront hotels. Huge monoliths of concrete, a reminder of the heady days and the good times of the 60s and 70s.

Andreas tapped Nathan on the arm, saying, 'Let's just go in here,' and pointing to the nearest apartment. All the windows and doors were missing so access was easily gained. The two men walked in through what used to be a patio door and found themselves standing in the lounge. The walls were bare concrete, any sign of plaster or paint seemingly piled up at the base of each wall. The dust and grit underfoot was considerable. The building was a carcass, with not even a window or door frames remaining. It had been totally stripped of anything that could be reused, or was it corrosion and decay that had taken its natural course? It looked as if only the outward-facing openings had been boarded up, which therefore became the Varosha perimeter wall.

'Let's go upstairs for a better view,' said Andreas. Nathan followed him as they walked up a set of concrete steps, which had been covered with bird excrement. As they approached the landing, they were greeted by a rusty old bicycle frame minus its wheels. The rust residue seemed to have leeched into the tile grout beneath it.

As they entered a bedroom that overlooked the oasis, there were pages of a Greek Orthodox bible strewn all around the room. The hardback cover with its spine still in place sat there in the middle of the tiled floor, having been stripped of its contents over many windy winters. There was a small balcony with an open view over the surrounding urban terrain. They walked towards it but remained just inside the room, which offered some semblance of cover. Nathan withdrew the map of Varosha from his combat shorts pocket and pointed out to Andreas the hotels on the coast road, the cul-de-sac, and the silo.

Nathan pointed towards the west. 'And that should be Ermou Street. Look, look,' he said excitedly. 'Between the two buildings, behind the trees … it's the silo.'

Both men were now looking at the large off-white construction that could be seen through the gap. Even from a distance they could see that it had a cylindrical shape, like no other in the area. Lines of rust seemed to pour from the riveted steel seams around its circumference.

'Let's waste no more time,' said Nathan. 'Let's get this drone up and head for our target.'

'Just beware,' said Andreas, 'there is actually a public viewing point not far from here, near that hotel.' He pointed to the large building, which seemed to be the first in a long line of hotels, stretching southwards all the way down the coast. 'I think if you stay relatively low, nobody will see it, as there are just too many buildings in between.'

'Right, I'll bear that in mind. I wish you had told me earlier though,' said Nathan irritably.

'Yes, sorry,' said Andreas very apologetically.

They prepared the drone for launch. It only took a couple of minutes before it was linked to the tablet and the controller and was ready to go.

'Do you want to fly it?' asked Nathan.

'Not particularly. I thought you were slightly better than me, and you pick things up more quickly than I do, so please, I will leave it to you.'

'Okay, no problem. Here we go …'

With the tablet clipped on to the console, which had a joystick at either side, Nathan stood up, while Andreas flicked the tiny switch on the drone, kicking it into life. The four propellors started to rotate with a dull humming noise, which increased as the drone lifted off the ground and hovered above the balcony, before heading in a westerly direction.

Andreas first stood behind Nathan watching the drone, then looked at the screen on the tablet. 'It is a great picture,' he said. Nathan nodded in agreement. The drone was transmitting pictures of a continuous scene of desolation and abandonment, flecked with the green images of nature forcing its way through roads and pathways. Some roads were completely overgrown, while others were clear. The same applied to the buildings, some crumbling as tree roots forced huge fractures and fissures to appear, increasing their instability, while some looked almost habitable from a distance.

Andreas picked up the map and tried to direct Nathan towards the silo. 'Are you going to go straight between the two buildings? Because, if you do, you are then going to have to turn right, on the assumption that the silo is at the end of Ermou Street. It means that we are going to lose sight of the drone and must fly it off camera.'

'Yes, I'm going through the gap. And yes, we'll lose sight of the drone, but there's no other way of doing it unless I fly really high and risk being spotted. I know Mav said never lose sight of it but what else can I do?' said Nathan.

'I agree. Fly by camera, nice and slow.'

The drone arrived at the gap. Nathan controlled it with extreme care, although he was anxious because his view didn't include what was above, he was only looking forward and down. He maintained a height of five metres. The drone was still in the sight of the two men but they knew it was about to get a little trickier.

The drone exited the gap and almost immediately in front of them was the silo. Larger than they expected, it appeared to be growing foliage from its roof, trailing down over its mass. At the base of the silo was a door, two metres in height and half as wide. Nathan carefully turned the drone to his right and there it was in all its glory – Ermou Street. Quite a long road with rows of shops and offices on either side.

Nathan reduced the drone's height slightly, then began to progress along the road. They were looking at the properties on the east side and stopped outside every building to see whether there were any clues leading to a shop or office with the name Mykanos. Most of the buildings were just empty shells, past the point of reclamation and destined for demolition at some point in the future.

Andreas tapped Nathan on the shoulder. 'What's that up ahead in the middle of the road?'

Nathan directed the drone to hover above something in the road ahead. As it approached, two large birds of prey opened their wings with slow flaps and left the scene, kicking up dust from the road in their wake. Lying on the road was the bloody carcass of a dead animal.

'It looks like a cat,' said Nathan. 'We'll have to crack on. Only ten minutes' battery life left.'

The drone moved towards the end of the street without seeing anything of interest, then as it was turning to take a reciprocal route, they came across a Datsun car showroom. Most of the vehicles looked to be in place but some had their doors and bonnets open, stripped for spares decades ago.

'I've seen pictures of that showroom on the internet,' said Nathan.

'Yes, I think it is one of those iconic images from that era here in Cyprus,' replied Andreas.

The drone progressed back up Ermou Street, this time concentrating on the properties on the west side. There was nothing of any significance, just a badly sun-bleached sign that read 'Chris Car Rentals'. As they reapproached the animal carcass in the road, a group of large rats were now feasting, no doubt having waited for the birds to leave before they approached, for fear of falling victims themselves. Suddenly, the drone shuddered and its camera angle changed. The last image they saw was the rapidly approaching concrete surface of the road, before the picture died.

'Shit, shit, no! What happened?' said a shocked Andreas.

'I don't know, it just died; it fell like a stone. It will be in a million pieces now. Something must have brought it down.'

'Mav will not be happy,' said Andreas.

'I'll give him the money for a new one,' replied Nathan impatiently.

'Maybe the footage will show what happened. We can look when we get back. Let's make a move before we get spotted.'

They headed down the stairs, out of the building and went through the alleyway between the two buildings.

Nathan could see through the fence ahead and was horrified at the sight of a white car with POLIS and a blue stripe down the side. It was parked at the end of the cul-de-sac. 'Get down,' he hissed. They both crouched low in the long grass.

'What is it?' asked Andreas.

'It's the police. They're at the end of the cul-de-sac. Just stay low and don't move.'

Nathan could see through the long grass and between the gaps in the fence. The police car was parked roughly where Andreas had parked earlier, so fortunately not too close to the fence. Suddenly, two police officers appeared along with a shirtless man with Union Jack shorts. He had a plethora of tattoos all over his body and was wearing bright red flip-flops. He was very unsteady on his feet and it looked as if they were taking him into custody. They pushed him into the back of the car, then one of the officers jumped in next to him, while the other stood outside, next to the door.

Nathan could hear the sound of raised voices coming from within the car but was distracted by a stinging feeling on his leg and back. He looked down at his feet and realised he had stood in a nest of large angry ants, which were now crawling up his legs and back and stinging in the process.

'Get back but stay low,' Nathan whispered to Andreas. They both shuffled backwards in a walking crouched position and headed back into the building. Nathan removed his T-shirt and shorts and started to rigorously shake his clothes. Standing there in his trainers and boxer shorts, he looked at Andreas, who was calmly patting himself down and brushing away any surplus ants.

'Do they not bother you, Andreas?'

'Not particularly. They sting a little but I am quite used to them.' Nathan looked at him in amazement before replacing his clothes.

'I've really had enough of this place. I don't usually suffer from feeling vulnerable but I am now and the thought that we can't just walk out of here is pretty unnerving,' said Nathan.

'I know what you mean. Let's just give it five minutes and hopefully the police will have moved on.'

What an absolute disaster of a day, Nathan thought to himself. *Not just the fact that we lost the drone, but we're no further forward. Unless the drone footage shows us something that we've missed with the naked eye, I think I'm going to accept defeat on this one and, to be quite honest, I hope I never see this inhospitable dangerous place again.*

Nathan snapped out of his despondency and went to check whether the police had moved on. He returned to Andreas. 'Okay, it's all clear. The police have gone. Follow me.'

They moved quickly between the two buildings. Nathan had the fence out and replaced within seconds, before the two of them casually walked down the cul-de-sac and across the car park to the waiting pickup, Andreas now

164

wearing his high-vis and carrying his spade across his shoulder.

The journey back was eventless, even crossing the border. The two men hardly spoke as they pondered the implications of the day's events. They made their way back up to Mav's place to inform him that his drone had been lost. They had already decided not to tell him that it had been lost in Varosha and thought it best to tell him they had lost control of it over the sea while looking back to view the coastline.

Needless to say, Mav wasn't happy. He shouted and cursed in Greek and at one point banged his fist on the table. Andreas said he had never seen him so angry. Nathan did, though, agree to suitably compensate Mav for the loss of the drone and the inconvenience of having to purchase another one. In the end, Mav shook hands with them both, before Nathan transferred the footage of the drone flight on to his smart phone and deleted it from Mav's tablet.

On the way back to the village, they called in at a couple of small shops to pick up some supplies for the upcoming barbecue. Andreas informed Nathan that Helena had agreed to do the preparation, as long as they did the cooking. He then dropped Nathan off at the villa.

'See you later. What time do you want me?' asked Nathan.

'Seven will be fine.'

Nathan waved as Andreas left in a cloud of dust, then opened the front door, where he found a few envelopes on the floor that looked mainly like junk mail. He picked them up and took them through to the kitchen, where he turned on the air conditioning unit, poured himself a glass of water and took it upstairs. He needed a shower.

In the bedroom, Nathan picked up the air conditioning remote and turned it on. As he was returning it to the bedside unit, he noticed a small piece of folded paper on the floor. He picked it up and realised it was the phone number of the girl from the bar. It wasn't clear to read and he certainly couldn't make out her name. He didn't remember asking her but he remembered her asking him his name. He turned the paper over and noticed on its edge an embossed symbol. He held it up to the light. It was circular and, in its centre, he noticed the double-headed eagle of Russia. There were some letters printed around the outside, which formed part of the circle. The letters were feint but he could make out U R A L S CORP.

Perhaps a large company from the Urals area of Russia, he thought, so he picked up his smart phone and quickly did a search for URALS CORP. He was astonished to find that it was a huge organisation, with offices in China, South America, Australia and, of course, Russia. There was nothing relating to landfill sites; on the contrary, it appeared that it was a mining company specialising in iron ore, nickel palladium, cobalt and lithium. *Cobalt and lithium. As far as I know these are an essential ingredient for batteries, in particular car batteries for all the new electrically powered cars. They could be attempting to purchase the land under false pretences. They're not a landfill company, they're a mining company.*

Nathan was shocked. *No wonder the Russians are desperate to get their hands on the land. If it contains lithium, or any other precious metals, it's worth an absolute fortune. Maybe the woman in the bar was a honey trap and she's been sent to find out whether the land papers exist and, if so, where they are. But there might be no connection between the two. It might just be my overactive imagination. It seems a bit of a coincidence though, and coincidences are not always what they seem to be. Does the municipal council know who it's dealing with? Do they really think it's going to be a landfill or are they part of the ruse? So many questions that need answers.*

He stripped off his clothes and jumped in the shower. *What's my next move? I should contact Detective Pavlos and inform him about the telephone number and the embossed mark. They should know, even if they can't do anything about it. They'll then realise that this needs to be taken more seriously.* After his shower Nathan was straight on his mobile phone. He rang the number on the card that Pavlos had given him. It was a recorded message, so he left the briefest of communications.

After dressing, Nathan made his way down to the kitchen, which had now been suitably cooled by the air conditioning. Standing against the kitchen worktop, he decided to look at the footage on his mobile phone of the events in Varosha. The video was very clear. The mixed feelings of deprivation, abandonment, desolation and isolation washed over him. The drone approached the rusty silo as it passed between the two buildings. As it turned to the right, it advanced down Ermou Street, overflying the carcass and scattering the birds of prey.

It was on the drone's return journey as it approached the carcass that Nathan noticed a swinging sign hanging from the front of one of the premises. He paused the footage. *Does that say Mykanos?* He zoomed in on the sign. The closer he got the grainier the image became. He zoomed out again and could clearly see the letters MYK but the rest of the sign had either deteriorated or the sun's reflection was making it difficult to read.

That's got to be it. Nathan reversed the footage and approached again. This time he could see a large opening where the front window used to be and right next to it a single opening that used to be the front door on to the street, a front door that hadn't seen customers in decades. He also noted a small entry to the side, next to the front door. It was difficult to see whether this went the full length of the building and separated it from the building next door or whether it was just a recess.

This is so frustrating; I just can't see enough of the building; I wonder whether there's a rear entrance. He continued playing the footage. As he passed over the carcass in the road, something caught his eye, moving in the top left corner of the screen, just before the drone's sudden dive and obliteration on the road below. He rewound the footage and watched it again and again, until he reached the spot where he could freeze the frame and zoom closer. It looked like a do-it-yourself watchtower. Four wooden pillars, a platform with sides, then a small square sloping roof. What was disturbing was the image of a person in the watchtower, holding a rifle aimed towards the drone. Nathan rewound and played the footage again and noticed a very feint flash just before the drone vibrated and then crashed down to the road. *The drone was shot down deliberately. Presumably the guy in the watchtower is a guard. Things just got more dangerous.*

Nathan sat down on one of the kitchen chairs, shaking his head. *I must be crazy to even think about going back in there. It's potentially a death trap. Anyone moving in Ermou Street would be visible to the watchtower. I would have to approach the building another way and hope I don't come across any other watchtowers. I can't believe I'm still contemplating doing this.*

He reviewed the footage numerous times until he was familiar with the layout of Ermou Street, from the silo to the car sales showroom. He was uncertain and starting to doubt once again whether or not to just give it up. He decided to give Loretta a call, regardless of the time in New Zealand. He knew that if she wasn't available, her mobile would pick up any messages.

12

LORETTA DIDN'T answer Nathan's call. It went to voicemail but he gave her an update anyway. He didn't like doing it but he lied about the fact that they had been into Varosha and that perhaps he was going to go back in to try to retrieve the documents. He did tell her about the Russians' interest in the land and the fact that they were trying to obtain it under the guise of a landfill company when they were actually a mining company. He thought it was a bit ironic that part of the business portfolio of the Mykanos Group was mining. He also didn't tell her about the attack at the villa.

Nathan was looking forward to returning to New Zealand but was concerned about how Loretta would react when he later told her that he had gone against her wishes. She had given him the number of the office in

Auckland, so when he was ready to return he was to call and they would arrange the return flight and any additional admin costs to be incurred. He felt like calling the office now and telling them to book the next available flight but he knew inside that he couldn't just walk away. He had to do something to help Andreas, his family and all the other families that they had met during their initial meeting. They were crying out for help; they didn't want to lose their homes and their livings.

~~~

Nathan was ready early and, after securing the villa, decided to call in at the village bar on his way to Andreas's house. As soon as he left the villa he was hit by the heat and humidity. *It feels warmer, even though it's early evening.* He had only reached the end of the drive before the perspiration was starting to form on his forehead.

As he walked along the dry dusty road, he suddenly felt very lonely. *I'm here in a foreign country, on my own with no real friends, no one to turn to for advice and no one on hand to help me if I get into trouble.* His mobile rang and he stopped under the shade of a lemon tree and took the call.

'Mr Mason, it is Detective Pavlos here.'

'Hi,' replied Nathan. 'Are there any developments from the other night?'

'I am afraid not. I have enquired at all the hospitals in the area on both sides of the border and no Russians have checked in with head injuries. None of their fingerprints gave a match and I am still waiting to hear from the lab about DNA and the blood results. I suppose it is just as well for you that your attacker has not come forward to press charges.'

'I acted in self-defence,' replied Nathan sharply. 'I'm the victim here … of armed robbery and assault.'

'I am just calling to keep you updated but perhaps you could provide me with a list of anything that was stolen, or anything that may be of interest,' said Pavlos, rather robotically and without any real concern.

'Er, yes, there is something I would like to give you; I was given it by the girl in the bar the other night, so it might be connected to my attacker.'

'Very well, I will be back on duty at nine in the morning. I will give you a call and let you know what time I will be at the villa.'

'Okay, that's fine.'

'Goodbye,' said Pavlos abruptly and ended the call.

Nathan mused, *I'm sure if it was the UK or New Zealand, he would have come around straight away, or at least sent someone around to see me. I'll just have to accept that they are more relaxed about things over here.*

He continued his walk and, as he approached the bar, he could see that there was nobody outside and that he had the pick of the tables. He made sure that his choice was suitably shaded by the overhead vines and he chose a seat with his back to the stone wall of the building so that he could watch all the comings and goings through the village. It was deathly quiet.

The bartender came out to him. 'Good evening, what can I get you?' he asked.

'A large, very cold Keo please.'

'Okay, I will be right back.' He returned almost immediately with some olives, oil and bread, then returned with a large bottle of Keo beer, which was dripping with condensation, and a pint glass.

'That's brilliant, thank you,' said Nathan. 'Can I just ask you something?'

'Of course.'

'Do you get many Russian visitors in the bar?'

'Ahh, you are asking about the beautiful girl from the other night?'

'No,' replied Nathan, starting to blush, 'not at all, just Russians in general.'

'Okay, yes, there are small communities of Russians but they are mainly on the Turkish side. They come here occasionally but I must admit there has been more activity recently. It is very good for business. They are very big drinkers, although they can be a bit unruly at times. The two girls that you were with the other night, they are Cypriot but they are always with the Russian men. It would be wise to stay well clear. I do not trust them. I do not know them but I still do not trust them. They could get you into a lot of trouble.'

'Why do you say that?'

'I have heard rumours that the Russians may be involved in attempting to buy the Anapetri Villa land. And that they are employing some unpleasant people for them to do so. They know who you are. I heard them speaking the other night. I can pick up the odd word. They know that you are here on behalf of the Mykanos company.'

'What else did you hear?' asked Andreas anxiously.

'That is it. I am afraid I do not know any more. I have only told you this because there is no one around to hear me. Now, can I get you anything else?'

'Yes, you can do me a favour. If you hear anything more from the Russians, about me or the Anapetri land, will you let me know?'

'Yes, I can do that. As much as I want their custom, I do not want it to be at the cost of our village being turned into a landfill site.'

'Thank you,' replied Nathan, as the bartender turned and walked back to the bar.

That's interesting. I thought the girl who was showing particular interest in me the other night was Russian. Either way, it doesn't matter what nationality she is if she's a honey trap. The important bit is that she's an acquaintance of the Russians. It's also interesting that the barman knows that it's the Russians who are interested in the land, and he thinks it's for landfill and not for mining. The last resort, if I don't find the documents, is publicising the fact that the company interested are miners and not a landfill company. That would cause so much grief for the council, the Russians and anyone else with a finger in the pie.

Nathan placed his large hand around the glass and poured the cold beer. Condensation started to form very quickly on the outside of the glass and he took a huge gulp. *A word to define this heavenly taste: nectar.*

He pondered the day's events. He was unsure whether or not he should tell Andreas about the armed guard that shot down the drone. He was frightened of putting him off and losing his support, even though he thought he had identified the Mykanos premises they were looking for. But he didn't expect Andreas to go into Varosha again. He would go in on his own but he just needed Andreas to be nearby in case he had to leave in a hurry.

Nathan finished his beer and some of the olives before paying his bill and making his way to Andreas's house. He started the short walk up the fruit road. It was a gorgeous evening, still very sticky. There was no breeze and the sun was yet to set. The swallows were busy in the road, diving to collect flies that had gathered around the squashed oranges, lemons and limes, which had been pressed into the road. Dragonflies seemed to be in abundance, as well as other flying insects that Nathan was unfamiliar with.

He suddenly became aware of a vehicle approaching from behind so he turned around to take a look but thought nothing of it as it passed by. Shortly after, he recognised the same black car coming back down the road. It was unusual because it was a make with which he was unfamiliar. As it approached, he took a quick look at the driver, and the driver and passenger took a quick look at him.

Nathan felt immediately uncomfortable. His senses were telling him that something wasn't right and he made a mental note of the number plate, AD 805, and the description of the thickset moustachioed driver. He turned to watch the car move slowly down the road and out of sight after it took a right turn at the junction. *That didn't feel right. Could they be following me?* He quickly stepped off the pavement and headed into the orchard immediately to his left. *I'm going to wait to see if they come back.*

He stood and waited in the cover of the trees but in a position that gave him a clear view of anything that passed. Sure enough, within a minute the same car cruised past. Nathan held his position and the car returned from the opposite direction.

They've been following me and now they're looking for me because I've slipped the net. It's the Russians, I know it is. What have I got myself into here? They're trying to frighten me off, or see me off. I certainly don't want them to see me going into Andreas's house, although I'm sure that they'll already know that he's a friend. What if they followed us today to Varosha and just lay in wait to see what we were up to? This whole saga is getting too big and out of control. I just want to go back to New Zealand but I can't. It's madness, I know, but I've got to see this through. If I'd have known, I wouldn't have got Andreas mixed up in this but without his help where would I be?

Nathan realised that the car must have stopped only fifty metres down the road. He heard both doors close, meaning the two men had got out. He could hear voices talking in Russian. He then heard another car pull up nearby and the sound of another two doors closing. *There must be four of them out there. I hope they didn't see me coming into this orchard.*

The four men were now all conversing loudly in Russian and it sounded as if it was becoming heated. Nathan considered withdrawing further into the orchard but was worried about making a noise and drawing attention to himself, so he didn't move. He thought to turn his mobile to silent just in case he received a call and notified all and sundry of where he was hiding.

The men continued to talk as the aroma of tobacco wafted its way through the orchard in Nathan's direction. He then heard the sound of footsteps on the pavement and someone stepped into the orchard, heading in his direction. *Shit, I'm going to have to gamble and back up or this guy's going to walk right into me.* Suddenly, the footsteps stopped and Nathan had to stay still as his movements would be audible. The next thing was the sound of a zip being opened and trickling water as the man relieved himself before re-joining the others. Nathan breathed a quiet sigh of relief. *That was too close for comfort.*

The men eventually finished their conversation, got back in their cars and drove away. Nathan knew only too well that he had to wait. It didn't take long before the large black car reappeared. It drove past the orchard, presumably to the top of the road before returning on a reciprocal route. Nathan waited a few more minutes until he felt confident that the car had gone, then continued the short walk to Andreas's house. By the time he approached and knocked on the front door, he was sweating profusely. He was mopping his brow with the front of his T-shirt when Helena opened the door. She was welcomed with a view of Nathan's impressive six-pack.

'Hello Nathan,' Helena greeted him.

'Oh, hello Helena, sorry about that,' Nathan replied, sheepishly lowering his T-shirt.

'Come on in,' she replied. 'It doesn't happen often, you know.'

'Sorry, I'm not with you.'

'A man turning up on my doorstep baring his six-pack.'

Nathan thought he felt his face blush yet again but realised it was probably red already due to him perspiring in the extremely humid air.

'Come through,' Helena said. They walked through the house and up the external stairs to the terrace. Andreas was just tending to the barbecue, which looked like an oil barrel that had been cut down the middle, placed on a leg framework and had a metal mesh placed on top.

'Welcome, my friend,' said Andreas. The two men shook hands as Helena returned to the kitchen. Andreas opened a cooler box and presented Nathan with a large bottle of Keo.

'Thank you,' said Nathan. He had barely sat down when Helena appeared with a large tray of plates containing skewered swordfish souvlaki, with mushroom and tomatoes, chicken and mushroom kebabs, salad, tzatziki, and hummus with pittas. She was carrying little George in a baby sling attached to her chest.

'Wow, this looks fantastic Helena,' said Nathan.

'Thank you, but you have the difficult bit, the cooking.'

'I may as well make a start,' said Nathan, standing up.

'I will get you an apron,' said Helena.

Andreas had lit the barbecue about half an hour earlier so the charcoal was now turning white, indicating it was ready. Nathan noted a large metal plate beneath the barbecues legs, no doubt to deflect the heat away from the timber terrace decking and to collect any falling coals.

Helena reappeared. 'Put this on Nathan, just in case you get any spits.'

Nathan put on the apron then realised the image on the front was one of a lady wearing stockings and suspenders. He looked at Helena and she just raised her eyebrows, as if to say 'it suits you'. Nathan noticed that she was in a particularly good mood and wondered whether she had made up with Andreas. She was certainly looking more attractive than on his previous visits. Her skin was nut brown in the evening sunlight and had a kind of glow that he hadn't noticed before. She appeared much younger and he suspected that she was wearing a little make-up.

As Nathan cooked and chatted and drank more wine, he couldn't help but admire the view across the orchards and the olive tree fields to the ocean. On such a spectacular evening he wished Loretta was with him.

The barbecue was a success, the food excellent, but by this time George was getting a bit grumpy, so Helena decided to retire to settle him down but not before giving Nathan a kiss on the cheek.

'We will go down, Helena, so we do not disturb you two,' said Andreas, pointing at the orchard.

'Okay, you go and enjoy a smoke,' she replied.

'How did you know?' said Andreas.

'Well apart from the smell on you and your clothes, quite often I see smoke billowing up through the trees. When it blows in this direction it is hard to miss. Anyway, goodnight,' she said as she walked into the house.

'Goodnight,' they replied in unison.

'Nice to see Helena in good spirits,' said Nathan.

'Oh, er yes, we made up,' Andreas replied shyly.

'When?'

'About two hours ago, while George was having a nap,' Andreas replied with a wink.

'Ahh, that's nice,' said Nathan with a smile.

'Yes, it was,' said Andreas, smiling in return.

The two of them made their way down into the orchard to Andreas's not-so-secret bolthole. When they had settled and Andreas had produced a bottle of wine, two glasses, a pack of cigars and a lighter, Nathan decided to tell him what he had found on the drone footage.

'I want to let you know about the footage from this afternoon,' Nathan said. 'It was more revealing than expected.'

'Oh, what does that mean exactly?'

'Okay, do you remember the carcass in the road?'

'Yes, of course.'

'Well, the drone flew over the carcass, went to the end of the road and did a U-turn at the car showroom. On its way back, just as it approached the carcass, there was a swinging sign attached to one of the shop fronts. I could clearly see the letters MYK. Andreas, I think we've found the building that we're looking for. The front window opening is clear, as is the front door.'

'That sounds very promising but what about—'

Nathan held up his hand to stop Andreas in his tracks. 'Unfortunately, the bad news is that the drone was shot down by a guard. He was stationed in a guard box over the road but further up towards the silo. I want you to watch this.' Nathan produced his mobile phone from his pocket and showed Andreas a clip that lasted about thirty seconds. It showed the swinging sign then the shooting down of the drone. It was clear and unequivocal.

'I warned you, Nathan. I told you how dangerous it is in there.' Andreas was becoming more animated by the second. 'We could have been shot ourselves. Who knows, maybe there was a sniper watching us.'

'Let's not go over the top, Andreas. We weren't shot at when we entered Varosha, which indicates that our entry point area is clear.'

'You do not know that,' said Andreas in a sharp, angry tone.

'I know that we're both here now and that we weren't shot at, which indicates they never knew that we'd entered.'

'I am not going back in there and I hope that you are not still considering it.'

'Actually, Andreas, I will be going back in there and I don't expect you to come with me. But I'd like you to be my driver.'

'Are you insane Nathan?'

'No, I'm not.'

'Are you afraid?'

'A little, but I'll have the advantage.'

'Have the advantage? How do you work that one out when there is a man in a guard post who will be prepared to shoot you if necessary.'

'There's my advantage. I know where he is but he doesn't know where I will be and, as long as it stays like that, I have the advantage.'

'What makes you so confident to think that you will not be captured or shot?'

'I have confidence in my abilities,' said Nathan.

'Why, what abilities?'

'I'm an ex-detective of the Metropolitan Police in London. I've been trained in surveillance and counter-surveillance techniques. There's a good chance that I can get in and out of there undetected, as we've shown today.'

'Maybe but, with all due respect, you will need to go a lot further into Varosha. All we did today was a quick in and out. And the fact that you are an ex-police officer, well, I will not hold that against you,' said Andreas with a wry smile.

'So, you'll be my driver?'

'Look, I appreciate everything that you are doing for us but—'

'Will you be my driver?' persisted Nathan.

'Yes, you know I will.'

'Well, there's something else that you need to know,' said Nathan.

'I do not like the sound of this.'

'Look, I think the Russians may have been following us.'

'What makes you say that?'

Nathan gave Andreas a rundown of his conversations with Detective Pavlos and the barman, plus the incident in the road near Andreas's house.

'Are you serious?' said Andreas in a raised voice. 'They could have been following us and they may know where I live. What about Helena and George? This is not good. I am putting everything at risk. I am an accomplice, for god's sake. It is okay for you, you can leave the country but, when you have gone, it is just us on our own against the hostility of the Russians. The police are not going to protect us; there are not enough of them as it is.'

Andreas now had his head in his hands. He was genuinely taken aback by Nathan's disclosures. 'I am not sure I can be your driver Nathan,' Andreas continued.

'This whole thing has got out of hand and I have now put my family at risk, the one thing that I promised to myself that I would never do. You know that you have made a bad situation worse by coming here and getting involved.'

'I agree,' said Nathan. 'But it's only going to get a lot worse for all of you, including the Mykanos family, if the Russians take this land and everything that's on it. Sometimes a situation has to get worse before it gets better, or would you rather roll over in submission like a puppy on its back with its legs in the air.'

'I am not going to commit to this. I have too much to lose.'

'But Andreas, you know I need you. Just drive me to Varosha, then go and park up somewhere and pick me up when I've finished.'

'No, I will not do it,' replied Andreas abruptly.

Not long after, the two of them decided to call it a night with very little further being discussed. Nathan said he would return to the villa using the shortcut over the rear fence and through the olive trees. Andreas advised him to be careful because of the prickly pear cacti that grew in the long grass. Nathan used the torch on his smart phone to light his way.

As he approached the rear of the villa a security light illuminated the patio and pool area. He looked down at his legs, which were causing significant discomfort, and saw that they were scratched and sore with mosquito bites and god knows what else. He stripped down to his birthday suit and jumped into the pool. It was like jumping into a warm bath but still felt refreshing against the hot, humid evening air. The bites on his legs stung slightly as they were washed over with chlorinated water. He grabbed a blue floating foam noodle, wrapped it around his waist and held it in place on his stomach. He was then able to float on his back and appreciate the fantastic ceiling of stars on display in the dark sky above.

As spectacular and relaxing as the night sky was, he felt angry and let down by Andreas. He was now in a position where he had to do this on his own or not at all. *Assuming that the Russians are following me, they'll be waiting for me, and as soon as I come out of Varosha with whatever I've found, they'll try to take it. So, unless I can get there undetected, there's no point in even trying. I feel like giving up, I really do.*

Nathan stepped out of the pool, dried himself with the towel and re-dressed himself with shorts and a pair of flip-flops, which he had left by the pool earlier. He was looking up at the light on the rear of the villa and was amazed at the number of moths and other flying insects that were attracted to it, some of them quite large.

He heard a loud knocking noise, which seemed to be coming from the front of the villa. Instead of going through the kitchen and hall to the front door, he decided to quietly go around the side of the villa. Quietly opening the gate, he heard the knock again and, as he peeped around the corner, he could see someone at the front door, although they were in the shade of the overhanging roof and he wouldn't be able to see them clearly until they stepped away from the villa.

'Can I help you?' asked Nathan.

He saw the person jump slightly at his question and then they stepped out into the moonlight towards him. To his surprise it was the girl he had met in the bar the other night. It was the honey trap.

'Oh, hi,' she said rather shyly as she walked a little closer. She was wearing a short black dress and stilettos. The belt around her waist accentuated her very petite figure. Her hair was long and wavey and her make-up looked immaculate. She was carrying a small black clutch bag.

'Why are you here?' enquired Nathan.

'Because you did not call me,' she replied.

'And do you expect everyone that you give your number to call you?'

'Yes, because I very rarely give it out and when I do I mean business.'

Nathan had that feeling again. She was here to get as much information out of him as possible and this could be the ideal opportunity to deflect some of the heat from him. He decided to play along.

'How did you know where I was staying?'

'It is a small village and the bar owner is very friendly.'

That's probably a lie, Nathan thought. *She would have known where I was staying if she really is a honey trap. I must box clever here.*

'Would you like to come for a drink on the patio?' said Nathan.

'That would be nice,' she replied.

She followed him around the side of the villa, through the gate and on to the patio, where she took a seat overlooking the pool.

'Can I get you a drink? A beer? A glass of red wine maybe?' Nathan

'A glass of red wine please.'

Nathan went into the kitchen, retrieved a bottle and two glasses, then returned to the patio. He placed the bottle and glasses on the table, poured two drinks and handed one to her.

She held the glass high. 'Yamas,' she said.

Nathan reciprocated, before adding, 'I'm sorry, I didn't catch your name the other night.'

'Georgia. Georgia Constantinou.'

'So Georgia, why are you here?'

'The other night I thought we got on pretty well. You never mentioned a girlfriend or wife, so I presumed you were here on your own.'

'I am now. My girlfriend has gone back to New Zealand. It's a good job she isn't here or she may not have been impressed with a young woman turning up at her door.'

'Oh, I would have talked my way out of it and made some excuse.'

Yes, I can believe that you were probably well prepared and totally disregarded the fact that I have a girlfriend. It wouldn't matter to you, probably, because you're here a mission.

'Are you a local? Do you live in the village?' enquired Nathan.

'No, the bar in the village is just one of the places that I and my friends like to come to.'

'So where's your home village?'

'You ask a lot of questions,' she replied, smiling.

'I know, I'm sorry. It's just good to speak to someone. I've had a bit of a stressful day.'

'Oh, do you want to talk about it?'

Now it's my turn to lie. 'Yes, I do. Would you like a top-up first?'

'Yes please,' she replied. Nathan could sense her sudden improved interest and eagerness for him to continue. He topped up both glasses and looked at her clutch bag, which was resting in her lap.

I wonder whether she's recording this conversation or someone's listening in. I'd better make this sound genuine. 'My girlfriend belongs to the family that owns this villa, all this land and all the other properties.' Nathan pointed in the direction of the small holdings. 'A lot of people make their living from this land. A lot of mothers and children are reliant upon what they can farm and grow here.'

'It is all good so far,' she interjected.

'Ah, but there's one major problem.'

'What is that?'

188

'All this land appears to have been acquired illegally. You see, in 1974 this area was ravaged by the war. Families were displaced and their land taken. It happened to the Cypriots as well as the Turks. It looks like the council has been looking into the legal ownership of this and other plots of land. It looks like the family may have seized it illegally in 1974.'

'But how do you know that?' Georgia asked.

'Well, the council, on the understanding that the land was illegally grabbed, want to take it back and sell it to a company as a landfill site. The council has asked the family to prove legal ownership and they've been unable to do so. I've spoken to the majority of the major solicitors and accountancy companies that have had previous dealings with the family in Cyprus and abroad, to see whether there are any relevant documents stored or registered. And there aren't. It's a disaster for all concerned. I'll be going to inform the council in the next day or two so that they can, unfortunately, start their eviction process.'

'This is all very sad. So not only are you a friend of the family, you are in their employ, and you feel like you have failed them and the people who live off the land here.'

'Well, yes, you've put it rather bluntly but you're correct,' replied Nathan.

'Having said that, if it was not their land, they had no right to—'

'I know,' Nathan interrupted, 'but the family has done so many good things here. They built houses with plots and let them out at reduced rates to local families who had been displaced after the war.'

'All the same …' she replied.

She's hard and cold this one but she's got what she wants, or so she thinks.

Georgia leaned over and placed her hand gently on Nathan's. 'Would you like me to give you a massage to release those stresses and strains?' she said, as she stood, hitched up her short dress and straddled him face to face.

'You're very beautiful but I'd like you to leave,' said Nathan with authority.

She glared at him with her large brown eyes, disbelieving at actually being rejected. After a moment she slowly removed herself, with as much poise as the situation allowed.

'At least you got some things off your chest,' she said. 'You have my number if you want me,' she added, before slowly walking away.

'Goodnight,' Nathan shouted after her, but she had already walked out of sight around the side of the villa.

Nathan jumped up quickly and went through the kitchen and into the hall, where he stood in front of the window and watched as Georgia walked to the end of the drive. She stopped briefly and turned left in the direction of the bar. She hadn't travelled far before a large shiny black car pulled up alongside her and she got in without a second's hesitation.

I think she fell for it and she'll be telling them there are no documents. With a bit of luck that will get them off my case. But I need Andreas as my driver. I'm not giving up. When he finds out what's happened tonight, he may be back with me.

Nathan tidied up the patio before locking up, having a shower, then going to bed. He didn't know how he was going to sleep, with the nagging possibility that he may get a visit from his Russian friends, so he went downstairs and returned with a golf club, which he placed under his bed before settling down and eventually drifting off to sleep.

~~~

Back in England, in the Cotswolds not far from Cheltenham. It was dark as he pulled the body into the pig pen. When the pigs realised that something had entered their domain, the adult males appeared from their sties. He closed the gate quickly but quietly and, as he walked away, he could hear the pigs grunting and gorging on the large luxurious slab of meat. Nothing would be wasted, down to the last bone or tooth. He walked away into the trees. He had blood on his hands.

The next thing he was in New Zealand and on the small hill in the Urupa. The warm air vented from the fissure in the earth's crust. He looked into the blackness and pushed the body in. He walked away. He stepped over the sign and washed his hands in a stream nearby …

Nathan awoke with a start and sat up in his bed immediately. He was perspiring profusely. He had his head in his hands. *Not the nightmare again please, please …*

13

IT WAS eight o'clock by the time Nathan awoke the following morning, although, after his nightmare, he had been fortunate to be able to get back to sleep pretty quickly. He lay in bed for a short while, then after getting up and completing several sit-ups, he had a warm shower and went down for breakfast. *Not very Mediterranean but you can't beat a bowl of muesli with cold milk*, he thought.

He carried his breakfast outside to the patio table and took in the smells and sights of yet another gorgeous summer morning in Cyprus. The sun was up but still low. He noticed the remnants of dew glistening on the pink fragrant flowers of a bougainvillea plant in the patio border. The sea was as calm as he had ever seen it in Cyprus. Out at sea, he could see a thin line above and parallel with the horizon. It looked like a line of cloud. He remembered when Andreas had described the signs of a very humid day to come, and these were the signs; it was actually a thin line of humidity. *Fresh now but hot and sticky to follow.*

After eating, Nathan went inside and made himself a cup of coffee, before returning to the patio. His thoughts returned to the previous night's conversations with both Andreas and Georgia. He hoped that he had successfully put the Russians off the scent and that they were now thinking it was only a matter of time before the land was theirs. But he desperately needed the help of Andreas, if only to successfully progress through the border and back again. He also wanted someone there to help him if he needed a quick getaway.

His concentration was disturbed by his mobile phone ringing. He picked it up it and saw that it was Loretta. Once again, he was very happy to hear her voice but he could tell by her tone that she was very sad for her father's rapid demise. She reiterated the fact that she needed Nathan by her side as she was finding the whole situation difficult to handle. Nathan agreed to call the office and arrange a flight out of Cyprus the following afternoon. Loretta shed a few tears before ending the call. Nathan called the office in Auckland and asked for his flights to be changed to depart from Larnaca the following afternoon.

The decision was made. If he was going back to Varosha, it had to be tonight or not at all. Nathan decided to give Andreas one final call. He dialled the number and Andreas picked up after a few rings.

'Hi Andreas,' Nathan said, with an optimistic tone.

'Good morning. I am just in the orchard at the moment.'

'Look, this won't take a minute. I just wanted to talk to you about our discussion about going back to Varosha.'

'You do not give up, do you?'

'Not easily, and there have been a few developments.'

'Okay. I have to go to the wholesalers, so I will call in at your place in half an hour or so.'

'Okay, great, see you then.' They ended the call.

That sounds promising, thought Nathan. *Maybe he'll be a bit more receptive when I tell him about Georgia.* He decided to call Pavlos to inform his about Georgia's visit. It went straight to voicemail so he left a brief message.

Andreas arrived about forty minutes later and went to join Nathan at the patio table to enjoy a cold glass of orange juice.

'Thanks for coming round,' said Nathan. 'There's a couple of things that I need to talk to you about.'

'Fire away,' said Andreas in a serious manner.

'I had a visit from Georgia last night, the girl from the bar.' Nathan noticed that he had piqued Andreas's attention all of a sudden.

'What on earth was she doing here?'

'I've told you already that I think she's a honey trap and she's trying to find out information about the land documents.'

'Yes …'

'Well, she tried it on with me last night.'

'And did you—'

'No, of course not, but I did feed her with some false information.'

'Such as?'

'In a nutshell, I told her that there were no land documents. I said the family can't prove ownership and I was going to inform the council of my findings in the next day or two, so that they could start their eviction process.'

'So, what was your thinking behind that?' enquired Andreas.

'I think it will put them off our scent. Why would you continue to follow someone when you've just found out that there's no point because the documents don't exist?'

'But Nathan, you are basing this on the fact that Georgia is a honey trap and is going to report back to the Russians.'

'Yes, exactly.'

'But how can you be so sure? Is it not a bit of a gamble?'

'Only a small one, and I think it's worth taking. I reckon that Georgia thinks she's done her job and got the information out of me that the Russians wanted, and I'm sure she went straight to them and told them. One other thing … I'm going back to New Zealand tomorrow afternoon. So, it's Varosha tonight or not at all. Andreas, I need you. If you can just drive me across the border, wait for me, then bring me back, that's all I ask. This is the last chance to see whether the documents are there. Just imagine if they are, Andreas. What a coup it would be for all   of   us.'

14

DETECTIVE PAVLOS was in his office at Palakori police station. The previous day he had sent a request for information about Nathan Mason over the Interpol network. He had done the same to his contacts in the UK and had received two emails in his mailbox.

The first was from an old friend in the Metropolitan Police, who had carried out a few enquiries on his behalf. Pavlos was surprised to see that there was a comprehensive file relating to Nathan that indicated that he was indirectly implicated in a missing persons case. The person in question had killed Nathan's parents by mounting a kerb while driving his car under the influence of drugs. He had killed them outright.

This had happened in Nathan's hometown of Cheltenham. There was only a suggestion that Nathan could have been involved in the person's disappearance, mainly due to the fact that he knew the offender. He was never officially a suspect and a body had never been found. Apart from that one incident, Nathan had an exemplary police record and had been due for promotion to inspector. There was just a brief note at the end to say that Nathan had been medically discharged.

Pavlos turned to the second email, from Interpol, which more or less repeated the previous one from the Metropolitan Police but had one addition from Police New Zealand. Pavlos skimmed through the Auckland report – the break-in at the church at Wellsford, the horrendous murders of three people. A man had gone missing in the hills and Nathan had found the missing gold and given it to its rightful owner.

He read about how Nathan had been interviewed on numerous occasions over the deaths and about the missing person but, once again, no further action had been deemed necessary. There were no arrest warrants or requests for knowledge of his whereabouts. *This guy has been either very lucky or very clever. Either way, when he is around, more often than not bad things happen*, Pavlos thought to himself.

Pavlos had also brought himself fully up to date with the situation regarding the Anapetri land. He had spoken to various council representatives about the current status of the dispute but tried not to voice his opinion or show any bias. Privately, however, he did have sympathy with the cause of the Mykanos family, the tenant farmers and all that Nathan was trying to do. The detective was a local man and, as such, cared about future developments, particularly if they would have an impact on the environment and village life. He was feeling conflicted between the question mark over Nathan's past and the good work he was trying to do now. *I have to stay impartial but there is something about this Nathan Mason guy … I cannot put my finger on it. If he is as clever as I think he is, I probably never will.*

Pavlos listened to his voicemails, including the message from Nathan saying he wanted to speak to him. He picked up the handset of the telephone on his desk and dialled Nathan's number. 'Mr Mason, it is Detective Pavlos here. I got your message and I will be passing Anapetri on a call shortly. Could I come and pay you a visit in about twenty minutes?'

'Yes, of course,' replied Nathan.

'Okay, see you then. Thank you, goodbye.'

A short while later, Detective Pavlos arrived at Anapetri Villa.

'Good morning,' said Nathan as they shook hands.

'Good morning,' replied Pavlos.

'Please come through to the patio.'

Pavlos followed Nathan through the hall and kitchen to the patio, where they joined Andreas, who was sitting at the table beneath the parasol. 'Good morning again,' said Andreas.

'Good morning.'

'Can I get you a drink?' asked Nathan.

'No, that will not be necessary. There was something that you wanted to speak to me about?'

'Yes, there is, and it's relating to the girl in the bar the other night. Before I left she gave me her telephone number.' Nathan retrieved a small, folded piece of paper from his pocket and handed it to Pavlos. 'As you can see, the number is written in ink on one side but if you turn it over you'll see a circular embossed stamp. A bit like an official company stamp. You'll notice that around the outside of the stamp the wording is URALS CORP and in the centre is the double-headed eagle of Russia. I made some enquiries on the internet and, sure enough, URALS CORP is a large Russian company operating in many countries throughout the world. It's not a landfill company but a large-scale mining company; we're talking about iron ore, cobalt and lithium, to name just a few modern-day treasures, and many of them are toxic.'

Pavlos eyed Nathan with no emotion. 'You are a good detective, Mr Mason, very explicit. It seems to come naturally to you.'

Nathan noticed a slight change in Pavlos's expression, an ever so slight movement around the eyes. *That look he just gave me and him mentioning me being a good detective. I think he's checked me out. I wonder how much he knows.* 'I'm very thorough in everything I do; I was born with an inquisitive mind,' Nathan replied.

'Indeed, Mr Mason, indeed. So, we have the girl in the bar. The attack on you here in the villa. And you believe them to be connected to URALS CORP. So, they want to buy this land from the council because it is believed to have been taken illegally by Mr Mykanos, which would make the council legal owners.'

'Yes, you've summed that up pretty well.'

'Thank you. I too am very thorough and very proud of the work of the Cyprus investigators. In fact, I believe we are among the best in the world, if not the best.'

He's trying to get a response from me. Well I'm not buying it, thought Nathan.

'If you do not mind, I will take this piece of paper and carry out a few enquiries back at the police station.'

'Not at all. Oh, and by the way, the name of the girl is Georgia Constantinou.'

'I know,' replied Pavlos immediately. 'She has come to our attention on several occasions.'

'Can you tell me more?' asked Nathan. 'Like who the men are that she associates with, and why?'

'I am limited in what I can say but what I will say is this. Her associates are mainly Russian and her connection to the men appears to be through business. How can I say it … she appears to look after her clients?'

'Do you mean a prostitute?' replied Nathan.

'No, I think the correct phrase is a honey trap.'

Nathan looked at Andreas and got an acknowledging nod in return.

'But I suspect that you already knew that Mr Mason,' Pavlos added.

'I suspected that was the case,' Nathan replied knowingly.

'Have you called her number?' Pavlos asked.

'No,' replied Nathan.

'Have you got any further information about the men who attacked Nathan?' asked Andreas.

'I am afraid not, and unless Miss Constantinou comes clean, which I do not think she will, I do not believe we will ever know. Do you have anything further for me?'

'I'm afraid not,' said Nathan. 'In fact, I'll be returning to New Zealand tomorrow afternoon.'

'I am sorry that you have been unable to locate the documents and that you have to accept defeat.'

'Well, I'll be doing my best from New Zealand to increase awareness of what's going on in Anapetri and what the future holds for this beautiful village.'

'It is no doubt a worthy cause, Mr Mason, but please be aware that you are still at risk as long as you remain here. Your attackers may still come looking for the missing documents, unless you tell the world that they have been lost or indeed never even existed.'

'That's a valid point but I'll be staying here tonight. This is my last night and I refuse to be run out of town.'

'Then I wish you well. I will ensure that any patrolling officers are aware of your situation. If there are any further developments, please keep me informed. If I hear any more I will be in touch.'

'Okay, thank you.'

'Goodbye, Mr Mason … and Mr Polycarpou.'

'Bye,' Nathan and Andreas replied in unison.

Detective Pavlos left, making his way around the side of the villa. Nathan looked at Andreas and asked, 'Did he seem more friendly? Like an attitude change?'

'Yes, a bit less severe,' agreed Andreas.

'I think he's probably checked us out, done a criminal records check, or whatever they call it over here. Do you have a criminal record Andreas?'

'No,' Andreas insisted. 'Why would you say that?'

'Because I need to know who I'm associating with. If we get stopped on the Turkish side and you have previous, it could prove problematic.'

'Two things. Firstly, I do not have a criminal record; and secondly, it would not be problematic because I am not going over the border with you, and you are going home tomorrow anyway.'

'Come on, let's give it one last try. Let's give it a go. One last try tonight. I need you Andreas.'

Nathan could be persuasive when he had to be.

15

'WHERE DID you say you were going to tonight?' enquired Helena suspiciously.

'I am taking Nathan to the old town in Famagusta, just to have a look around. He wants to buy some gifts to take back to New Zealand.'

'When is he going back?'

'Tomorrow afternoon.'

'And what about the papers? What is going to happen to us when he has gone?'

'He has not given up,' Andreas assured her. 'He has a few more people to see before he goes.'

Andreas knew that if he was honest with Helena about what their plans were for this evening she would most probably erupt and call him irresponsible and reckless, and it would escalate into one of their full-blown arguments.

He was feeling nervous and anxious enough about helping Nathan tonight as it was.

'What are the chances?' asked Helena, with a serious look on her face.

'Chances of what?' replied Andreas.

'Of these papers miraculously turning up and saving us all from god knows what.'

'I will be honest, it is not looking good. I know he is planning to start some kind of campaign when he gets back to New Zealand.'

'What sort of campaign?'

'An awareness campaign. Contacting the government, the council, the environment department and other such organisations, I presume. He has not gone into any details. He is in a rush to get back to see Loretta and his father-in-law. He seems to be very ill and with not long left in this world.'

'It is very sad but we can only concern ourselves and our neighbours with what is going on here. Our future and our livelihoods as a family are all at risk,' said Helena.

Andreas put his arms around her. 'I know. Try not to worry.' They kissed passionately.

Before Andreas left, Helena informed him not to come home late, smelling of wine. But she did suggest that she would be in bed waiting for him and she had a glint in her eye when she said it. He made a mental note not to be late under any circumstances.

~~~

It was early evening; Nathan was just finalising his kit for the venture into Varosha. *I'm so lucky that I could change Andreas's mind. If he'd stuck to his guns, I really don't know what I would have done. I just hope the risk is worth it. What's the chance of finding a very secret safe in the basement of a dilapidated real estate agency that was ransacked in 1974? In a couple of hours, I'll know.*

Nathan had a very small backpack, loaded with a few tools from a garden lockup container. It was difficult to know what he would need or indeed which tools he would be able to use, bearing in mind the close proximity of the guard in the lookout post. He would have to keep noise and light to a minimum, so he had procured himself a small claw hammer, a masonry chisel, a collection of screwdrivers, a small LED hand torch and a head torch.

He was wearing a black T-shirt and a pair of khaki cargo pants, which he had brought with him, although realising that the likelihood of wearing long trousers in Cyprus was slim. The only thing of concern were his grey trainers. The soles were thick and, although no longer white, they still stood out as if he had stepped in a paint tray. He had already tried to camouflage them with a mix of mud made from the clay-coloured soil that was prevalent in Cyprus. It had at least removed the luminosity aspect, until it started to dry, crack and fall off. He needed trainers though; he had no option. He needed the agility and degree of safety that they gave compared to a pair of plimsoles or flip-flops.

With his wallet and mobile phone in his backpack, Nathan was ready to go. He took a small bottle of water from the fridge and went and sat on the patio. A short while later, Andreas arrived and made his way through the side gate, walking over to sit opposite Nathan.

'Would you like a drink?' said Nathan.

'No thanks,' Andreas replied.

'Is everything okay?'

'I will be quite honest; I am a bit worried about tonight. Worried that we are going to be followed by the Russians … the police … I do not know. I am just a little nervous, I guess.'

'So am I, and there's nothing wrong with feeling like that. It's only natural. Let's go over the plan so we know exactly how things are going to work.'

'Okay,' agreed Andreas.

'I'm going to use the same entry point into Varosha as last time. I need to go in there at nightfall so I can get a clear view of my route just before it goes too dark. It's only when it goes dark that I'll make my move. I'll be slow and methodical until I get to the location, then I'll pick up the pace. As you know, I have to find the basement and search for the so-called hidden safe. If I do find it, with or without its contents, I'll be leaving as quickly as possible after that and hopefully doing a reciprocal route back to the entry point. I need you to be in a position to see me when I come out so you can pick me up at the end of the cul-de-sac. But make sure that you don't make it obvious that you're waiting for someone. If you can go to the café, the one that we went to last time, and sit at a table with a view of the cul-de-sac, but make sure you have your Isuzu parked nearby so that we can make a sharp exit.'

'I can see that you have thought it through,' said Andreas.

'Yes I have. It's a one-shot opportunity to find these documents. If they're there, I'll find them.'

'Our lives are in danger as it is. If you do find them, that danger is increased considerably,' said Andreas.

'You're right,' said Nathan, 'but I want you to try to think positively now. Your future and that of many families, a whole village, will be secured if we're successful, so let's work on that basis. We're going to succeed.'

'Okay, let's go for it,' said Andreas. 'But if I can make a suggestion.'

'Of course.'

'It does not start to get dark until about nine-fifteen, so we have a couple of hours to kill. I was thinking if we could go now and get the Isuzu in position, leave it and go for a walk around old Famagusta. It is completely surrounded by old stone walls, a bit like a fortress. The good thing is it is only a stone's throw from Varosha, plus I told Helena that is what we are doing tonight, sightseeing, as well as looking for a gift for you to take back to Loretta.'

'Apart from killing two birds with one stone, you're not lying to Helena. Very crafty, Andreas, very crafty.'

'We Cypriots, we are very clever when we want to be,' Andreas said with a wry smile.

'If you don't mind me asking … Helena seems to be in a very good mood of late. What actually changed?'

Andreas suddenly looked embarrassed and his face started to redden.

'You don't need to give me all the details about your sex life,' added Nathan. 'I just wondered what started the improvement in your relationship. Something must have happened initially …'

'Oh yes,' Andreas suddenly looked reassured. 'She found out about some online stuff that I was doing, that's all. I promised I would quit.'

'Andreas, you've not be looking at porn by any chance.'

'No, definitely not, what sort of person do you think I am?' Andreas was getting annoyed.

'Okay, I'm sorry for being nosey. Let's leave now and go with your plan.'

'Have you got your passport?' asked Andreas.

'Yes, it's in my backpack. I'll just go and fetch it from the kitchen, then I'll lock the villa and see you out front.'

After securing the villa, Nathan left through the front door, double-locking it just in case. Andreas was already in the Isuzu and Nathan jumped in.

'Gambling,' said Andreas, unexpectedly.

'Look, we've already spoken about this. You need to stay positive and think—'

'No,' Andreas interrupted. 'That is what I have been doing online … gambling.'

'I'm sorry to pry into your private life like that.'

'It is okay, I do not mind telling you about it. After all, I may never see you again after tomorrow.'

'Well, I have some bad news for you, my friend. In the words of Arnold Schwarzenegger … I'll be back.'

Andreas laughed.

'Everything that you say to me will be in confidence, don't worry,' said Nathan reassuringly.

Andreas spilled the beans on his gambling habits, while Nathan listened but, at the same time, observantly watched what was going on around them, in particular to see whether they were being followed. Before they realised it, they were at the border. A quick glimpse at Nathan's passport and they were through. After a short distance, Nathan asked Andreas to pull over.

'Do you have any of your little cigars?' Nathan asked.

'Yes, why?'

'Let's just get out and have a smoke.'

'No problem.'

They lit a cigar each, then Nathan looked at Andreas. 'Thanks for telling me all that personal stuff. It's certainly got your mind off the evening ahead.'

'Well, it had until now. Do you think we are being fol-lowed?'

'I don't know, that's why we pulled over. There isn't much traffic but it gives me the opportunity to have a look at who's passing and whether anyone's interested. It also gives me chance to memorise some of these cars in case we come across them further up the road. They may pull over and wait for us to catch up.'

'You are very conscious about what is going on around you. I presume this is due to your police work in the UK.'

'Yes, you're right. In fact, one of the best courses I ever completed was the surveillance and counter-surveillance one. It was carried out in central London. We were given a target to follow. We trawled through department stores and backstreets, following a male who we'd only seen on a series of photographs that morning. In the afternoon, we ended up in multiple vehicles travelling through the Surrey countryside, following the same man. That evening, we all ended up back at Southwark police station. When we were finally introduced to our target, he knew that he'd been tailed for the day but he didn't recognise any of our team of four. We were delighted.

'However, there was a second guy sitting next to him. He'd been shadowing our target, as a kind of lookout, and his job was to identify any potential followers of the target. And he recognised all of us. We were busted. We were all focused and concentrating on one man that much that we weren't aware of someone potentially watching the target's back and, therefore, watching us. It was a harsh but good lesson to learn. We hadn't failed the course, we just moved on to a more advanced stage where we had a lookout, looking for lookouts. You can imagine how complicated it can get, the more people that become involved, and you end up in a watching me, watching you situation.'

'Fascinating, it really is, but maybe such skills will not be required in this case and, anyway, you were convinced that the so-called honey trap would tell her other team members to back off, now that you told her that there are no documents.'

'That's what I'm hoping.'

'Hoping? What do you mean?'

'That she believed me.'

'You were pretty sure last night,' said Andreas anxiously.

'I still am.'

'Then why all this counter-surveillance stuff? It freaks me out. I can feel my anxiety levels rising.'

'Calm down Andreas. It's just me being ultra-cautious. Don't worry.'

'It is easy for you to say. Here we are, on the wrong side of the border. I feel exposed.'

'So do I, my friend.' Nathan briefly put his arm around the shoulder of Andreas in a gesture of reassurance. 'Just a few hours and we can go back to where we feel comfortable. We can do this. Let's give it a try as agreed.'

'Okay, but can we move on now? I just feel the Turkish police are going to get suspicious.'

'Okay, let's go.' *I'm not too worried about the Turkish police,* Nathan mused. *It's Detective Pavlos I'm worried about. I suspect he's been showing an unhealthy interest in me and my past.*

212

There were no suspicious vehicles parked up ahead and, as far as Nathan was concerned, there was no evidence that they were being followed. They made their way to the café car park adjacent to the entry point into Varosha. This time Andreas parked behind the café but in a position that gave a clear view of the cul-de-sac.

'This is a good location,' said Nathan. 'When you leave the café to collect me, you should be able to see if there are any police in the area, either on foot or in vehicles.'

'Okay,' replied Andreas, who now had a steelier-eyed appearance. His movements were more positive as he got out of the vehicle. 'Let's walk in that direction, towards the large open archway in the wall.'

'That's fine,' replied Nathan.

As they approached the old city, the height of the perimeter walls loomed over them. Nathan was briefly reminded of a book that he had read in London when he was recuperating from his stroke. It was testing his memory somewhat. *I'm sure the Christians, including the Knights Templar, escaped here after the defeat by Saladin in the Levantine city of Acre in the thirteenth century. Since then, it's been ruled by the Ottomans, the British, the Greeks and now the Turks, to name just a few.*

As they walked through the large stone archway they were greeted by a plethora of activity. Shops, cars, stalls, cafés and, of course, people. There was a man walking around barefoot, carrying a tray of Turkish flags, who seemed to be approaching as many people as he could, trying to sell his wares. There was a café on the corner, with two tables and chairs outside, occupied by two men puffing on a large hookah pipe, the bowls of which were placed on the pavement besides their chairs. As Nathan and Andreas walked by, the smell of scented tobacco and burning coals surrounded them.

Nathan stopped to look in a shop window. It was displaying a large selection of leather goods – shoes, bags, belts, jackets – more or less everything and anything.

'Fancy a bit of leatherwear to take back to New Zealand do you Nathan?' asked Andreas.

'No, not really, just window shopping,' Nathan replied nonchalantly.

They continued to walk around the dusty streets. Nathan was engrossed in the small shops, the cafés, the music and the smells. It was as if they had crossed into another continent when they had walked through the archway. They approached a small pavement café and decided to take a seat. The waiter came out to serve them. They ordered a Turkish coffee each and the waiter returned quickly with two coffees and two glasses of water.

'This is amazing, Andreas; it's like another world, so chaotic, but it works and has a certain charm. I know it's difficult, with you being a Greek Cypriot.'

'It is and I have to agree, it is a bit of a culture shock.'

I think that was meant to be a derogatory comment towards the Turks, thought Nathan, while eyeing the street in the direction they had just travelled. He couldn't help himself; he was people-watching but in a different sort of way – who was loitering, watching, waiting, observing? The only person paying any sort of attention was the waiter, who had probably heard Andreas's earlier comment about it being a culture shock and wasn't too impressed to hear it from the mouth of a Greek Cypriot.

After that had finished their drinks, Nathan paid the bill and they walked to the end of the street, approaching an intersection with another road. Above them on the perimeter wall was a raised platform. They walked up a set of stone steps to the vantage point. The view was spectacular. Out to the east was the sparkling Mediterranean Sea and, as they turned around, they had a view across the old town and walled city of Famagusta. There was smoke rising from small low-level chimneys and barbecues belonging to the street vendors, cafés and restaurants. They were all busy preparing meat feasts for their paying customers. There were more people out on the streets now, looking for their evening meal. Nathan scanned the immediate area. *There could be multiple observers out there.* It was almost impossible to identify any candidates.

'If you look to the south along the coast, you will see Varosha,' said Andreas. Nathan turned to look. His first impression was of a large bay with a sandy beach and the high-rise hotel blocks as far as the eye could see. It was only when he looked closer that the deprivation became apparent. The remnants of wind-blasted wooden parasols. The skeleton of a small boat. Buildings with huge cracks on their frontage, with foliage protruding. Hotel after hotel after hotel, all damaged beyond repair.

The beach had been partitioned so that the no-go area was clear and obvious to see. Rolls of barbed wire, intermingled with planks of wood, pallets and even car tyres. The perimeter fence was speckled with red warning signs showing a picture of an armed soldier. The lookout posts were difficult to see but you knew they were there. The fact remained that if you entered Varosha you were then fair game to be shot as an intruder.

The task ahead was daunting but Nathan was confident in his abilities. *We've come this far, everything is in place, nearly time to give it a shot.* 'Let's go and do some shopping,' he suggested. 'I just want one gift to take back for Loretta. Can you point me in the right direction?'

'There are some nice souvenir shops just across the way,' said Andreas, pointing. 'Let's go and take a look.'

'I'll follow you … no … let's just wait a second,' said Nathan.

'What's wrong?'

'I'm probably being over-cautious but there's a young guy on a blue Vespa scooter. He's been past us three times since we've been up here. He's got one of those black-and-white-checked Turkish scarves around his neck, the ones with the tassels.'

'You mean a shemagh,' said Andreas.

'Yes, that's it.'

'He could be just running around doing errands for restauranteurs – changing cash, making deliveries, that sort of thing,' suggested Andreas.

'Fair point but the next time we hear his scooter I'll be at the base of the steps. I'm going to head for the next viewpoint on that platform.' Nathan was pointing about one hundred metres along the perimeter where there was another set of stone steps ascending the wall. 'I want you to watch him from here, to see if he makes any phone calls or changes his route so that he can follow me. So just observe, okay?'

'Yes, no problem, but you better hurry as I think he is on his way round.' Andreas made a gesture with his hand cupped to his ear.

Nathan made his way down the steps, just as the man on the Vespa appeared at the intersection. He casually walked towards and ascended the next set of stone steps, which were only a short distance away. When he reached the platform, he called Andreas on his mobile. 'Did you notice anything? Did he pay any attention to me?'

'He never even looked at you; he just carried on doing whatever he is doing,' said Andreas.

'Okay, possible false alarm. Let's go and do some shopping. I don't know about you but I'm getting a little hungry.'

'I wish I was,' said Andreas. 'My stomach is in knots.'

'I understand,' said Nathan. *What else could I say? I could tell the truth and say so is mine and make him feel even worse.*

They made their way to the street that Andreas had suggested. It was chaotic. There were men sitting at small pavement tables, drinking strong coffee and playing a board game amid the surrounding mayhem. All the way up the street the pavements on both sides were occupied by shop displays and artisan tradesmen and women displaying their crafts. Every available space was being used. The shopkeepers began to retract their window canopies, which in some cases nearly touched the canopy of the shop opposite, creating a covered walk-through. But now as the sun had gone below the building line, there was no need for such a luxury.

Andreas led the way towards a large well-presented shop. As they stepped across the threshold they were greeted by the mixed aromas of mint, tea, spices, coffee, leather and burning incense. The shop was crammed full of everything, although textiles, leatherware and jewellery seemed to be prominent.

Nathan walked over to a large display cabinet full of yellow-gold jewellery. There was a multitude of gold necklaces, rings and bracelets. *I'm not sure what type of necklace she would like*, he mused. *I'm not sure of her finger size for a ring, so that leaves a bracelet. If I go for a plain gold bracelet, surely I can't go wrong.* It took him all of ten minutes to select a beautiful and very fine gold bracelet, complete with a safety chain in the event of clasp failure. He purchased the bracelet after a little negotiation with the vendor.

They left the shop and decided to eat at the café by the entry point to Varosha. They slowly made their way back. This time their route took them past several derelict Christian churches and other ancient buildings, some of which had been vacant for centuries and some only since the Turks had invaded in 1973. Any slight breeze that there had been earlier in the day had now completely gone. The air was sultry and very humid. The sky started to glow as the sun gradually fell towards a shimmering sunset. A very warm evening and night lay ahead.

As they approached the café, Nathan retrieved his backpack from the rear of the Isuzu. He then deposited Loretta's gift into the glove compartment, along with his mobile phone. He didn't want to, but the fact that the area was bristling with phone masts would make him easy to track. He certainly didn't want to leave a footprint in Varosha. They sat down at a table with a perfect view of the cul-de-sac and ordered lamb salad pittas and a cold drink. They enjoyed their meal but the time for action was approaching.

'It's nearly time,' said Nathan. 'So I need to be through that fence before it goes completely dark. Fortunately there isn't much activity at the moment so I'm sure no one will notice me. If you think I've been spotted by anybody, let's not risk being caught by the police or military. I'll look at you before I lift the fence and, if all is okay, just behave normally. Alternatively, stand up to stretch your legs and we'll abort.'

'Okay, I'll be staying here with a drink and a smoke. As soon as I see or hear from you, I'll come and get you.'

'You won't be hearing from me.'

'What do you mean?'

'I'm not taking my phone in; it will be traceable and leave evidence that I've actually been in there. I've left it in the Isuzu.'

'I understand … but to go in with no contact with the outside … what happens if you have an accident?'

'Best I don't have an accident then,' replied Nathan.

Andreas pondered for a second. 'Please tread carefully … and good luck.'

The two men shook hands. Nathan stood up and headed for the cul-de-sac.

16

NATHAN WALKED away from the café. However, instead of going straight to the cul-de-sac, he approached from the right, making sure that all was clear before quickly darting in the direction of the removeable fence. As he approached the fence, he turned around quickly to see whether anyone could have possibly spotted him. He could see Andreas in the café, he could see the other people adjacent to his friend, but they all seemed to be deep in conversation. Andreas was still in his seat, so he was clear to go in.

Within a matter of seconds Nathan had lifted the fence panel, squeezed through and relocated it behind him. He was in the space between the two buildings. He made his way to the end, turned right and stepped on to the patio of the apartment block. This was his last opportunity to observe the lie of the land before darkness fell. He looked in the general direction of the silo but was concerned by a series of obstacles such as fences and tree growth that he hadn't paid attention to on his previous visit. He looked in the direction of Ermou Street but, from his location, he was looking at the rear of the buildings. It was on the other side that the guard post was located.

His first objective was to reach the silo. He could see it in the distance but nightfall was turning into darkness, so he had only a matter of minutes left. He had to make a move. His first hurdle was an easy one, a one-metre-high concrete wall that formed the perimeter to the gardens of his starting location. He was able to step over it comfortably but immediately on the other side was a large prickly pear cactus. By the time he saw it, it was too late. As his leading leg hit the floor, his inner calf grazed along the side of a large spiny branch. The pain was immediate. As he stepped out of the plant, he bent over to feel his leg and noticed that blood had already leeched through his trousers. *Great start! I hope it's not too deep. I'm carrying on regardless.*

Having moved on a few metres, there was now a tree with a thick trunk in front of him. The land around the tree had sunk into a large circular trench, the bottom of which he couldn't see because of the lack of light and also because it had a peculiar type of vegetation growing within it. It rustled under his weight, like stepping on dried autumn leaves. He was unsure what was hidden within it but he had no choice, as the alternative was to try to scale a couple of randomly positioned rolls of rusty barbed wire.

Nathan carefully made his way around the tree. He could see the two buildings up ahead and knew the silo was lined up more or less between them. He also knew that when he reached the silo he was in play and potentially visible to the guard. He walked on slowly, step by step. *Feeling exposed in this open space. I need to get to those buildings asap.*

He was now in what felt like an area of very long grass, which was tall enough to nearly reach his waist and he could feel the seed heads at the end of the stems. Suddenly his foot hit something very hard, which nearly sent him into a forward roll. He just about managed to keep himself upright then knelt down and touched a large rubber tyre, which had presumably at one time belonged to a lorry. *Something to bear in mind. One of many types of trip hazard that are randomly placed.*

Nathan continued and, a couple of metres later, came across several oil drums. Some of them he could push to move but some felt as if they were anchored to the ground. They also appeared to have been chained together, which made them not only a tricky object to get by but also a noisy one. *The only way over this is to try to stride over it … but slowly.* He went to step over a barrel, hoping there were no nasty surprises on the other side, but his leg span was not as long as he thought. He was unable to keep his feet on the ground either side of the barrel, which resulted in a small but significant roll of the obstruction. There was a clang as the chain moved inside the rolling barrel. Nathan hurriedly pulled his trailing leg over and stood deathly still, listening. *Damn it, that's all I need now, an armed guard on the prowl looking for an intruder.*

He waited but there was no indication that anyone was coming towards him. He was now far enough away from any traffic or human activity. It was deathly quiet. On that principle, if anyone was looking for him, he should hear them coming. He moved onwards slowly. The humidity and the tension caused him to sweat profusely and, with that, the night's flying insects were delighted with the salty treat. He was mortified.

He finally reached the opening between the two buildings. The silo was a stone's throw away. There was a terrible stench in the air. Now he had to be ultra-careful. He knew that fifty metres down Ermou Street, to the right, there would be a guard in his box. Nathan crept carefully along the building line with his back to the wall, step by step, until he came to the corner. Peering around the corner, down Ermou Street, he looked up and sure enough the guard was in his box, his face illuminated by a bluish light. It was difficult to tell whether he was on his mobile or had a small television with him. Either way he was distracted so Nathan inched towards the foot of his perch.

By Nathan's calculations, the Mykanos building should be approximately a further fifty metres, on the opposite side of Ermou Street. He was now edging along the building line. He looked up and could see through a gap in the floorboards into the guard post. The man didn't look like police or military. He was heavy-set, wearing blue jeans and a dirty white T-shirt. He had a full black bushy beard, and a cigarette sticking out of his mouth. By the commentary coming from the post, it sounded as if he was watching football on his mobile phone. What was more disturbing was the fact that he had two rifles up there with him. Nathan thought he may even have a handgun on his belt, on the side that was hidden from view. *He's armed up to the teeth but this is as good an opportunity as ever to get across this road.*

Nathan continued down the building line until he was opposite what he believed to be the Mykanos Real Estate agency. He looked up at the guard, whose head was looking in a direction that was about ninety degrees from the location where Nathan was going to cross the road. But Nathan had an advantage as he could see the guard but he doubted the guard could see him.

He slowly and with stealth crossed the road and was now looking up for the swinging sign that he had seen on the drone footage. But it wasn't there. He would now have to move from his position and search for it. Rather than head east back towards the guard, he headed west. With short steps, looking up and alternately watching where he put his feet, he moved along, hugging the walls, until he realised that he had gone too far. He turned around and came slowly back. It seemed to take an age. Then there was a noise up ahead. The guard was now standing in his box and leaning over the side. He sounded like a pig as he took a large intake of breath through his nose, then spat the contents of his mouth over the side. He sat down and resumed his viewing.

Nathan continued in an easterly direction, squinting upwards, looking for the swinging sign against the night sky. He had approached the spot where he had originally crossed and only a few metres later could see a swinging sign above him. He was about to make his next move when he kicked a rusty old watering can that he hadn't seen in his path. It sounded like a gunshot. He looked up at the guard in his box, who was out of his seat in a flash and looking in Nathan's direction. He couldn't see Nathan, who was far enough away and in the dark, but Nathan knew he had to take cover before the guard produced his flashlight.

He slipped into the nearest opening that he found, not realising that he was in the small alley between the Mykanos building and its adjoining premises. The guard illuminated the area with his large heavy-duty lantern-style flashlight. From his position, Nathan could see that he was scanning up and down Ermou Street and, by the angle, it meant that he had stayed in his box.

Nathan just had to wait it out but the guard gave up very quickly and resumed his position, watching TV. As soon as Nathan was happy, he went out on to the pavement. The next opening he came to, right below the swinging sign, was the entrance to the Mykanos Real Estate agency. He stepped inside, then looked for his LED hand torch. It had a narrow beam but was perfect for this kind of work.

He appeared to be in the main office. It was full of dust, plaster, some bricks, a pair of very old desks and another car tyre. *I don't get it with these tyres; where do they all come from?* At the rear of the office, he could make out another opening, so he walked over, trying not to kick up too much dust. He stuck his head around the corner and got the shock of his life. All he saw was a dirty set of white, fanged teeth very close to his face. He fell back on his backside in a heap on the floor. *Shit! What was that?* He could feel his heart pounding rapidly in his chest. *Looked like a wild dog, and a big one at that.*

Nathan hoped that the episode hadn't caused enough noise to disturb the guard. *How am I going to get past that thing quietly? Why is it here? Maybe it's a stray that's made its home here.* However, he was determined that he wouldn't be deterred by a dog, but the fact remained that he had to get the dog out before he could go down the stairs. He had to take another look, this time with his torch outstretched in front of him so he had a better view. But as soon as his torch appeared in the doorway, a horrendous deep guttural growl came from the blackness. It looked as if the dog was lying on the landing area at the top of a set of steps. Then there were different noises emanating from the space, high-pitched noises, like a whimper. *I wonder if its injured or in pain.*

Nathan took another quick look. This time the animal was less aggressive and he was able to recognise it as a dishevelled black German shepherd. He realised immediately why it had been aggressive. She was feeding four tiny pups. She was lying on her side and the pups were suckling her. It was a heart-warming sight but all Nathan could think about was the fact that he had to get past an angry bitch that was protecting her pups. He had to try to win her trust. He looked in his backpack. *If only I had some food to give her.* Then he saw a small bottle of water that he had packed earlier. *I could somehow try to feed her this.*

With his torch in one hand, he unscrewed the lid and filled it with water. He moved closer to the opening, offering the lid to the dog, which just growled. However, Nathan persisted. The closer he put his hand to her mouth, the angrier she looked. Then suddenly the look in her eyes softened and a large pink tongue shot out of her mouth. When she realised it was water, her tongue movement became more rapid.

Nathan leaned in and carefully refilled the lid. With a tongue so large, the dog emptied it in a single lap. She was definitely more receptive and Nathan spotted a couple of tail wags. He decided the only way to do this would be to feed her the bottle. He approached her mouth and the tongue shot out like a huge receptacle, so he poured the water on to her tongue and into her mouth. Her tail wagged in sheer joy and appreciation. *I wonder how long it is since she had a drink, and how is she feeding those pups? Hopefully, she's now on my side. I'm going to be a bit vulnerable but I'll have to try to step over her.*

He had no choice. With his torch in his left hand, he positioned and held his backpack in place to protect his more vulnerable areas, namely his groin. He stepped over her very carefully and slowly, keeping eye contact with her and avoiding the pups. Once his feet were firmly on the ground on the other side of the dog, he sighed with relief. He slowly descended, with his small torch illuminating the steps in front of him, although he couldn't really see what was ahead. He walked through numerous spider webs, which clung to his skin. He wiped his face and head with his backpack just in case there was something in the webs that could sting him.

He reached a small half-landing, which indicated that the steps were turning off at a ninety-degree angle. At this point he removed his headtorch from his backpack, packing away the small hand-held torch. He put on the head torch and switched it on. It provided a much better illumination and now his hands were free.

Suddenly there was a very low fluttering sound on the wall by his right ear. As he turned to look, the light must have startled a small group of praying mantises that had gathered on the wall. A couple of them flew at him and landed on his face. The shock caused the immediate reaction of swiping them away. In the panic he had crushed one of them and its stomach contents were running down his face towards his mouth. He quickly used his T-shirt to wipe away the mess. *That was horrible. Two shocks in five minutes. I wonder what else this hell hole has in store.*

Nathan proceeded down the steps, where the room opened up in front of him. It was a five-metre-square basement room with a bare concrete floor that looked as if it had once been tiled. There was an old rusty filing cabinet, a rotten ancient desk and, amazingly enough, yet another car tyre, which someone must have rolled down here years ago, just for fun and because they could. The walls were covered in cream-coloured glazed tiles, each one about the size and shape of an English house brick. *It's like being in an old public toilet in London.*

Nathan carried out a quick survey of the room, looking for any potential pitfalls or predators. Happy it was safe to go forward, he walked into the centre of the room. Directing his head torch, he scanned the walls for any obvious giveaways that could indicate a safe. The good news was there were no giveaways, which meant it could still be in situ. The bad news was that he had to try to find it and he had to do it quietly.

Working on the principle that the safe had to be accessible, he ruled out all the tiling above his head height. He then concentrated on one wall at a time, starting opposite the steps because it was immediately on view when one entered the room. Using the handle of his screwdriver he religiously tapped every tile, looking for a different noise that may indicate a hollow or a safe, or anything different. There was nothing that stood out. In fact, all the tiles on that particular wall looked as if they were as solidly fixed as the day they were installed by the tradesmen.

It wasn't looking good but Nathan knew that there was a safe down there behind one, two, three or maybe even four tiles. He had no idea how large it was going to be. The tiles couldn't have been adhered to the safe door because there would have to be a tell-tale sign on the tile, such as a keyhole, which would make it a not-so-secret safe. And it would probably have been looted anyway.

The sweat ran down Nathan's body from head to toe. He was saturated and under pressure. He decided to try the wall immediately to the left of the steps. Again, starting at head height, he tapped his way along and down, level by level. He came to one tile, about waist height, which sounded slightly different when tapped, more hollow this time. Down on his knees now, he looked at the tile closely. There was no discolouration in the grout and it didn't look loose. In fact, it looked like all the others, in line and on parade. He pressed the tile on one side and it gave way slightly into the wall. Then as he slowly released the pressure, it sprang back out to its fixed position. *You would have no idea that was there but I believe I've found the safe.*

This time Nathan pressed the tile in and released it quickly. It was spring-loaded and opened on a small hinge on the right-hand side. Buried in the wall was a small safe door with a keyhole. *Brilliant, so well disguised.* Nathan's heart rate was accelerated, not for the first time that day. He pushed the end of his screwdriver into the keyhole and applied some outward pressure. The safe was locked. 'Damn it,' he said quietly under his breath but knowing it was a good sign. He tapped the safe with the screwdriver. It was solid steel and it was thick.

Because it was so small and the steel used was so thick, Nathan knew this was a very robust safe. He pondered whether he would be able to remove it from the wall with minimum noise but knew it was going to be impossible. He looked closely at it but there wasn't much to see. However, when he checked the hinges he was encouraged. The makers of this safe were reliant on the disguise element and not the physical security of its hinges, which would normally be inside the safe. But this one had been made with external hinges on the door, which might mean that the pins running through the centre of the hinge could be manipulated or drilled out. Nathan stared at the pins. *I think they've corroded. Could be that they were made of a different type of steel and there's been a chemical reaction between the metals.*

Using the screwdriver and the hammer from his backpack, Nathan tapped at the top of the hinge in an attempt to force the pin out. Gradually it started to appear from the base of the hinge. It was also crumbling into a powdery dust, which Nathan had inhaled. He managed to suppress the urge to sneeze, although it left him feeling as if he had inhaled a handful of pollen spores.

He started on the bottom hinge and had pretty much the same effect, slowly working the pin downwards as it crumbled to dust. Then the pins were no more but the door was still in place. The interlacing hinges didn't want to move, which was understandable. Nathan pulled out a small metal chisel of the type usually used on masonry. He had now used all the tools in his backpack, so if this didn't work he would never find out what was in the safe, if anything.

He wedged the chisel between the safe door and its frame on the hinge side. He tapped the chisel in different directions and slowly the interlaced hinges separated until they were no longer aligned. The door was now held in place by the bolt that was operated by the key, so he grabbed the door and pulled it. The lock bolt simply slid out of the keep in the locked position.

Excited now, Nathan placed the safe door on the floor and looked inside. There were documents that had been rolled and tied with a red ribbon. There was a small cardboard box to the rear. There was also a hole in the rear wall, which looked to have been caused by corrosion. He put his hand inside to take the box. Immediately a Cyprus scorpion, sensing the disruption, crawled out of the document roll and on to his hand. He froze in shock. *Shit! What do I do now? I don't know how poisonous this thing is but I know that if I pull my hand out it may strike with that nasty-looking tail.*

Nathan was in limbo. He was kneeling down in front of the safe, with one arm inside, scared to move and fearing the worst. He was in a very dire and uncomfortable position and, for once, was unsure what to do. *I could try to pull my arm out quickly but if the scorpion's hanging on to my skin the shock is going to make it sting me. I suppose I could use my other hand to swipe it off but if it sees my hand coming it could strike.*

He was considering his options when the scorpion made a move. It relinquished its grip and started to walk very slowly. It crawled on to his middle finger as the sweat just oozed out of his pores. He concentrated on staying as still as possible. The scorpion approached his nail, stepped off and disappeared through the hole in the back of the safe. The relief was immeasurable as Nathan removed his arm and briefly allowed his head to slump. He let out a huge sigh. *I do hope that there are no more nasty surprises in store. I can't take much more.*

After taking a minute, Nathan removed the document roll carefully and gave it a shake to make sure there were no more nasties clinging on inside. He wanted to unroll the documents to see whether they were indeed the missing records but what he wanted more was to get out of the hell hole called Varosha. So, both document roll and cardboard box were thrust into the side pocket of the backpack, the tools going into the main compartment. He swapped the head torch for the small hand torch, checked that everything was packed away, then started the slow ascent of the stairs.

He reached the half-landing without incident and continued towards the exit. As he approached the landing he expected to see the dog with its pups. To his surprise he could see in the moonlight that the dog was now lying out in the road and each of the four pups had a teat. Nathan was about to make his exit when to his horror there was a sickening thud and he was sprayed with warm blood from the German shepherd bitch. It was shocking. But worse was to come as each pup was hit with its own thud, that of a high-velocity rifle round. It was a nauseating sight and Nathan was now dripping with blood, sweat and tears.

Someone was approaching. *That murdering bastard of a guard.* Nathan positioned himself below the top step so he could just about peer above it. Suddenly the guard came into sight. A large man with a substantial belly, a large beard and a lust for blood. He picked the German shepherd bitch up by the tail and dragged her off. Nathan watched as the guard took her towards the silo, opened the door and with one hand grabbing the skin of her neck and the other her tail, threw her inside like a bag of rubbish. Then he walked back, picked up the remnants of the pups and despatched them in a similar fashion.

Nathan was expecting the guard to return to his post but he was heading back towards Nathan's location. He resumed his position on the steps. *If he comes in here I won't be responsible for my actions.* However, the guard casually started to cover the huge amount of blood that was soaking into the detritus that covered the road. After kicking around a bit of dust, sand and mud he eventually returned to his post and, as if nothing had happened, turned on his mobile phone and resumed his viewing of the football match.

Nathan was now standing in the entrance to the Mykanos building, out of the guard's line of sight, but watching him through what was once the front window. He was seething with anger at what he had seen but he had to remain focused. If he could get past the guard post and then the silo, he could make it. He only hoped that it was, indeed, the land documents in his backpack.

He had to take time to compose himself again before stepping out to cross Ermou Street. But the situation was made a little more difficult because the moon was now a little higher and was shining brightly down the street. He was in two minds whether or not to head west and cross further down the street, staying well away from the guard. But there was just as much chance of him being seen hugging the wall as he moved. He was going to be in peripheral range of the guard, so instead of sprinting across the road he was going to walk across very slowly and try not to catch his eye.

Nathan stepped out of the building and slowly crossed the area where the German shepherd and her pups had been savagely murdered only a few minutes earlier. He made it across and headed in the direction of the guard post. As he approached, he could hear the commentary of the football match in what he presumed to be Turkish. He walked beneath the post, but then the situation changed. He heard the guard firstly turn off his mobile phone, then heard his feet shuffle as if he had stood or was about to come down from his throne. It was the latter. Nathan took the opportunity to gain a few metres before ducking down behind a bush that had grown out of the pavement adjacent to the silo.

The footsteps were coming in his direction. *I haven't got enough cover here. I'm screwed.* The security guard was now standing over him. He lifted the butt of his rifle and brought it down with extreme force towards the side of Nathan's head. Fortunately it was only a glancing blow but the intention was there.

~~~

A few minutes later Nathan was on his route back from the silo towards the exit. As he approached the barrels he tripped and fell to the ground. His elbow shattered a piece of glass that was lying in the long grass. He lay there in complete silence. He didn't move because he could hear another voice not far away. *Two, possibly three people. It could be a patrol.*

Some of the surrounding buildings were briefly illuminated as the men swung their torches around at random. Nathan was unsure whether they were searching for him but they were getting pretty close. He managed to crawl up to one of the barrels and lie flat on the ground. They offered excellent cover. He could hear voices on the other side of the barrels and they were moving closer. Nathan lay still as torchlight seared through the gaps between the barrels.

Someone moved up ahead and Nathan watched as a man sitting on the side of a barrel swung his legs over and carried on walking, illuminating the grass as he went. Then, as Nathan feared, someone approached the barrel he was hiding behind. They pushed the barrel, which rolled the short distance into Nathan's back, briefly winding him. He lay stock still up against the barrel as two legs swung over and found ground immediately next to his torso. The area was illuminated by torchlight as the man stood and continued on.

Nathan lay there for another ten minutes before daring to move. He was on his knees now, looking above the tall grass for any sign of torchlight. He could see some reflections in the distance and decided it was time to make a move. He now had to use his own torch to illuminate the path in front of him as he navigated his way around the trees, undergrowth and other traps that were lying in wait.

He approached the low concrete wall, which indicated he was not far from the exit point. Suddenly he heard a voice up ahead. For a second he thought it may be coming from outside of Varosha but, as he looked more closely, he could see there was a guard sitting on a couple of cement blocks on the terrace next to the exit point. He, like the other security guard, seemed to be watching football on his mobile, which illuminated his head with a flickering light. It looked as if he had a rifle over his shoulder. *I hope he's not planning on staying there all night. There's no way I can get past him unnoticed.*

It was another waiting game, although only for another five minutes before the guard just upped and left. Nathan was over the wall in a flash and heading for the exit point. As he walked through the gap between the two buildings, he approached the moveable fence. He checked to see whether Andreas was in his position, which he was, but he was standing up. *Something isn't right. Can't see anything from here but he has an overall view from his location.*

Andreas could only stand and pretend to stretch for so long. It was starting to look odd. All he could do was pick up his cigar and drink, then walk just a few yards from his seat before returning. A waiter approached him to check that everything was alright. Nathan could see Andreas holding his back and feigning some sort of complaint in the lumbar region.

What Andreas had seen was a police car parked just on the outer edge of the cul-de-sac. It was just out of Nathan's sight and if he appeared in the cul-de-sac now he would surely be arrested on the assumption he had just exited Varosha. Andreas watched Nathan, while Nathan watched Andreas. It seemed a lifetime but was probably only about ten minutes before Andreas finally sat down. The police car had driven away.

Andreas then watched as Nathan calmly moved the fence, squeezed through and relocated it. Andreas left payment on the table, with a suitable tip for the waiter, then headed for the Isuzu. Like a military operation he arrived at the entrance to the cul-de-sac, where he collected Nathan just as he appeared at the junction. If all went well, their next stop would be the border crossing.

'You look terrible,' said Andreas. 'Did you find any documents?'

'Yes I did. I don't know if they're the right ones, I just grabbed them and threw them in my backpack. I think we should stash them before the border crossing just in case they decide to do a search.'

'I cannot see them doing that but it is better to play it safe. If you look under your seat you will see a first aid box. You can hide the papers in there.'

Nathan removed the papers from his backpack and pushed them into the spider-infested first aid box.

'You need to remove your T-shirt,' said Andreas. 'It looks like you have been involved in a bloodbath.'

'I have,' replied Nathan, as he stripped his T-shirt off and pushed it under the seat. 'The guard, he shot a dog while it was feeding its pups. It happened right in front of me. It was horrendous, a nightmare.'

'What happened to your head?' enquired Andreas.

Nathan lifted his hand and gently touched the right side of his head. There was a large lump and a small amount of blood had matted in his hair. 'I'm not sure. It was a bit like an assault course in there. It must have happened on the way out.'

'You will need to cover it; it really does look like you have been involved in a fight. We do not want them seeing that at the border crossing. There is a baseball cap on the back seat. Put it on. It should cover most of the blood.'

'Okay, thanks Andreas.'

'So, tell me all about it. You obviously found the safe because you have some documents.'

'Yes, I did, but if you don't mind, my head aches and I feel dehydrated. Could we wait until we get back to the villa?'

'Okay,' said Andreas, as he produced a bottle of water from the door pocket and passed it over.

Nathan gulped down most of the bottle but saved some to pour over his face. *This tastes like the best champagne ever.* The water ran down his neck, chest and stomach.

Andreas pointed at Nathan's stomach. 'Where do you get a stomach like that anyway? It is ridiculous, all this six-pack nonsense. You see the guys on the beach parading up and down. In fact, you even see women with them, although not as pronounced as yours.'

Nathan laughed. 'You sound jealous, my friend,' he said teasingly.

'No, not at all.' Andreas smiled.

'I've been lucky. I've never carried much belly fat, not yet anyway. But I do sit-ups whenever I can. I guess it started in the police, playing rugby and keeping fit.'

Andreas noticed that Nathan was keeping an eye on a single headlight, which seemed to be following them from a distance. 'Do you think it could be our man on the Vespa?' asked Andreas.

'I'm not sure. Let's pull over and have one of your smokes, but do it abruptly so as not to give him the chance to turn off.'

They were approaching a section of the road that had a disused junction. Andreas slammed on the brakes as he pulled to the side of the road. Unfortunately, he had created so much dust behind them that they were unable to see anything. They jumped out of the car, expecting a motorcycle or scooter to come by, but nothing. As the dust settled they could see back up the road. There was a car heading towards them but no sign of the single headlight.

'This means one of two things,' said Nathan. 'He's back there waiting for us to make a move or he simply lives off one of the side roads and has returned home.'

The two men stood there deliberating what to do. 'What do you think?' asked Andreas.

'I think he's sat back there waiting for us to pull away, so he can continue following us.'

'Well, if that is the case, it could all unravel at the border. If it is a Turk or Russian following us, there could be a reception committee waiting up ahead.'

'And if that's the case, Andreas, we can't afford to be caught in possession of these documents, because if they're what we think they are, they'll take them by force and without regard to us. But, by the same token, we can't afford to just sit here like fish out of water. I suggest we double back. Let's see if he's waiting back there. At the very least it could throw their plans into disarray.'

'Okay, if you are sure,' said Andreas hesitantly.

'I'm not sure but let's do it anyway,' Nathan replied.

They jumped into the Isuzu. Andreas spun the vehicle around in yet another cloud of dust as they headed back down the road.

'You watch your side of the road and I'll watch mine,' said Nathan.

There was no sign of any motorcycle or scooter either on the road or parked up. They searched approximately one mile back towards Varosha before Nathan said, 'Turn around.' Andreas did so without question.

'Let's just go for the border crossing,' suggested Nathan. 'I just have the feeling that this isn't the Russians. It seems too small-time; it doesn't fit right.'

'It could be the Turkish police,' said Andreas.

'I think it's more likely them than the Russians but I don't understand why, if it is them,' replied Nathan.

As they approached the border the tension in the vehicle was palpable. Severe halogen lights on tall steel posts illuminated the area, which in turn attracted thousands, literally thousands of flying insects, such as moths and mosquitoes. They pulled up slowly to the checkpoint. The clicking noise of the cicadas filled the air.

The border guard looked at Andreas, took a quick look at Nathan, who was brandishing his passport, and waved them through. They both breathed a sigh of relief from the tension but it was short-lived. As they pulled away, to the right at the side of the road there was a young man wearing a shemagh. He was smoking a cigarette while sitting astride a blue Vespa. He eyed them as they passed.

'Is that the same guy as earlier?' asked Andreas.

'Oh yes, I'd swear that's him, but it doesn't mean he was the one who was just following us, unless of course he circumvented the border crossing to get in front of us,' said Nathan.

'I do not think it is particularly difficult to do that,' replied Andreas.

'He has Greek Cypriot plates on. I never noticed before.'

'We never really got close enough,' replied Andreas.

'Let's just see if he follows us.' Nathan watched the rear-view mirror but there was no movement. 'Okay, as we round the next corner, pull over and switch the lights off.'

Again, Andreas pulled over without question. A matter of seconds later, the blue Vespa came by. The rider was now wearing his shemagh across his nose and mouth, no doubt to protect him from the insects of the night and all the dust kicked up from the road.

'I think it's safe to say that guy was following us,' said Nathan.

'It certainly looks like it.'

They watched as the scooter continued on its way and its rear light faded into the distance.

'Let's carry on back to the villa, but keep your eyes peeled,' said Nathan.

Andreas seemed to wince at Nathans words. 'You have used that expression before. It makes me cringe at the thought,' said Andreas.

'It's not one that you use in Cyprus then?'

'Peeling your eyes? Are you serious?'

Nathan laughed. They continued back to the villa without any further incident or sightings of the blue Vespa.

~~~

As they pulled into the villa driveway, Nathan wondered whether they were being watched. He loaded the items from the first aid box into his backpack. 'Are you coming in?' he asked Andreas.

'Are you serious? Of course I am coming in. I would not miss this for the world.'

Nathan unlocked the front door and Andreas followed him in through to the kitchen. With nervous excitement, Nathan pulled out the scroll of documents and placed them on the kitchen worktop. He slowly untied the piece of ribbon. As expected over such a long period of time, the documents had retained their rolled-up shape, but other than that they seemed to be in a decent condition.

The first document to be unravelled was a small blueprint. It looked as if it had retained all its original markings, measurements, plot numbers and key. It was written in Greek but they both knew that they had hit the jackpot – it was a plan of the Anapetri land. It showed just one building on the whole site, which was roughly were the current villa stood.

'Bingo,' said Nathan excitedly.

The next couple of documents related to a series of invoices from solicitors. Then Andreas clutched a more official-looking document. His hands were shaking. 'Look at this,' he said. 'It is a bill of sale for the plot of land to Mr Mykanos, and you will not believe who the seller was.'

'Who? Tell me,' insisted Nathan.

'It was the council.'

'Well, well, well. All it shows is how dishonest they are then,' said Nathan.

The two men looked at each other before undergoing a long hug and pats on the back.

'We did it Andreas, we did it.'

'No, you did it Nathan. It is all down to you and your persistence.'

'I couldn't have done it without you, my friend.' They hugged and patted again.

'So, what's next Nathan?'

'Let's photo each one of these documents first, then tomorrow I'll forward the photos to the solicitor and the originals I'll deliver by hand to him in Nicosia. He can then deal with the situation on our behalf.'

'I cannot wait to see Helena's face, and our neighbours for that matter. Their future is secure. And the relief that I feel inside, knowing that it is not stolen land. The council has a lot of explaining to do.'

'Yes they do,' said Nathan. 'And they'll worm their way out of any corruption allegations. But as long as the land is secure for the future, that's all that matters.'

Once the documents had been photographed, Nathan gave Andreas a full rundown of the events in Varosha. He included the assault course he had to overcome, both going in and coming out, the armed guard, the dog and pups, the praying mantises, finding the safe, the contents and the scorpion. When he had finished, Andreas stood there open-mouthed. He praised Nathan for his bravery and endurance, then abruptly informed him that he 'stank like a pig', and that he desperately needed a shower. He also said he needed to get home, as Helena was expecting him earlier this evening. They agreed to talk in the morning.

17

NATHAN enjoyed his shower. He was, though, sur-prised at how many injuries he had received in Varosha. His leg was badly gashed by the cactus, his head had received a significant blunt-force trauma and the knuckles of his right hand were particularly badly grazed. He also had several mosquito bites, mainly to his face, neck, arms and head. He applied a tube of bite and sting ointment to the handywork of the mosquitoes but any other injuries were left open to the elements.

He looked through the documents again, before placing them in the safe behind the mirror. He knew that it wasn't the best place to keep them but it would do for now. He then went downstairs, grabbed a bottle of red and a bowl of olives and made his way out to the patio, where he made himself comfortable. He felt absolutely elated but at the same time exhausted as the evening's activities now caught up with him.

It was ten o'clock, so he decided to call Loretta to give her the good news. As she answered, Nathan couldn't contain himself. 'Loretta, we have the documents, we have the proof that your father purchased the Anapetri land legally!'

'Oh Nathan, that's fantastic news. How did you get them?'

'I think it would be better if I gave you and your father a full explanation on my return to New Zealand.'

'I'm not even sure he'll be here when you return. His deterioration is rapid.'

'Well, I hope that he is. But, just in case, let him know that we have the documents. It may give him a little lift and, apart from all that, I'm sure it would please him.'

'I'm sure it will, and it's very good of you to think about him. I can't wait to see you back here in New Zealand. I miss you so much.'

'Guess what, I can't wait to see you either. I'll be on that flight tomorrow afternoon.'

'With regards to the documents, can I suggest that you deposit them at Stakis in Nicosia and let him deal with it?' suggested Loretta.

'That's the plan for the morning. Also, I've photographed them and they're sitting in the cloud.'

'I'm impressed, and I want to know all the details, but I'll wait for you to tell me in person. In the meantime, can you message the photographs over to me?'

'Of course, no problem.'

'How are you and Andreas getting on, by the way?'

'I really like him. He has his funny ways, as we all do, but, overall, a good man, and I couldn't have done any of this without him.'

'That's great news. We're so lucky, having a local on our side, and what's his wife like?'

'Formidable,' replied Nathan immediately.

'In what respect?'

'Well, she can be a bit fearsome. She isn't afraid to mince her words and she keeps Andreas on a short lead.'

'Why's that?'

'He has had a bit of an online gambling problem but he's reassured her that he's finally quit. This is all private stuff … and what's with the questions anyway?' enquired Nathan.

'I've been working on a plan. Sitting hour after hour with my dad, I've needed a distraction, purely for my mental health. The plan depended on you finding the documents. So that's one box ticked. But I wanted to discuss it with you first. I was thinking of using Anapetri Villa as a holiday let just for our employees. No matter in which part of the world they're based, they could use the villa for their holidays. All they would pay for is the utility costs and, of course, their travel costs. What do you think?'

'I think it's a great gesture and another perk for Mykanos employees, but why the questions about Andreas and Helena?'

'Well, what do you think about them running it, the whole thing … bookings, maintenance, cleaning?'

'It's a great idea and I suspect that Helena would be doing bookings, housekeeping and cleaning, while Andreas would do the maintenance and probably cleaning too. So, yes, I think it would work. This would be a philanthropic gesture to all concerned, which has got to be a good thing. And I feel good too, because finding those documents has released so many good intentions. So many people are going to benefit. I think it's brilliant.'

'Okay, so if you don't mind speaking to them about our plans and asking them whether they would be interested in the role. Tell them we'll be in touch.'

'Yes, okay I will. I have a feeling that they'll be delighted.'

'But make sure that you let them know that it depends on the council confirming that they're giving up their crazy land grab idea.'

'Yes, of course,' agreed Nathan.

'Thank you again, Nathan. I don't know what I would do without you.'

''You've said that before.'

'Well, I mean it. You've done so much … and now this. So, come on, I don't think I can wait until you get back. Tell me … how did you find the documents?'

'I came across them in Famagusta.'

'I don't believe you; you've been into Varosha haven't you!' said Loretta angrily.

'I did it for you, for us, for Mykanos, the company. I did it for Andreas and all his neighbours, and I did it for the village of Anapetri and everyone who lives there.'

'But I told you not to go in there because of the dangers involved,' said Loretta in a cold and distant voice.

Now Nathan was getting angry. He was overtired and wasn't up for criticism. 'Loretta, there's something that you need to know about me. I don't always do as I'm told. It's been that way since I was about sixteen; in fact, probably earlier, and please bear in mind I'm not an employee of yours.'

'No, I know you're not, but it still has to do with my family and our business.'

'But you asked for help. I even got the job done.'

'I think it's more than that; it's a trust issue,' said Loretta.

'How the hell has it become a trust issue? Have I ever given you a reason not to trust me?'

'No, you hadn't, not until now.'

'So how does me not being a yes man suddenly become a trust issue? I don't get it.'

'Nathan, my father's dying and you're on the telephone wanting to argue with me—'

'No, not at all, it's just that—'

'Leave it Nathan. I'll see you when you get back. Bye.'

'Bye,' replied Nathan as the line went dead. He put his head in his hands. *Was that my fault? Maybe I'm just angry because I'm tired, but if Loretta wants a yes man, then I'm not her man.*

He stripped off and jumped into the pool. He needed to calm himself down or he would be sat up all night wringing his hands. He swam length after length of breaststroke and gradually his mood lightened. He could hear his mobile ringing and, thinking it could be Loretta, he jumped out, ran over to it and answered the call. To his disappointment, it was Detective Pavlos.

'Mr Mason, Detective Pavlos here. I am nearby so could I possibly call in to see you?'

'Well, it's a little late but come around the side. I'm on the patio.'

'Okay,' Pavlos replied before ending the call.

A short while later Pavlos appeared. Nathan offered him a seat and a drink. To his surprise Pavlos accepted a glass of red wine and was the first to speak. 'Have you had any more problems?'

'No, all quiet,' Nathan replied.

'Then why do you look like you have been in the wars?' Pavlos took a large gulp of wine before firing his next question. 'Have you found the documents?'

Nathan hesitated before saying, 'What if I said yes, I have found the documents?'

'Who else knows?'

'Why do you ask?'

'Look, I have a vested interest in this village. My parents grew up here, I grew up here, so it is dear to my heart. When I heard what the council had in store with regard to the Russian mining company, I was devastated. So, you see, anything to do with this village means everything. If you are miraculously now in charge of the documents, then I and my colleagues will give you all the help that you need to bring closure to this whole horrid affair and secure the future for this plot and this village for future generations. So, please, if you have the documents, I need to know who else knows that you have them. Andreas Polycarpou and Loretta Mykanos perhaps? I assume that Andreas helped you find them this evening?'

'Firstly, this is nothing to do with Andreas. He just happens to be my friend. Secondly, what makes you think that they were found this evening?'

Pavlos swallowed hard. 'Well, earlier today you did not have them.'

'That's true but I could have still got the documents this morning or this afternoon, so why did you say this evening? Has someone been tailing us?'

Again Pavlos swallowed hard. 'Very well. You have been truthful with me, so I shall be the same. Yes, I have had you followed this evening to the old town and back. You have to realise it was more for protection.'

'What do you mean? I don't need protecting,' said Nathan.

'Oh yes you do.'

'Then tell me something I don't know.'

'The likelihood is that your mobile phone calls, messages, texts, emails, WhatsApp, or any other communication method are all being intercepted. Now, assuming that you have informed Miss Mykanos by whatever means that you have found the documents, the Russians will know and they will be coming for you. This land is so valuable that they will risk life and limb, a small taste of which you have already been the recipient of.'

'I don't really know what to say. Have you been listening to my calls?' said Nathan.

'No,' Pavlos replied with certainty. 'If you have the documents you need to plan their safekeeping. If you like, I can take them to police headquarters at Palakori. They will be safe there.'

'No, the documents stay with me.' *Still don't know how much I can trust this guy*, Nathan thought.

'Then what are your plans to secure them?' Pavlos asked.

'I'll be taking them to the solicitor's office first thing tomorrow.'

'And does anyone else know about your plans?'

'Only Loretta. Shit! I told her over the phone. I never thought that there was even the remotest of possibilities of my telephone being tapped. I should have known better.'

'Can I suggest that you change your plans, both for the safekeeping of the documents and that of yourself.'

'Yes, I'll take your advice.'

'Can I ask what your plans are? I can provide security for you en route.'

'That's very kind of you but the fewer people who know the plan the better,' said Nathan.

'Under normal circumstances I would agree, but in this case we are dealing with an unknown number of Russians with unknown resources. We really do not know how far they may take this. Like I said before, that piece of land is so valuable to them.'

'So, you think I'll need all the help that I can get?'

'I would say so,' replied Pavlos.

'Very well. The plan is, or should I say was, to deliver the documents to Stakis solicitors in Nicosia as soon as they open tomorrow. We were going to ask him to act on our behalf, as he has in the past.'

'Well, Stakis are probably the number one solicitors in the country, with a fine reputation, and they are honest. I speak from experience. I also know for a fact that they have off-site access to secure banking vaults. I do not know of anyone in Cyprus who has these same facilities.'

'So, what do you suggest we do?' asked Nathan.

'You need to throw the Russians off the scent.'

'Okay, understood, but I still want to use Stakis for all the reasons that we've just discussed. So, I need to put it out there that I'm using an alternative solicitor, maybe one in Larnaca.'

'I think that would be a sound idea. It would attract some of their resources to Larnaca and give us a run to Nicosia. But let me make another suggestion.'

'Okay …'

'We join the A3 at Ayia Napa. We travel west and, instead of joining the B2 north of Larnaca, we turn off near Aradippou. We go off track, so to speak, on some of the smaller roads and head north to Nicosia the back way,' suggested Pavlos.

'And why is that a good idea?'

'I have known them in the past to work the motorways, particularly the A1 and A2. They could have lookouts or cruisers ready to spring into action. So, even though you may have thrown them off the scent and attracted some of their resources to Larnaca, the likelihood is that there will still be lookouts. This is Russian organised crime; it is how they operate and, unfortunately for us, it is big in this country, although not as big as it is north of the border.'

'Can you suggest a company in Larnaca that we could use as a decoy?'

'Yes, Chloros and company, they are quite a big name and in the centre of town. We come across them pretty regularly. They often have a representative in Palakori police station.'

'Okay, Chloros and Co. it is,' agreed Nathan. 'I'll ring Andreas in the morning and hopefully the Russians will be listening in.'

'I thought you were leaving him out of it,' said Pavlos.

'I am. He won't be coming with me. He's been a good friend and hopefully will be rewarded. I'm just keeping him up to speed. He'll be the group spokesperson over here when I've returned to New Zealand.'

'Okay. What time will you be leaving here in the morning?' asked Pavlos.

'I'll be leaving at the latest at seven-thirty.'

'Okay, I will be here before then. There will also be two other detectives in an unmarked car. Tonight we are leaving an unattended patrol car on your drive, just for show. Maybe it will help to keep the Russians away.'

'I hope so. That's very kind.'

'Just before I go, and before I set these wheels into operation, I will need to see the documents as proof.'

'Let's go into the kitchen and I'll fetch them to show you,' said Nathan.

Pavlos was satisfied upon seeing the documents. He left just as a police patrol car was deposited for the night on the villa's driveway. It was getting late and Nathan was feeling tired but his mind wasn't slowing down. *The business about listening in on my phone calls, it could all be supposition, total fabrication. There's no proof but I have to err on the side of caution. I have to assume the worst.*

Unable to settle, he removed his shorts and took another dive into the pool. He lay there on his back and the thoughts of the dog and its pups exploding in front of him returned. The anger he felt was mixed with the feelings of jubilation upon finding the documents.

He climbed out of the pool, dried himself, tidied the patio, locked up and went to bed. With the air conditioning on in his room, he was asleep as soon as his head touched the pillow.

~~~

In the heart of England, somewhere near Cheltenham, Nathan grabbed the body and pulled it into the pig pen. When the pigs realised that someone had entered their domain, the adult males appeared from their sties. He closed the gate quickly but quietly so as not to make too much noise. As he walked away, he could hear the pigs grunting and gorging on the large luxurious slab of meat. Nothing would be wasted, down to the last bone or tooth.

He walked into the forest. He had blood on his hands. Suddenly, he was in New Zealand, on a small hill in the middle of a forest. A sign read URUPA Māori burial ground. The warm air vented from the fissure in the earth's crust. He looked into the blackness of the crevasse, then pushed the body in. He walked away, stepped over the sign and stooped down to wash his blood-soaked hands in a small stream. He splashed the ice-cold water on his face.

Now he was in Varosha, Famagusta. As the butt of the rifle came down in his direction again, he grabbed and twisted it with all his effort. With one motion he rammed it into his assailant's face. The guard fell backwards and his head cracked open like an egg on the rim of an oil barrel. He was forcibly loaded into the silo and joined dozens of animal carcasses. The door was closed behind him with a thud.

Nathan's body shuddered as he awoke from the repeating nightmare. *Oh, fuck! No, I didn't kill the guard, did I? Surely not. I would have known, I would have remembered. I remember he hit me hard with the rifle butt but I don't remember anything after that, until I left Varosha.*

Nathan checked his watch. It was five-thirty. He decided it may be early but he was going to make the best of his time. After his sit-up reps, he was in the shower. His skin was stinging, on his legs, arms and head, thanks to cacti, mosquitoes and a rifle butt. He dried off and went downstairs to make himself a traditional English breakfast without the fried stuff. Tea, toast and a glass of fresh orange juice. *Just as well that I'm going home today. I seem to have run out of food. In fact, I've run out of everything.*

He took his breakfast outside on to the patio. Yet again, another hot and humid day was in store. After he had finished his breakfast he went back into the kitchen and realised that his backpack was on the kitchen seat from the night before. As he picked up the bag with the intention of packing it away in his suitcase, he suddenly remembered the small box from the safe in Varosha. He put his hand inside and withdrew the box, took the lid off and saw what appeared to be several discoloured cotton wool balls. As he pulled them out, things fell from them on to the kitchen worktop. *What the … they look like diamonds.*

Nathan scooped them into his hands and looked at them closely. There were six finely cut substantial diamonds sitting in his hands, just glistening. They were absolutely magnificent. He couldn't believe his eyes. *They must belong to Stelios. He must have stored them in Varosha, no doubt bound for one of his many jewellers shops. I would be surprised if Loretta knows about these. I wonder if she practises finders keepers. I very much doubt it. I'd better pack them in my suitcase, although I'm sure there's some sort of tax to pay or importation laws attaining to diamonds. Anyway, I can't just leave them here. I bet Stelios was beside himself when the Turks took over Varosha. I wonder if he ever thought he would see these again. I wonder if he was bothered. Perhaps there are many more undetected safes in the basements of buildings. I guess all it takes is a metal detector. All the same, I won't be going back.*

After washing the dishes, drying and placing them in the kitchen cupboard, Nathan started to gather his things to pack. He had made a subconscious decision that after the documents had been delivered he was heading for the airport. His time in Cyprus was nearly over. All he wanted was to get back to New Zealand.

18

AT SEVEN am Nathan called at Andreas's house for a quick coffee. He explained the situation and that when he returned to the villa he was going to ring him and inform him that the documents were being taken to Chloros and Co. in Larnaca. He also told him that it would be a decoy call, probably intercepted by the Russians, with the intent to throw them off the scent.

'You think the Russians are still following us then?' asked Andreas.

'Detective Pavlos thinks that my mobile phone may be tapped or being listened into. And I happened to mention to Loretta last night that I'd located the documents and will be taking them to Nicosia today. They still will be going to Nicosia but I want them to think that I've changed plans and am now taking them to Chloros and Co. in Larnaca.'

'That is probably a shrewd move. You do not know if your calls are being listened to anyway,' said Andreas.

'The detective might be wrong though,' added Helena.

'I know, but I have to play it safe and work on the assumption that the Russians know what I'm up to,' replied Nathan. 'But listen, just before I leave, I have a proposal for you two.'

'This could be dangerous Helena,' said Andreas.

'Well, if it is, you are not going,' she replied with her stern look.

Nathan explained. 'This plan depends on the council dropping its land grab proposal for the Anapetri plot. If I can get these documents lodged in a safe place today, with a solicitor instructed to deal on our behalf, then we're ninety-nine per cent there.'

'So, what is the plan?' enquired Andreas.

'Loretta wants to turn Anapetri Villa into a holiday let solely for Mykanos employees. She'll want someone to look after the bookings, maintenance, cleaning, repairs, all the usual types of stuff. The thing is, she wants you two to run it. It's madness, I know. I told her you wouldn't be interested but she insisted that I ask you,' said Nathan, teasing them.

'Of course we are interested,' said Helena in a high, excited tone. 'Aren't we Andreas.'

'Oh yes, of course, if it means that we have a steady income all year. That would be amazing and something that we have never had before. But what makes her think that we are suitable and can do the job?'

'I haven't got a clue,' said Nathan, smiling.

Helena suddenly leapt towards Nathan and flung her arms around him, saying, 'Thank you, thank you.'

'Like I said, it's all a plan at the moment and depends on the council dropping its action, but if I can get the documents to a solicitor without any hiccups, it should be plain sailing.'

Andreas stepped forward. 'We appreciate everything you have done for us,' he said. The two of them shook hands. 'Can I give you a hand today, even if it's just for company?'

'Thank you for the offer but stay with your family. I've got support from Detective Pavlos and his colleagues. They're going to be helping me to get the documents delivered.'

'Can you trust him?' asked Andreas.

'I didn't at first but, when I found out how invested he was in saving the village, yes, I think I do trust him.'

'We will be praying for you today Nathan, and the detective and his colleagues,' said Helena.

Nathan leaned in and gave her a peck on the cheek. 'I must go now. We're leaving shortly and I'll be going straight to the airport afterwards. I'll keep in touch and let you know how I get on. Take care you two.'

'Same to you,' they replied.

When Nathan returned to the villa he loaded his suitcase and other belongings into the rear of the Hyundai. When he was happy that he was leaving it in a decent state, the last thing he did was to place the precious documents in a large clear zip-up bag and locate them beneath the driver's seat. He wanted to email Stakis solicitors but realised from a security point of view it was a ridiculous idea. He then made the decoy call to Andreas.

While waiting for Detective Pavlos to arrive, Nathan was deep in thought. *I wonder whether the Russians are going to fall for this. I've never made an appointment with Chloros in Larnaca but neither have I made one with Stakis.*

Pavlos pulled into the drive in a white Ford estate. There was another man in the passenger seat. They both got out of the car and Pavlos introduced his passenger as a colleague from the office. Nathan didn't catch his name.

'I have a route planned,' said Pavlos. 'As we discussed yesterday, we will be heading towards Larnaca on the motorway but will divert on to the side roads near Aradippou and head for Nicosia. It is a long journey that will take a few hours. I will be the lead car, and behind you at a distance there will be a patrol car, very similar to mine. The police patrols in the areas that we are going to be passing through are aware of what we are doing. If we need backup, it will be available. So do you have the documents and are you ready to go?'

'Yes, I'm good. Just got to lock the villa.' Nathan walked round and checked all the doors and windows before locking the front door and depositing the key in the key safe on the external wall. 'Okay,' he said, waving to Pavlos. They jumped into their cars and drove down the driveway, passing the patrol car that had been left there overnight.

As soon as they pulled out on to the village roads the dust was up. It was okay for Pavlos, who was at the front, but Nathan was driving through a cloud of fog and backed off slightly. *I pity the third car when it joins us.* As they left the village on the improving roads, a police patrol car suddenly appeared in his rear-view mirror and stayed well back. Nathan felt reassured that backup was there.

The convoy of three headed to the holiday resort of Ayia Napa, where they joined the A3 heading towards Larnaca. The roads were very quiet as it was still early morning but the further they progressed along the A3 the busier it got. Nathan noticed that the police car behind was travelling much closer now, so as not to allow too many cars between them. He decided to do the same and get a little closer to Pavlos. The traffic around Nathan now slowed to keep to the speed limit because of the patrol car in attendance behind. He suddenly felt hemmed in as the cluster of cars around him drew closer. *I feel like I'm being boxed in, or is it my imagination?*

He called Pavlos on his hands-free phone. 'Pavlos, it's Nathan. I don't know if this is me but I feel that I'm being boxed in. It could be the patrol car that's causing it. Could you ask him to either drop back or come out ahead in front.'

'Okay,' Pavlos replied. Within a minute, the patrol car shot past the traffic until it was barely in sight. It had the desired effect, as the traffic in the immediate area increased speed and left Pavlos and Nathan cruising along on their own. The patrol car had left the motorway at the next exit and, as Pavlos and Nathan passed the junction, it re-joined behind them.

They made their way along the motorway, past a couple of junctions until they approached the turn-off for Aradippou, where they pulled off the motorway and approached a large roundabout. Pavlos indicated that he was turning right and heading north. Nathan did the same but, instead of turning off, he stayed on the roundabout. He did two full circuits, checking his rear-view mirror. He also observed vehicles that entered the roundabout, before turning off to follow Pavlos's route.

Pavlos had slowed, as if he was about to turn around and go in search of Nathan, whose phone then rang. He pressed the button on his steering wheel to answer. It was Pavlos. 'Why did you do that?' the detective asked.

'Can I suggest that we keep conversation to a minimum to secure our location,' said Nathan.

'Very well,' was the reply.

The patrol car reappeared in Nathan's rear-view mirror, presumably having followed him on his circuit of the roundabout. Nathan couldn't decide whether this was a good thing or bad. Either way they were on the move and now heading in a westerly direction. After another turn they were heading towards Ayia Varvara. The roads were now minor ones and, as such, apart from dust and dirt, there were no pavements, plus an abundance of potholes.

It was slow, hard going and Nathan and the patrol car found themselves dropping further and further back, just so they could see the road in front of them. The dust had settled on the trees alongside the road and given the leaves an unusual sheen that Nathan hadn't seen in Cyprus before. They passed a line of small stone cottages, one of which was displaying a clothesline full of fine Cyprus lace. It appeared to be dripping with water. Nathan looked in his mirror and saw the door flung open and an elderly lady came out shaking her fist, no doubt at the amount of dust that had been created. He assumed they didn't get vehicles coming up here very often.

At the next village, Pavlos indicated and pulled over at the side of the road. He gestured out of his window for Nathan to follow suit, as did the patrol car. The five men came together at the side of the road.

'Let's go for a coffee or a cold drink, whichever you fancy,' Pavlos said, addressing them all.

Almost opposite where they had stopped was a road-side café. The men sat at two of the three white plastic tables. The blue checked gingham tablecloths that covered them were held in place by large heavy-looking glass ashtrays and salt and pepper shakers. A top-opening freezer displaying the name Wall's was located against the front of the cottage, under a parasol that offered some semblance of protection from the heat.

The two patrol officers sat at their own table and ordered fresh orange juices and jam doughnuts from a man who Nathan presumed was the owner. He who wore a white vest, and braces to keep his dark trousers up around his ample waist. Nathan ordered English breakfast tea, while Pavlos ordered Cyprus coffee and his passenger an orange juice. The owner looked quite flustered with this sudden influx of customers with their differing orders.

Pavlos was looking as if he had something on his mind. 'Is everything okay Pavlos?' asked Nathan.

'Yes, all is fine. We have had no notifications about our adversaries in the Russian criminal underworld being up to anything in particular. In fact, it is all too quiet. I do not like it.'

'Presumably you have patrol officers looking for suspect vehicles on the motorway network. Haven't they seen anything?' said Nathan.

'No reports,' said Pavlos.

'Do you think that we'll have a clear run through to Nicosia?' asked Nathan.

'Yes, so far it looks like it. But there could be a reception committee at either Larnaca or Nicosia, if they are not sure where we are going to turn up.'

'Okay, so let's assume the worst and not be predictable. Will they be expecting us to turn up at the front of Stakis in the centre of Nicosia and me to walk straight through the front door, documents in hand?'

'I do not know but I bet they will be preparing for that eventuality.'

'Then can we not get local foot patrol officers and detectives to hover in the area and then all converge just as we arrive?' suggested Nathan.

'Yes, we probably could but I think it may be better to wait until we get nearer. See how the land lies and then make a decision.'

'That's fine by me. And I think that from now on we don't use our mobile phones for fear of letting our location out of the bag.' Pavlos and the third man nodded.

Pavlos looked over at the two patrol officers. 'You two, radios only from now on. Channel three, okay.'

'Okay Boss,' they replied.

'What's channel three?' asked Nathan.

'It is an alternative channel to the everyday one. It is much harder for people from outside to access it.'

Suddenly one of the patrol officers jumped up and, with his hand on his firearm, was shouting a warning at a man who had just stopped next to their car. The man was stooping over and feeling the rear tyre of his bicycle but the patrolman had seen more. He removed his side arm and pointed it at a middle-aged man with tanned leather skin and extremely hairy arms. The man stood with his hands in the air. The patrolman approached at pace, throwing the man across the bonnet of his car and handcuffing him from behind. Pavlos rushed over, shouting, 'What's the problem?'

'He stuck something under my wheel arch.'

'Are you sure?' asked Pavlos.

'Definitely.'

Pavlos crouched down and ran his hand around the inside of the wheel arch. 'I can't feel anything,' he said.

'I saw him do it. It will be there, whatever it is. It may be magnetic.'

Pavlos continued his search and came across a small square box about the size of a matchbox. He could feel the draw of the magnet as he removed it from its anchor point. He stood up and looked at the box then looked at the man in handcuffs. 'Why are you attaching a GPS tracker to a police car?' he said with menace.

There was no reply. Pavlos got close to the man so they were face to face. The spittle from Pavlos showered the man as he shouted, 'Why are you attaching a GPS tracker to a police car?'

Again, there was no reply. The patrolman started to go through the man's pockets, where he found a further four tracking devices.

'You will be going to the cells. I will give you a choice. You can go to Dali, the local police station, or you can go to Paphos on the other side of the island,' said Pavlos.

'Dali, where else?' the man replied.

'Then tell me who supplied these to you and for what purpose,' said Pavlos.

Silence.

'Then you will be taken to Paphos in the back of a van and interrogated there,' warned Pavlos. 'If you are released it will be up to you to find your own way home.'

'Please do not do this to me. I have a very sick wife at home. I have to look after her and I have no money to get back here from Paphos. Please do not do this to me.'

'I will not if you answer my questions,' said Pavlos. 'Who supplied these GPS trackers to you and for what purpose?'

The man hesitated; his resistance waned as the thought of trying to get back from Paphos became a reality. 'I do it for the money.'

'Who for?'

The man visibly squirmed but he couldn't help the words from coming out of his mouth. 'The Russians.'

'Why are you helping the Russians?'

'Because it is the only way for someone like me to earn any money. It is how I survive.'

'Who gives you the trackers?'

'The Russians.'

'Which ones?'

'Cherishev.'

'Who is Cherishev?'

'I have never met him.'

'Then how did you get these trackers?'

'They call it a drop. Just a place somewhere that you can go and collect a delivery from them.'

'Why are you attaching this tracker to this police vehicle?'

'Because I was told to.'

'By who?'

'Cherishev.'

'How did he tell you?'

'I got a phone call.'

'How did you know to fix it to this patrol car?'

'Because he gave me the registration number. He also told me it would be passing through my village with two other cars very soon and, if it stopped, I had to attach the GPS to it.'

'And what are these other trackers for?'

'Any other cars that are with it.'

'And why are you attaching these?'

'Because Cherishev told me to.'

Pavlos looked at the patrolman and ordered, 'Put him in the back of your car and hold him for a while.' The patrolman obeyed.

Nathan took hold of Pavlos's arm and nodded for him to go to one side. 'There's something seriously wrong here,' he said. 'There are two patrolmen, one diligently doing his job while his partner stands back and does nothing. He's probably responsible for supplying information to the Russians, right down to the registration plate on the car. Not only does he do nothing but I also saw him send a very quick message on his phone while you were searching for the tracker. It must have only been two or three words long. Pavlos, I believe we have a spy in the camp. You have to get those two off this case.'

Pavlos looked Nathan in the eye. 'Yes, if what you say is true, then I think you are correct. I just have to make a call, so I think I will use the phone in the café.'

A few minutes later Pavlos returned and pointed at the patrolmen. 'Right, you two, return our Russian sympathiser to Dali police station. There will be someone there to receive all three of you. Go straight there, do not stop.'

The diligent patrolman said, 'Very well Boss, but we are supposed to be part of the protection team.'

'Yes, you were,' replied Pavlos sharply. The patrolman knew not to argue and his colleague didn't utter a word. 'Before you leave, open the bonnet of your patrol car.'

'Open it, why?' asked the trusted patrolman.

'Just do as I say,' said Pavlos.

The patrolman pulled the lever near the footwell and the bonnet sprung open. Pavlos inserted his hand to release the catch and lifted the bonnet. He lifted the plastic lid on a small fuse board positioned near the bulkhead. He removed a fuse, pressed the cover closed, then released the bonnet so it slammed itself shut.

'Okay, now you can go,' said Pavlos.

The patrolmen loaded their prisoner and got in the car, which did an about turn and left in a cloud of smoke.

'What did you do?' Nathan asked Pavlos.

Pavlos showed him a small fuse in a plastic fuse carrier. 'I have just disabled his police radio. I know they will have their own mobiles but it will stop them from listening to us on channel three and finding out where we are. So, we can still keep in touch on the radio.'

'That's great thinking but I suppose we need to crack on and get to Nicosia asap. God knows who else may be listening to channel three. Let's make sure we keep communications to a minimum and don't mention our location.'

'I agree,' replied Pavlos.

Pavlos went to the men's room to relieve himself, while Nathan took the opportunity to speak to the third man, who was just finishing his drink. 'Sorry, I didn't catch your name earlier,' he said.

'It's Dionysus, but just call me Dion,' he replied.

Nathan noticed that other than being nearly as tall as he was, Dion looked like he took care of himself. His white shirt fitted him well but was slightly tighter across his biceps and chest. There was no evidence of any excess weight. He had strong features, with a slight scar through one of his heavy black eyebrows.

'How did you come to get involved in this, Dion?' asked Nathan.

'I work in the same office as Detective Pavlos. I am, if you like, his junior, but I think the main reason that he selected me for this job is because I was born just outside the village. I live in Palakori now but am passionate about Anapetri. When I heard what could be going on there I was horrified. So, between you and me, I am part of a small group trying to raise awareness of what is going on. When I heard that a Russian so-called landfill company wanted to purchase the land, that is when I joined them. The police do not know about this. I do not see why I have to tell them.'

'Does Pavlos know?'

'He knows that I am, shall we say, busy on that front, but he never asks any questions. I think if he was not as high-profile as he is, he would probably join us.'

'I guess it doesn't affect your working relationship, does it?'

'No, not at all.'

'It's nice to know we're all on the same side, unlike some of your colleagues,' said Nathan.

'I was just observing the incident with the patrol officers. You could be right about one or even both of them. Unfortunately the tentacles of the Russian crime mobs spread far and wide. We have just seen an example of it in this tiny village and it is occurring recently in our own police service. I should imagine it is much worse on the Turkish side. As for corrupt police officers, there is nothing worse. There will be a big investigation into them now and, if the evidence is there, as a minimum one or both will lose their jobs.'

Pavlos reappeared, then approached the owner and paid for the drinks before walking over to Nathan and Dion.

'Pavlos, thanks for the drink,' said Nathan.

'Yes, thanks Boss,' added Dion.

'Maybe the next one will be a celebratory one,' said Pavlos.

'If so, I'll be buying,' Nathan replied.

'Can I just show you this,' said Pavlos, directing them over to his car. He spread out on the bonnet a road map of Cyprus. It was quite obvious that the part of the country that they were currently in had very few roads and those that were in existence were in some cases more like tracks. Pavlos pointed out their current location just to the west of Dali. They were heading for a village called Tsari, which was about thirty minutes south of Nicosia.

'Once we get moving, I will radio up ahead,' said Pavlos. 'I have asked for a presence in the village to make sure it is all clear. It may only be one man in a car but he should be able to let us know if there is any additional activity that may indicate a potential problem. After that, hopefully it is plain sailing to Nicosia.'

'Okay, let's go. We have some documents to deliver,' said Nathan.

The two cars pulled away. *I don't feel any more vulnerable now that the patrol car isn't behind me*, thought Nathan.

They were making good progress and there was no chatter on channel three; all seemed to be going well. They were on a narrow single-track road, which was very quiet. The aspect was open across untold acres of scorched land, where goats roamed freely and any kind of irrigation would be at a premium, except during the winter months. To the west in the shimmering distance of a heat haze, there was a large mountain range, which eventually led to the beating heart of Cyprus, the Troodos mountains.

The journey to the outskirts of Nicosia was a tense one. Hardly a word had been spoken but there was plenty of thinking being done. Then channel three activity increased, although it was just a case of local units making each other aware that all was quiet.

They soon reached Strovlos, on the outskirts of the city, where traffic was busy, although moving steadily. They approached the centre of Nicosia on Chilonos Street, slowing to a snail's pace at a junction by a multistorey car park. Nathan knew exactly where he was. Stakis solicitors was only a few hundred metres away. He was nose to tail with Pavlos and blew his horn, before gesticulating for them to turn into the multistorey.

The two vehicles eventually found places adjacent to each other on the top floor. The three men got out of their vehicles and walked towards the edge of the car park. They were high enough to enjoy a spectacular view over a small part of the city. Opposite was the rear of a row of shops, the frontage of which were directly opposite the Stakis building. They could see over the shops and could identify the front of Stakis, although the shops prevented a view of the road.

Nathan's leadership skills suddenly came to the fore. 'We're very close to Stakis. Thanks for leading the way Pavlos. Dion, if you keep your eyes on anyone that comes up the ramp to this level – type of car, occupants, etcetera. If you're suspicious just let us know. Pavlos, I'm just going to watch the area below from this vantage point. Stakis is just around the corner from that building.' He was pointing at a modern three-storey office block. 'I just want to see if I can spot anyone doing any surveillance or maybe just loitering around the general area.'

It was busy in the centre of the city and in late morning there were lots of young mothers pushing prams, while elderly couples sat at the tables of the pavement cafés. There were also a couple of businessmen, who Nathan assumed had popped out of their office for some fresh air. There were, after all, numerous banks and financial institutions in the immediate vicinity. However, Nathan was cautious and said to Pavlos, 'I'm not sure about the businessmen. Let's just watch and see what they do.'

The more they watched, the more people came into the frame. Nathan decided that there were at least five potential persons of interest, who he pointed out to Pavlos. 'Do you recognise any of them as police officers?' he asked.

'No, but do not forget we are a couple of hours away from my division, so the chances of me knowing any of them is slim anyway. The problem is that we cannot see who is in Emba Street. There are some pavement cafés on this side hidden from view.'

'Yes, I remember from my last visit,' replied Nathan. 'It's tricky. There are numerous places to carry out surveillance.'

'What makes it worse is that there are flats above the shops, and they have balconies,' said Pavlos.

As he observed, Nathan thought about the next steps. *There would be a problem at the front door, from the time of pushing the button on the intercom to actually gaining entrance. Meanwhile, I'm left there like a sitting duck, in the wide open with valuable documents in my hand. It would be easy for someone to approach me with a weapon. We could always go mob-handed, say six of us approach the front door at the same time. Would that be provoking a shootout? Do I really want to put other lives at risk? There has to be another way, a safer way.*

Nathan could see the rear of a row of shops, a small road that entered Emba Street, then another row of shops, the end one with the signage *SO FRESH FOOD TO GO*. *We could get the documents delivered by So Fresh hidden beneath the packaging or in the base of a box. It's still putting someone in danger but surely there would be no need for the Russians to gun down a delivery boy or girl just doing their job.*

'Pavlos, Dion, what do you think of this? I go to So Fresh, order a breakfast to be delivered to Stakis and secrete the documents within the delivery with a message from me. They'll have to know what we're doing to a degree but it seems a good way of getting the documents in there unnoticed. I know it's simple and no doubt been done many times before, but it could work, particularly if we can cause some kind of distraction at the same time.'

Pavlos was deep in thought and contemplation, when Dion spoke up. 'I think it is a great idea. But I do not think you can go to the shop. You will stand out, even with a baseball cap on. The Russians know what you look like and when they see your blonde hair beneath your cap they will know it is you. Look around, there is no one here that has hair as blonde as you. I will go to the shop if that is okay with you two.'

'Dion is right,' said Pavlos. 'You cannot go down there. They would easily recognise you.'

'Okay, thanks Dion.' Nathan walked over to his hire car. He retrieved the documents from under his seat and wrote a note on a piece of paper that he found in the glove compartment.

Dear Dimitri

Enclosed is the documentary evidence that the Anapetri land was purchased lawfully by Stelios Mykanos. It goes without saying that the documents are confidential and need to be secured in a vault for fear of falling into the wrong hands. Going forward, can you please act on our behalf to ensure that the compulsory reclamation of the Anapetri Villa land is quashed.

Many Thanks

Nathan Mason

On behalf of the Mykanos Corporation

Nathan placed the note with the documents inside the plastic envelope and walked over to Dion. 'Dion, inside the envelope is a note explaining everything. It needs to be delivered to Dimitri Stakis. I need you to go and place a breakfast delivery. Explain to the manager that these documents need to be covertly delivered with the breakfast and that there's an element of danger involved. If you come up against too much resistance, just withdraw and we'll think of something else. If you're successful in persuading them, stay in the shop to see that the documents aren't interfered with.

'I also need you to make sure that they're adequately hidden within the delivery and to stay and watch it as it goes out through the door. As soon as the delivery leaves the shop we'll be able to watch the approach to the Stakis building. Make sure that whoever takes the delivery, when they get to the front door of Stakis, they must not mention a food delivery, because they probably won't even get access. Just say delivery for Dimitri Stakis.'

Dion took the envelope and looked at Pavlos for reassurance. Pavlos nodded in approval and passed to him a folded newspaper that he had just retrieved from his car. 'Place the envelope in here, and good luck,' said Pavlos.

The envelope slotted nicely in the fold. Nathan then handed Dion a €20 note. 'For the breakfast,' he said. Dion folded the money into his trouser pocket. 'Thanks for doing this Dion,' added Nathan. Dion made his way to the staircase and gave Nathan a thumbs-up sign. Nathan and Pavlos returned to their observation post.

'Thanks for all your help with this Pavlos,' said Nathan.

'You know how I feel about Anapetri. I am obliged to help wherever I can. The same goes for most of my colleagues, with the exception of the ones who have passed over to the dark side. I am sure they will be dealt with appropriately.'

Pavlos had a steely look in his eyes but suddenly looked at his mobile, which had been vibrating. He had an incoming call from Georgios, his liaison officer in Nicosia.

'Hello Georgios … yes, thank you for your help on this … no, do not say anymore,' Pavlos said in a raised voice, looking more angry by the minute. 'They could be tracing or tapping the call for Christ's sake.' Pavlos hung up.

'What's wrong?' asked Nathan.

'He has only gone and given away our location. We have three men on Emba Street, he said. Jeeze, I cannot believe that guy. It is just incompetence. If the Russians are listening in, they know exactly where we are now.'

'The wheels are in motion, so we can't stop Dion now,' said Nathan.

As they looked down from their position, Dion had just exited the car park via a single door and was heading in the direction of So Fresh.

'We've probably only got a few minutes to think about this,' said Nathan. 'When the person making the delivery appears, we could do with causing some sort of distraction, just to take the heat off the front door of Stakis.'

'Well, other than going down there and causing some sort of disturbance in Emba Street, I cannot see what we can do,' replied Pavlos.

19

D ION APPROACHED the front of the So Fresh
shop. He had a quick look down Emba Street
towards Stakis & Co. Nothing stood out but it was only a
quick glance, for fear of attracting attention. He walked
into the shop, where there were three small tables against
the right wall, two of which were occupied. There was a
glass counter to the left, which displayed an array of cakes
and pastries. There were two young women behind the
counter, each wearing a bright orange polo shirt and
baseball cap, both with SO FRESH emblazoned on the
front. One appeared to be taking orders over the
telephone, while the other one was doing general duties,
wiping shelves and rearranging the food displays.

Dion walked up to the counter, where it was the latter assistant who approached with a smile. 'Can I help you?' she asked.

'Yes, can I speak to the manager please.'

'Yes, of course, she is just on the phone.' She looked at her colleague beside her. 'Is it something that I can help you with?'

'Possibly, but if you do not mind I will wait to speak to her.'

'Okay. Can I get you a coffee?'

'A small glass of orange juice please.'

'If you want to sit at the table, I will bring it over.'

'Thank you,' replied Dion.

A short while later the manager brought Dion his orange juice. She was an attractive woman in her mid-twenties, with shiny olive skin and the typical extremely dark eyes that you would come to recognise in a local Cypriot woman.

'Here is your drink,' the manager said. 'Is there something that I can help you with?'

'Yes, but can we go somewhere private please?'

The manager wasn't too inclined to agree to Dion's request until he produced his police identification.

'Okay, if you follow me, we can go into the back.'

Dion followed her past a series of stainless-steel worktops, where food was being prepared by another two members of staff. Just before the rear staff entry and exit door there was an office on the right. Dion followed her in and didn't waste any time in explaining to her what he needed. 'There is a business down the street called Stakis and Co.'

'Yes, I know it,' she replied.

'I need to get some documents into the building disguised within one of your deliveries.'

'Sorry, I thought you were the police.'

'I am.'

'Well, if you are, what is to stop you from delivering it yourself?'

'The thing is, we believe the premises is being watched by some undesirable people who may try to prevent the documents from being delivered.'

'Oh, I see, so it is dangerous, and rather than putting a police officer at risk, a member of the public is preferred.'

'It is not like that and, believe me, it would be a great advantage for us all if we could get these documents in there unnoticed.' Dion opened the newspaper to reveal the plastic wallet.

'I guess I do not get to find out what the wallet contains.'

'I am afraid not. All I can say is that it is a matter of national importance.'

'Well, I am afraid that I am not prepared to put any of my staff at risk.'

'Erm, okay.' Thinking on his feet, Dion added, 'Have you got a uniform that I can borrow? I will deliver it myself.'

'I am afraid not one big enough for you. Like I said, I am not prepared to put any of my staff at risk but I will do it myself.'

Dion smiled. 'Thank you so much.'

She presented him with a delivery menu. 'You will have to pay for this, you know,' she said.

'I know.'

'But seriously, how dangerous is it?'

'If you just act naturally and go about your business, there should not be any problem.'

'What if I get stopped by one of your undesirables?'

'We have to make sure that the documents are well hidden, so that you have nothing to worry about. Also, it is important to make sure that you deliver direct to Dimitri Stakis in person and let him know that there are hidden documents.'

'What if he is not in or he cannot see me?'

'Then just make sure that whoever you deliver to knows that there are hidden documents for Mr Stakis.'

'Okay, what would you like me to deliver?'

'Oh, just some feta cheese toast and blueberry porridge. If you can bring it to me when you are ready to go, so I can hide the wallet.'

'Yes, okay, if you wait here I will be back soon.' The manager left the room with a nervous look on her face.

She reappeared about five minutes later with a box that was very similar to a pizza delivery box but slightly deeper.

'I have put a liner in the bottom,' she said. 'I thought that perhaps your plastic wallet would fit underneath.'

She placed the box on the table and opened the lid. There were two rounds of feta cheese on sliced toast, plus a portion of porridge in a see-through sealed bowl. She lifted the contents out on to a cardboard base liner. 'Now put your wallet in there,' she said.

Fortunately, the wallet fitted nicely in the box and she was then able to replace the base and its breakfast contents before closing the lid. 'Okay, I am ready to go.'

'Please, before you go, what is your name?' asked Dion.

'Ariadne.'

'Ariadne, when you get to the front door, there is a door intercom. Press the button and say delivery for Dimitri Stakis. Do not mention a food delivery because they may not let you in. I will pay at the counter on the way out. And, Ariadne, a big thank you for doing this.'

Ariadne smiled and, without saying a word, slipped out through the rear exit.

20

PAVLOS AND Nathan were still high up on their observation point in the multistorey car park.

'Pavlos, look, that could be our delivery.' Ariadne had appeared on the corner by So Fresh and was now making her way across the road in the direction of Stakis & Co. Pavlos ran to his car, jumped in, locked the doors and activated the alarm system. It was loud. Birds left their perches and took to the air. He repeated the process with Nathan's car, so there were now two going off.

Ariadne approached the front door of the solicitors and pressed the intercom. The wait was excruciating but eventually the lock buzzed and she pushed the door open. She was in. Nathan signalled to Pavlos to turn off the car alarms. He did so, then rushed over to where Nathan was standing.

'She's in, Pavlos, she's in.' The two men shook hands and smiled with relief. Nathan continued to observe Emba Street. The suspicious-looking characters that he had his eye on earlier seemed to have melted away. Everything looked surprisingly normal. The door opened and Ariadne reappeared.

'Look, Pavlos, here she comes.'

She made her way casually across the street towards So Fresh. Crucially, this time she was empty-handed. A few minutes later Dion appeared by the shop on the corner of Emba Street. He was making his way back to the car park. When he appeared at the observation point, he confirmed that Ariadne had delivered the documents directly to Dimitri Stakis. The three men shook each others' hands and Pavlos smiled for the second time that day. They all agreed that on the occasion of Nathan's next visit they should have a get-together for old times' sake, each of them knowing that such a regroup, with all the best intentions, very rarely occurs.

~~~

Pavlos and Dion needed to report to the local police station to join the debrief of the morning's events. Nathan decided to make his way to the airport at Larnaca as originally planned. Pavlos and Dion asked him to keep them up to date on developments, particularly if and when the council decided to withdraw its compulsory reclamation order on the Anapetri land.

Both cars left the car park, Pavlos going left and Nathan right. Nathan was on his own now and had to make his way from Nicosia to Larnaca airport, going through the city and joining the A1 motorway on its outskirts. He could take his time; it wasn't yet 11am and his flight wasn't due to depart until 4pm, which gave him time to think and consider what had actually happened during the last week.

We came for a holiday and I became embroiled in a fight for survival. I searched for hidden documents in a forbidden city, which if not found could have led to a natural disaster for the island, never mind the region. We were pursued by the Russians, who had hired a local to fit a tracking device to one of our cars. And, once more, on top of that, I'm returning with a fistful of diamonds. I could pen a book about this experience; it's quite incredible.

Nathan made good time and, before he realised, he was approaching Dali. He followed the signs for Larnaca and was on the A2 motorway, where he began to see signs for the airport. Although he was quite relaxed while driving, he became aware of a BMW and an Audi that had been behind him for quite a while, maybe even rotating and sharing the load so as not to be obvious. *It's nothing; just me being over-cautious. All the same, I think I'll go round the roundabout to see if it follows.*

As Nathan approached the roundabout, the BMW was still behind but had dropped back considerably. He indicated right and the BMW did the same. Nathan made a circuit of the roundabout before leaving at the airport departure sign and, sure enough, the two cars followed suit.

There's definitely someone following me, possibly two cars working as a team, but I don't want them to know that I'm on to them as that would make me vulnerable. I have to stay ahead of the game. Why are they still following me, though? Could it be just for revenge, some sort of payback? I did make a mess of that guy the other night. He was becoming anxious about what lay ahead. *Oh no, I bet it's the diamonds they're after now. They could have a hidden camera or two in the villa and saw the diamonds when I poured them out of the box and on to the kitchen worktop. If that's the case, then I've got problems.*

As Nathan approached airport departures he spotted a sign for car hire return. The BMW and the other car were keeping their distance but were still there, following. He was now driving along a car park perimeter road, where he saw another sign pointing left for the car hire return. He turned in and was confronted by a car park barrier and a metal digital keypad on a post. He remembered that the hire company had written the four-figure access code on the front of their rental docket, so he looked inside the glove compartment.

He was now very conscious that his followers were not far behind him. He grabbed the docket, read the handwritten code and quickly typed it into the keypad. The barrier rose and Nathan was through. He noticed in his rear-view mirror that the barrier was on its way down as the BMW arrived. It was just too late for the BMW, or it was one of those barriers that doesn't allow any tailgating. Nathan breathed a sigh of relief, then wondered whether they had anyone else in the car park or even in the terminal building. *I'm so tired. When is this nightmare going to end?*

Nathan parked the car as near as he could to the car rental kiosk. He cleared the vehicle of his suitcase and belongings before dropping the key into the dedicated key return box on the front of the kiosk. Fortunately, there was a luggage trolley nearby, so he loaded his belongings on to it and started walking towards the departure building. *I'm better getting into the building quickly. There will be more protection for me in there, I hope.*

He was about to cross the road to enter the terminal building when he noticed to his left that there were three men approaching at a fast pace. Nathan stepped out into the road, trolley first, in front of a taxi, much to the disgust of the driver, who sounded his horn for a ridiculously long time. A second car followed suit. The three men were a matter of metres behind. Meanwhile, the noise of the horns had alerted a couple of police officers, who were on patrol in the departure hall. They exited the building immediately in front of Nathan, just as he was about to have to start fighting for his life again.

The three men, noting the appearance of the police, feigned a conversation with each other and passed around a pack of cigarettes. Nathan walked past the police officers as they stood there menacingly surveying the scene at the front of the building. When they realised there was nothing to see and that it was far too hot outside the air-conditioned terminal building, they turned around and walked straight back in.

Nathan, now inside, looked up at the departures display screen. *Check-in desk 42. Once I've checked in this luggage I'll feel a lot better.* The check-in desk happened to be right down the other end of the hall and there were a lot of people milling around, not knowing which way to go. It was a slow process and, while he was in the thick of it, he was approached by two suited men. 'Which check-in do you want?' one of them said with a strong unknown accent.

'Sorry, who are you?' asked Nathan.

'We are just airport helpers; we help people with their luggage to check in.'

'I don't need any help, thank you. I can find my own way.'

'You do not understand. You have to come with us.'

'No I don't. And I'm not going to.' Nathan, already wearing his backpack, picked up his suitcase from the trolley. The two men closed in and stifled him for space. They slowly shuffled him to the rear of the hall but he refused to let go of the suitcase.

Suddenly an opportunity arose and Nathan kneed one of the men in the groin, very hard, and he went to the floor in agony. Nearby, women and children screamed in panic. The second man took the opportunity to grab the suitcase, as well as pull a knife from his waistband. People around were now screaming in terror as a man brandishing a knife was making off with a suitcase. Nathan was following him but at a safe distance.

Just as the man approached the sliding doors and the exit from the building, he turned and ran for it. He only made a few metres outside before Nathan rugby-tackled him and brought him to the ground. Remarkably, the man was still holding his knife and was now coming back at Nathan. In the melee, Nathan tried to get his suitcase back but the man lunged at him with the knife. Nathan was able to sidestep the blade and, as the man drew nearer, he struck him with great force in the Adam's apple with the side of his open hand. The man doubled up, gasping for air. Nathan quickly grabbed his suitcase and made for the check-in desk. As he stepped back inside the building, acting as if nothing had happened, the two police officers rushed past him, guns drawn.

Nathan was relieved to eventually see his suitcase on the check-in desk conveyer belt, where it disappeared into the baggage-handling area. He grabbed his ticket, boarding pass and passport, then headed through to the departure security area. He felt so relieved, even though he still had all the laborious security checks and passport control to go through. But once he was in the business class lounge he really began to relax. He found a table in the corner and, after a chicken salad with warm bread and a couple of glasses of wine, he suddenly felt really sleepy. He set the alarm on his mobile phone to notify him an hour before the flight departure. He wanted to call Loretta but, once he had settled into one of the easy chairs in the lounge, he fell asleep.

In the heart of England, somewhere near Cheltenham, Nathan grabbed the body and pulled it into the pig pen. When the pigs realised that someone had entered their domain, the adult males appeared from their sties. He closed the gate quickly but quietly so as not to make too much noise. As he walked away, he could hear the pigs grunting and gorging on the large luxurious slab of meat. Nothing would be wasted, down to the last bone or tooth.

He walked into the forest. He had blood on his hands. Suddenly, he was in New Zealand, on a small hill in the middle of a forest. A sign read URUPA Māori burial ground. The warm air vented from the fissure in the earth's crust. He looked into the blackness of the crevasse, then pushed the body in. He walked away, stepped over the sign and stooped down to wash his blood-soaked hands in a small stream. He splashed the ice-cold water on his face.

Now he was in Varosha, Famagusta. As the butt of the rifle came down in his direction again, he grabbed and twisted it with all his effort. With one motion he grabbed it and rammed it into his assailant's face. He fell backwards and his head cracked open like an egg on the rim of an oil barrel. He was forcibly loaded into the silo and joined dozens of animal carcasses. The door was closed behind him with a thud.

Nathan awoke, startled by the nightmare. Although severely distressed, he didn't show it. Not in the middle of the business class lounge. The nightmare was occurring more often and now it included the guard in Varosha. It was getting more and more disturbing. There was nothing he could do about it.

He walked over to the coffee machine for a cappuccino. On the way back to his seat he selected a slice of lemon drizzle cake from the sweet counter. Suddenly his thoughts were all about Loretta. He loved her so much and there was nothing he could do about that either. But for some reason he was still unsure whether or not they had a future together. He decided he would call her from the plane, no matter what the time was in New Zealand.

Nathan's flight was called and he made his way from the lounge to the gate. Next to one of the bookstores there was a large TV high on the wall that waiting passengers could watch from the seated area. Something on the screen caught his eye. It was footage from Varosha. He stopped and read the subtitles at the foot of the picture. A thirty-five-year-old security guard has been found dead in Varosha. It was believed that he had been attacked and killed before being loaded into a nearby construction silo. Enquiries were ongoing. Nathan continued to the departure gate and boarded the plane.

21

THE FLIGHT had been good for Nathan. After boarding his connection at Doha he was able to catch up with some well-earned sleep. He managed to have a brief conversation with Loretta but the signal was poor. The good news was that they didn't argue and Loretta actually apologised to him for her abruptness during their last call. She was going to collect him on his arrival. After the phone call, he flushed the SIM card from his mobile down the toilet on the plane, just in case he was still being tracked when he arrived in New Zealand.

On arrival, Nathan became increasingly worried about the diamonds in his luggage. As he passed through immigration and made his way to the luggage hall, he was half expecting to be apprehended by customs and asked to 'come this way'. Although he was an ex-police officer, he had no idea whether what he had done was illegal. Was he going to be accused of theft? If they did find them, how would he explain where the diamonds came from and how they came into his possession? Who did they actually belong to? It would take some explaining. It could also put him in the frame as a potential suspect for the Varosha murder if he had to tell them where he had been.

The wait by the baggage carousel seemed to take a lifetime. Bags, suitcases, pushchairs, golfclubs, all seemed to pass by as Nathan anxiously waited for his one suitcase. *Something's gone wrong. I'm sure mine should have passed through by now. Some of these have been around three or four times and there aren't many people left from the flight.* Then a blue Samsonite suitcase appeared through the black rubber draft curtains and was slowly making its way around the carousel towards him. It looked like his but he wasn't sure. Someone else picked it up, lifted it off the carousel, checked the luggage tag and then placed it back on. As the case came closer, Nathan realised it was his. He pulled it off the carousel and checked the luggage tag. *Well, it isn't damaged and it doesn't seem to have been forced open.*

He made his way through to arrivals nervously but without any further incident. He breathed a sigh of relief as he finally entered the arrivals hall and was overjoyed when he saw Loretta waiting for him. He had never seen a woman in a pair of faded blue denims and a white T-shirt look so beautiful. She was as happy to see him as he was her.

They held each other and kissed briefly, then she took him by the hand and said, 'Let's go, the car isn't far away, and give me your backpack.' He handed it to her and she flung it across her shoulder.

As they made their way to the car, Nathan asked, 'How's your dad?'

Loretta welled up almost immediately. 'He hasn't got long left. At least he's at home and is comfortable in his own bed. I haven't told him about Anapetri and the fact that you found the documents. I thought I'd wait so that you could tell him. It's a bit of a risk but I thought it may give him a boost.'

'I've definitely got something that will give him a boost.'

'What do you mean?'

'Apart from the news on the documents, how about half a dozen, quite large cut diamonds.'

'Diamonds? How?' Loretta replied excitedly.

'Believe it or not, they were in the safe in Varosha, in a small box filled with cotton wool.'

'How do you know they're the real thing?'

'Well, I think I do. I thought maybe your dad would be able to confirm.'

'This is fantastic, but he's never mentioned them before.'

'Maybe he's just forgotten over time. He must have handled lots of stones and jewellery, with him being in the trade,' said Nathan.

'Yes, you're probably right.'

'And, of course, you must bear in mind that only a person that you could trust would be handing them over. I could have pocketed the lot.'

'Okay, I get it, and I'm sorry that I doubted your trust. I've been regretting saying it ever since. But it was a stupid thing to do.'

'It had a measured risk with significant reward,' replied Nathan.

'Yes, whatever. Anyway, I have good news that you may want to hear. While you were flying back from Cyprus, I had a call from the office to say that Dimitri Stakis has forwarded a copy of the land documents to the council and that the originals have gone to a secure vault. Apparently, it's a foregone conclusion that the council's action will be dropped.'

'That's fantastic. The damage that the Russians were going to do to that island … I meant to ask, what sort of mining are Mykanos involved with?'

'I believe it's mainly aggregate and stone, nothing nasty, so you don't need to worry about it. Anyway, you're my hero.' She kissed him again as they reached her car. They left the airport and headed for her parents' home.

'By the way, did you ask Andreas and Helena about possibly taking over the running of the villa?' Loretta asked.

'Yes I did.'

'And what sort of response did you get?'

'A very good one. They're both up for it and very excited. I told them that we would let them know as soon as the land and everything is secured.'

'Oh, that's great to hear. I think that could work out really well, don't you?'

'Yes, it's a great opportunity for them to learn new skills and secure the future for little George. And a big bonus is that it will be available to Mykanos employees and their families, all of which should secure loyalty and make Mykanos a company that people want to work for. Not that they don't already, but you know what I mean,' said Nathan.

'Yes, I think it's a big plus for us and may help to tip the scales in our favour in the search for quality employees,' Loretta replied. The rest of the journey was filled with small talk, then they were soon pulling into the drive of the Mykanos home.

'You may be shocked when you see him,' Loretta said.

'Okay, I'm prepared.'

They parked up and Loretta went to open the front door with her key. Maia was waiting in the hallway with hugs and smiles for both of them. Eventually they went through to the bedroom to see Stelios. It was a shock to Nathan. Stelios was in bed lying flat on his back. He was under a duvet and his neck was exposed, revealing a huge swelling on the front of his throat. He lifted his hand to wave as they entered the room. Nathan sat on a chair adjacent to the bed, while Loretta and Maia busied themselves within the room.

'I'm sorry to hear about your illness,' said Nathan.

Stelios didn't reply. He just waved his hand.

'How is he today, Mum?' asked Loretta.

'I'm afraid his voice has gone completely now. That's why he isn't speaking to you Nathan. He'll just wave his arms and give hand signals.'

'That's okay,' said Nathan. 'Just listen to me Stelios. I have a story to tell. You knew about the plans for Anapetri and turning it into a landfill site.' Stelios gave a thumbs-up. 'Well, they didn't want the land for landfill, they wanted it for mining. They were lithium miners and their excavations would have ruined and poisoned the whole area. The good news is that I found all the documents that prove that you purchased the land lawfully back in the seventies. The documents are in the hands of Dimitri Stakis in Nicosia and he's made representation to the council to stop the land reclamation claim.'

Stelios smiled and weakly punched the air. Then tears began to slide down his cheeks and dampen the pillow beneath his head. Maia and Loretta approached to comfort him in his happy distress.

Nathan continued. 'Stelios, there's something else that I must tell you. In the safe in the basement in Varosha there was a small box that was filled with cotton wool. Wrapped in the cotton were six quite large cut diamonds. Do they belong to you?'

Stelios gestured for Nathan to come closer and in a very low and hissing voice said, 'Yes, they were for an investment, but I forgot about them. I had too much money in those days. I want Loretta to have them, to do as she so wishes.'

Nathan repeated Stelios's comments to Loretta.

'Thank you Dad, thank you so much, but maybe you should be giving them to Mum.'

'No dear,' said Maia. 'Your dad knows what he's doing. I'm not in the slightest bit interested in diamonds and I certainly don't need the money. Listen to your dad.'

'Thanks Mum.'

'You're welcome dear.'

Stelios was gesturing for Loretta to go over. She placed her ear next to his mouth. It was said very quietly but Nathan heard it.

'The diamonds will pay for your wedding and a new home.'

Loretta blushed and Nathan pretended he hadn't heard anything. 'Okay, thank you Dad.'

Stelios now made a general wave with the back of his hand, indicating that he wanted to be left alone. The three of them left the room and reconvened in the kitchen.

'So, it sounds like you've been having an exciting time in Cyprus,' said Maia.

'Yes, you could say that,' Nathan replied.

'How did you know where to go in Varosha? And how did you get past security?' Maia asked.

'Lots of research. Then we put a drone up to identify the street and the building. But it was shot down by the security guard.'

'And you still went in, even after that?' said Loretta.

'Yes, the drone was up long enough to gather important information for us, such as the road, access points and the location of security guards, for example.'

'It's all very interesting. I would like to hear more but would you like a drink first?' said Maia.

'No, if you don't mind, I'd rather be on my way. I feel a bit jet-lagged. I promise I'll come back and tell you more.'

'I understand,' said Maia.

'Okay, point taken, let's get you back,' said Loretta.

On the journey to Loretta's, Nathan cemented his decision not to tell her about the attack at the villa. It just seemed to be the wrong time; he didn't want to upset the applecart with her. He wanted things to be smooth and for their relationship to progress and improve. He certainly didn't want to be arguing with her about the close shaves that he suffered in Cyprus. He also didn't want to look too much of a risk taker, although it was blatantly obvious that he liked a challenge.

When they were back at Loretta's apartment, Nathan showered and unpacked his bag and suitcase. Loretta was now keen to take a look at the diamonds so Nathan went through his suitcase, emptying it slowly. However, to his shock and horror, there was no box. It wasn't there. Then he started to feel through individual garments. He had nearly emptied the suitcase when he remembered that when packing he had put the box into the zip-up section inside the lid. His heart began to return to its normal speed and rhythm as he unfastened the zip and produced the box. He took Loretta over to the dressing table, removed the lid of the box and poured the contents on to the glass top.

Loretta's eyes were fixed on the light being reflected from the immaculate stones. 'They're the biggest diamonds I've ever seen,' she said.

'I've been meaning to ask you,' said Nathan.

Loretta suddenly turned to face Nathan and looked at him directly. 'Yes, go on,' she said, smiling, and with a look of interest.

'Do you believe in finders keepers?'

'Oh yes, you find and I keep,' she replied, smiling.

Nathan laughed out loud, realising that she was too quick for him today, most days in fact.

'I love them. Thank you for bringing them back. They're worth a fortune.'

'Yes, I thought they may have been, that's why I kept the biggest ones for myself.'

'Ha, ha, very funny.'

Nathan took her in his arms and kissed her passionately, then out of the blue she stopped him and pushed him away.

'What's wrong?' asked Nathan.

She had that very serious look in her eye again. 'Nathan, I need to know how you feel about me.'

'That's funny because I need to know how you feel about me.'

'I asked first,' she said.

Nathan rolled his eyes. 'Okay, how do I feel about you? You're the most beautiful woman I've ever set eyes on. You have a fun personality but can be a bit too serious sometimes. You're intelligent, you're wealthy, you have a great future, you have great parents and I love the ground that you walk upon.' Nathan had thought he would never hear himself saying such things but the truth of the matter was that he was madly in love with her.

Loretta stood there, open-mouthed and with a tear in her eye. She eventually composed herself and, with her infamous serious face, she said, 'I don't know how to follow what you've just said to me. But I know that while we've been apart, although I've been looking after Dad, I was thinking about you every minute of every day. I can't help it; I love you Nathan Mason.'

'I love you Loretta Mykanos, and I was thinking … can't we get one of the diamonds made into a ring, because I'd like you to be my wife.' *Oh no, what am I going to do if she says no?*

'Yes I will. I love you. I want to be your wife.' Loretta cried more tears of joy.

22

SADLY, THE following day Stelios Mykanos died in his bed at home. He was happy in the knowledge that the business had been rightfully handed over and that the future of Anapetri Villa and its land were secure. But, more importantly, he was overjoyed that his beloved daughter had found the love of her life, had announced her engagement to Nathan and her future looked positive.

Three weeks later, Mykanos head office received a call from Dimitri Stakis in Nicosia. They had been informed that, in light of the evidence that confirmed that the Anapetri land belonged to the Mykanos family, the council had dropped any plans for a compulsory reclamation.

Not long after, Andreas and Helena commenced their roles as caretakers and managers of Anapetri Villa. Nathan had asked Andreas to look at the possibility of employing a specialist to carry out an electronic bug sweep to check the villa for hidden cameras and microphones. Andreas employed the services of a professional from Nicosia, who found one hidden camera in the form of a screw head in the kitchen. Nathan was now convinced that was how they knew about the diamonds. He suspected the camera may have been fitted on the night of the break-in and subsequent attack.

Once the news about the lawful ownership of the Anapetri land broke, all the future plans of URALS CORP mining company melted away, with all the menace and threat that came with them. In addition, no one ever made a claim of assault at Anapetri Villa.

Today, the diamonds are still in the possession of Loretta Mykanos and are said to be worth many millions of pounds. One of the stones was finely cut to make an engagement ring for her. Six months later she married Nathan in a low-key church wedding in Auckland.

Loretta now employs a management team to her liking. She's still learning about and visiting some of the businesses of which she's now the owner. Nathan works on a freelance basis for Mykanos and travels all over the world. He visits the company's different retail outlets and deals with any security issues, whether staff-related or a premises-related problem. On the odd occasion, Loretta goes with him.

No one was ever arrested for the murder of the security guard in Varosha. There are no suspects but the file remains open. Meanwhile, a government investigation is ongoing into the conduct of officials at the Palakori council and whether or not there are any corrupt or fraudulent issues to be taken into consideration with regards to their dealings with the Russian company URALS CORP.

The police patrol officer was accused of bringing the force into disrepute and released from his duties as a police officer. Meanwhile, Detective Dion is now in a relationship with Ariadne, the manager of Go Fresh. Detective Pavlos is restoring an old stone house in the village of Anapetri, where he is looking forward to his retirement.

Nathan no longer deals on the stock market. He sold the remainder of his shares to his brother-in-law to add to his portfolio. He still suffers from the recurring nightmares. He considers this a matter for himself and no one else. That's the way that he intends it to remain.

Afterword

Thank you for reading *Nightfall in Famagusta*. I hope you enjoyed this book.

If you want to know when I release my next book, please join my mailing list at www.jacksonbeck.com

You can also follow me on Facebook, Jackson Beck
Or on Instagram @jacksonbeck66

And, if you have a moment, please review *Nightfall in Famagusta* on any book retailer site, such as Amazon, Google, BookBub, Book Depository, Goodreads, Waterstones, Blackwell's, or any other social media networks, and inform other readers why you enjoyed this book.

With thanks
Jackson Beck
www.jacksonbeck.com

Printed in Great Britain
by Amazon